PRIMITIVE ANARCHY

PRIMITIVE ANARCHY

DAVID
LAWRENCE

ILLUMIFY
— MEDIA.COM —

Contents

Prologue/2016

"In the past man has been first. In the future, the system must come first."

— Fredrick Winslow Taylor, 1911

October 28, 2016

Agent Ryu Murakami sat stoic outside the operating room. His body felt like he'd slept in a rock tumbler and the stapled gash above his eye ran all the way to the top of his head. It stung and he was losing sight. His sweat soaked clothes had all dried to a crispy salt-stained suit that felt like it was made of old cardboard. No one had updated him. There had been no other information. The clock was still speeding towards 8:00 a.m. He knew the US Government and the Pentagon had to make a choice: Submit to BurnBear's demand or face a completely new type of weapon.

Neal Walcott had designed this choice almost thirty years ago. It was binary.

1

Anonymous Human Potential/1991

"Genome engineering will allow us to become ever more diverse, enhancing our prospects for survival."

— George Church, 2012

Jinnah International Airport, Karachi Pakistan
June 2, 1991

Within minutes of disembarking their international flight, the Walcott Labs Research team had been discreetly approached in the crowded terminal by an innocuous little man in a grey nehru suit.

"Hello doctors," The man said as he approached and spread his arms wide like a bird of prey.

"My captain had requisitioned interviews with you prior to your clearance into Pakistan. If you could come this way with me, please." He gestured to an unmarked door inside the terminal where three armed soldiers in full military uniform were already awaiting their intake.

The group of six scientists were escorted down a long windowless hallway and separated into interrogation rooms. One by one the soldiers peeled them off. Dr. Taeng Chairasit, Prof. Neal Forest Walcott's moon-faced chief medical officer and wife, stayed in sight of her husband as long as she could, but eventually, she was inserted into a room and Neal was led deeper toward the immense mahogany door at the far end of the hall.

Dr. Chairasit was brought into a small formal office where a secretary with a stoic countenance sat next to a dictation machine coded in Urdu. They waited for the captain while Taeng continued to focus on full relaxed breaths and regulating her heart rate. Taeng and Neal had been working toward this expedition for a little over a decade. They both knew everything, but in anticipation of being detained they had kept the four other researchers completely in the dark. All they knew was what was on the official itinerary.

A soldier opened the door and an impeccably dressed Paki man holding a small paper file and a pristine pitcher of cool clear water stepped into the room followed by two attendants carrying Taeng's checked luggage.

"Dr. Chairasit my name is Captain Fazian. I am the customs chief for Internationals here in Karachi."

"کیا آپ کو اردو، کپتان میں بات کرنا پسند ہے؟" Taeng said.

It was hard for the captain to place the accent, but it was more than passable Urdu. Taeng watched as the captain and Secretary shared a quick micro expression, redesigning their approach to this interrogation on the fly.

There is a plan in place here, thought Captain Fazian.

"Actually, I would prefer French," the captain replied with genuine good humor. "It is such a beautiful language, and I have so few opportunities to practice. English… I get a lot of practice with English," he said. "So, let's speak that."

The captain reached for a short crystal glass on the desk between them and poured the woman some water.

"Please state your name and occupation," he instructed as he offered her the glass.

"I am Dr. Taeng Chairasit. I am a medical researcher and the chief medical officer at the Walcott Labs at CalTech."

"And how long have you been at these positions?"

"About two years. Prior to that I was Chief Surgeon at Bumrungrand Hospital Neuroscience Center in Bangkok."

"Those are a long way apart. What prompted such a drastic change?"

"I met my husband. He is a professor at the university. It's his lab. So, I moved."

"It is good for a woman to do this for her husband."

The captain noted that the subjugating jab did not faze the doctor, and he moved on.

"And what does your lab do?"

"We study the connection between the brain and the human genome."

"Why? What are your lab's goals?" the captain inquired as his brow began to furrow.

"Someday our research will help those with neurological, genetic and brain disorders."

"I see. Please tell me about your travel."

"Today and tomorrow the Walcott Labs team and I are visiting LZS Mainframe here in Karachi. An old colleague of mine from Bangkok chairs the genetics lab at Peshawar Medical University and he's meeting us there to discuss building a searchable genetic database for South Asia."

The creases in the captain's forehead deepened.

"Seems odd there would be a genetics lab at a university focused on getting basic medical care to the tribal lands."

"Not at all captain," Taeng countered. "Peshawar Med has three sister campuses in Hyderabad, Uganda, and Northern India. If a gene base existed here, we could help transform medicine for billions of people in this part of the world."

The captain smiled. "You speak English beautifully, doctor. Quite eloquent."

"I grew up in California. I left when I went abroad for med school. I only just returned to the States a couple years ago."

"I see. And after Karachi where do you go?"

"We will be headed North. Touring the base of the Himalayas."

"Why exactly?" asked Captain Fazian.

"A sense of spiritual rebirth, I suppose," Taeng said cryptically. "I don't know if I'll ever be back. We wanted to bear witness to one of the highest majesties on the planet while we are all here."

The captain motioned to one of his officers who pulled Taeng's full body hard shell cold suit from her suitcase and held it up.

"Just staying at the base of the mountains?" he asked incredulously. "Everyone has packed such substantial cold weather gear."

"Well, the weather in California thins out the blood pretty quickly," Taeng parried. "Better to be over prepared than under, don't you think?"

"Of course, doctor. And after you've glimpsed Allah's mountains?"

"We'll be attending a tech conference happening across the east for the next month or so. And then it's back to the university for the Fall."

The captain nodded to the customs attendants to repack the cases.

"Such a journey doctor. Please refresh yourself. My secretary Mindah is here to assist your ease and comfort. I believe we'll be able to conclude these interviews shortly, and I personally want to apologize for inconveniences. Wait here now."

The captain closed the door behind him and stood in the hallway calculating. Everyone had the same story. They were part of CalTech's research faculty working at the recently minted Walcott Labs which was focused on the data architecture of the human brain and genetic code. They were on their way to DataEast Computer Summit '91 which was spread out from Seoul to Shanghai over the next month. But the combination of the Meals Ready to Eat his customs officer had found which were for American soldiers; and the communications tech they had found next, just rang too many alarm bells for a man who had never trusted Americans, especially smart ones. And the man he was about to question in the next room had apparently won a Nobel prize. He knew well that the world doesn't like their prize scientists fooled with. Fazian had been part of the security team that shepherding Pakistan's nuclear weapons into existence and had seen firsthand the value applied knowledge. Governments are nothing but words and money without scientists and engineers. If he had to officially detain the group it would be an international incident, but if he let them loose into Karachi and something happened it could cost him his life.

The captain composed himself. He was good at interrogations. He genuinely liked people, which often made his subjects decide to trust him long enough to explain why they were truly in his country. In the end he decided to play the encounter by ear instead of strategizing. He needed to be in the room with the man to get a better read on him. He'd go in and do some other business first and let the electricity of beginning dissipate. It would give him a chance to breathe in the ring for a moment before they began.

Start with something simple, he told himself and turned the knob on the door.

The captain had intentionally spoken to everyone else first while Neal Walcott had been left alone for nearly three hours. The professor would be more likely to repeat key phrases of any rehearsed group lies. The captain entered and walked to the opulent oak desk at the far side of the room and sat down. A momentary thought about how important props are to interrogation wandered through the captain's mind and he pulled his cigarette case from his jacket pocket. He casually pulled a cigarette from the middle of the row, lit it with a wooden match, and took a long satisfying drag while pretending he needed to glance at the detainment file in front of him before they began.

Fazian's initial impression of Neal Walcott was unassuming until he looked up and met the professor's gaze. Neal's expression was perfectly still and calm, but the captain felt like all the power had drained out of his body. Something in the energy and presence of Neal Walcott was deeply intimidating.

This is why you decided to do something else first before you start talking to him, the captain reminded himself. He gave his best impression of being unfazed and he broke the initial moment and reached for the phone on his desk. Captain Fazian placed phone calls to his superiors and various third parties, in an attempt to regain some semblance of control in the two men's personal dynamic.

This man is remaining far too calm, thought the captain as he waited on hold for a representative of the AsiaEast conference to come on the line. He had detained innocent business travelers suspected of mischief before, and they had unanimously met the allegations with an emotional blend of fear, hysteria, and Western indignation. But this man, who has something to do with the future of global computer systems, hadn't batted an eye through the entire process.

He doesn't have the affect of an academic, but he's not a spy either, thought the captain. Spies have the sense to fake their incredulity. If he was a diplomat we would have seen papers immediately. I wonder…

There was a click in the captain's ear and a woman's voice came over the line. She was the production coordinator for AsiaEast and she was not happy. It was quickly ascertained that the man sitting in front of the officer was in fact Neal Walcott, the headlining lecturer at AsiaEast this year and Nobel prize winning faculty at California Institute of Technology. The woman confirmed the group's identities and itinerary before softly threatening to come to Pakistan herself if the Walcott Labs research team wasn't released immediately.

The captain hung up and looked again at the man's credentials. Prof. Neal Forrest Walcott PhD Advanced Mathematics, Information Architecture.

"You are traveling with a lot of doctors for a mathematician professor," Captain Fazian noted. "Please explain the association."

"My research deals mostly with chaotic events and the organization of their data," said Neal.

"Chaos isn't an English word I like very much professor. Please explain further. What is it you will be speaking about at your DataEast conference?"

"My lecture is on the phenomenon known as Collapse and Replacement in the Truth of Occurrence."

Neal paused for a moment. Captain Fazian gave the impression that he was unimpressed.

"It just means that truth evolves."

"Truth is truth precisely because it is eternal, professor."

"No captain," Professor Walcott corrected him. "Truth is truth because it is factually accurate in accordance with reality. As reality changes, so too does the truth."

"It sounds like you've made math out of the hubris of Man," the captain scolded, intentionally letting his disdain for Western secularism show before continuing.

"And the medical doctors? What do you need them for?" the captain asked. "What field of endeavor is this professor? What do you teach?"

"I don't teach anymore," said the professor. "I'm at my lab full time. The university and I have an agreement—CalTech is my silent partner, and they pay for everything, but I don't have much to do with the school."

"I am not interested in the specifics of your professional situation, professor. What exactly do you research now?"

"I've reoriented my research from technical computer science and data storage to the massive data sets those systems and computers can interpolate. Mostly the data of the human brain and genome, and I have no expertise in either which is why I have a staff of MDs. Neither endeavor has yielded much yet."

That was a lie. For the last decade Neal Walcott had secretly been taking quantum leaps in both fields.

"I've been stuck for almost ten years," the professor continued.

"Stuck…?" queried the captain.

Neal noticed as his interrogator leaned across the desk toward him caught by genuine interest.

"It must be quite a thought you're attempting to have, professor."

Neal liked the captain's turn of phrase, and a subtle smile bloomed on his face.

"The thought is attempting to have me, captain."

Captain Fazian chuckled in spite of himself and finished his cigarette, tapping the smoldering butt into the clean brass ashtray on his desk.

"You have pooled many resources for a man who claims to be, as you say, stuck. Please tell me about this grand attempt at thought."

"We are trying to answer the question of what we do with data sets that are constantly changing and too big to compute. The vastness of the data in either the fields of neuroscience or genetics have remained stubbornly beyond our ability to compile and synthesize. So, the university gave me a new lab and research team to help me attempt a breakthrough. So far, it's been frustratingly slow going. This is the reason for my staff and the CalTech endowment. I've come to a scientific and technical impasse."

Neal thought for a moment before adding, "But perhaps this trip will lead to a breakthrough."

They both knew the customs office was out of time. Any longer with such high-profile western scientists and the captain risked diplomatic retaliation. The door to the interrogation room opened with a loud echoing clack. A soldier took one thick booted step inside.

"You've been cleared into Pakistan professor," said the captain. "Please come with me and I will return you to your group."

The officer handed Neal his passport which had already been stamped and brought him to the group which was released, but the customs officer was determined to make sure the detainment was as costly as possible for the group, and they were hobbled by the confiscation of food and much of their equipment. The captain and customs office's thoroughness had threatened to significantly raise the traveling group's profile which was not something they could afford. The group toured LRZ Mainframe that afternoon, tailed by plain clothes police in unmarked cars, but by nightfall when the group had checked into their hotel, the police had gone. The Walcott research team decided to abandon their itinerary, and Neal and Taeng grossly overpaid the group's handlers to drive through the night heading straight for Kathmandu at the western border with Nepal.

That was almost three weeks ago. Since then, there had been nothing but water and noise and blindness.

═══════

Border of Nepal and Kingdom of Bhutan, Northeast Asia
June 21, 1991

The dark green rover skid and clawed its way up the narrow mountain trail. During the Monsoons, the unrelenting rain and fog bore down on everything below the mountains' tree line. After four weeks of traveling to the far side of the world, Carol Nyken had found the rainforests at dawn in the distance of the Himalayas to be the most disorienting and forsaken condition. The team's dossiers had waxed poetically about a Hindu belief the mountains were Shiva incarnate in repose, and Carol's imagination had conjured a lush exotic cacophony of color and organic soundscape, but once inside the actual rainforest ecosystem, even the light from the rack of Halogen lamps bolted across the rover's frame did almost nothing to penetrate the veil. The only thing the six scientists and their Bhutanese guides had heard for the last week had been the pounding white noise of the deluge. It was like being in an endless rainstorm inside a cavernous mine.

Another planet.

Carol could hear the air intake on their transport beginning to strain as the atmosphere around the convoy thinned. She could feel the increase in altitude. There was less oxygen, and the temp was dropping sharply on the layer of sweat encasing her body. She had watched for the last three days through the small plastic window in the back of the converted LR Defender as the vegetation surrounding them had thinned. Carol had learned a good deal about trees in her life. As the expedition cleared thirteen thousand feet, she identified the tall strong cedars were giving way to grand Himalayan fir trees. She knew they were getting close.

Carol and the other five travelers had upended their lives of immense privilege in the highest echelons of science and medicine, first to join Professor Walcott's new lab at CalTech, and then to join this clandestine pilgrimage East. They each had their reasons. What they had in common was that they had been true to their word. They had followed the professor to the other side of the earth without knowing why. Neal had been singularly focused since Pakistan. As patient and calculating as a machine. Any other snag and they were risking catastrophe. Neal's blank expression had been staring off into the great middling blur for days. His labored movement gave the impression of a marionette performing admirably on its own, while the puppeteer tended to more important matters.

Since clearing six thousand feet they had been dealing with icy nonexistent roads and much of their cold weather gear had been confiscated. The rain had arrived weeks early and the snowpack was high which had slowed them down considerably. Because of the secret nature of their travel, Neal had insisted purchasing a retail expedition was not possible. They could not risk drawing attention to themselves. Now, so many days later the rain and swings in temperature had kept the group dehydrated and mentally fatigued. They had been forced to buy new rations in Nepal after their food was confiscated in Pakistan, and Ang Zhao had become diuretic and was deteriorating into dysentery, but everyone knew how close they were. Finally, a change would come this morning.

From an early age Carol Nyken had believed she could learn anything. Do anything. Over the years she had developed a well-earned sense of self-confidence and balance around chaos. She possessed focus and determination and relied on these attributes as a scientist.

But as the air thinned around her, she was hitting a breaking point. She wanted comfort and quiet and relief. Her lungs craved the oxygen reserve tanks rattling in the mesh gear hold above their heads, but there was none to spare. The tanks had been prepped and ready for the next phase of the group's covert mission.

At six a.m. two canteens were passed along with cold Tsampa balls as the group jostled and pitched on the bench seats in the back of the Rover. It's hard to drink water when you feel like you're drowning, like trying to breathe smoke in a burning building. The body naturally wants to reject it. But you can't swallow Tsampa without water.

Two hard raps on the cabin wall.

"It's time," Neal said.

He pulled the bags he had kept in his possession during their detainment with Pakistani Customs from the gear-hold and set them aside. He then reached back and began unwrapping the triple wax cloth around a large ugly green suitcase. The six travelers stripped completely naked as Neal passed each of them a bath towel triple wrapped in white plastic garbage bags. All the layers of careful preparation coming to bear. The dry towel on Carol's skin was a visceral comfort. The group wiped themselves dry and began applying their base layer.

Carol opened her pack and pulled her thin thermal underwear from the tennis ball canister she had packed it in and put on the black tank tucked into black thermal shorts and thin foot drying cotton socks. Carol looked up and for the first time ever they were all wearing the same thing. They had left as individuals, and right that second, they looked like a unit, but as they each put on their more external layers the individualism returned, and the militaristic effect vanished.

The rover pitched hard, and the windows filled with clouds and lightning, like an airliner that catches a strong gust of wind and takes a sudden dip of one of the wings. Carol thought they had fallen off the mountain as the sensation passed the momentary jolt and continued into the seizing terror of real falling. A moment later the rover's front landed on solid terrain and began the last few hundred yards. The scientists were rattled, but as they put on their full thermal jumpsuits, the sound of the rain stopped. After so many days of unceasing noise, now the lack of it was otherworldly. The rover pushed hard up into the last few feet of cloud, and a strong silent white light came in through the windows. While everyone else in the group for at least a moment had reveled in the new light and silence, Neal already had his dark tinted snow goggles on.

Neal spoke. "I need you all to know some things that I have kept from you."

He paused and turned toward Taeng.

"Dr. Chairasit and I started a for-profit corporation. We have another lab which is quite different from the one at CalTech. And it's why we're here. We're bringing something back with us."

Carol looked around the vehicle, but the other three scientists shared only a stoic moment's eye contact with her as they finished zipping and buttoning their outer layers.

Two hard thuds landed from the driver's cabin, and Neal pulled his fur lined hood up.

"Use your oxygen when you need it. We start the ascent in five minutes."

The transport came to a hard stop and Walcott walked to the aluminum double latch doors at the tailgate. He pulled the latch open and put his shoulder into the door. A hard icy wind rushed into the cabin and one by one the group exited the rover. Carol stepped to the door and focused her attention on the ground of broken rocks in front of her. She landed surely and cleared out of the way.

Time seemed to slow as Carol looked up towards the south facing side of the Himalayas and took in the expanse before her. Steep and treacherous, but far from vertical, the exposed rock stood in front of them as both obstacle and path. The sherpas were already several hundred feet above the group laying lead line and securing first ropes with Neal and Taeng on the ground. Beyond that, wise reverent peaks with clouds above and clouds below. Neal finished securing his line and turned to the group, calling out above the wind.

"Masks on. Tanks open. Final checks."

Carol turned to Dr. Gregory Langstone, and they checked final ropes and harnesses just like they had practiced dozens of times on the porch of Neal's farmhouse. Foot to head, every gauge, buckle, lace, or strap was double checked and cleared. They each hooked into the lead line and to their safety line partner and a few moments later the ascent had begun.

Finally, Carol thought. This will all make sense.

The march up onto the south face of the mountain lasted all day. Progress was slow. The sky at dusk was a neon euphoria as the sun dropped behind the Himalayan peaks. The exhausted trekkers had moved into a cloud bank what seemed like hours ago. Carol performed the automatic reach out with the left hand always in search of the lead rope, over and over again into the coral lit hue blocking all shape or inference of the landscape. The elevation had grown steadily steeper throughout the day. And here on the last push as Carol labored to breathe, she could feel the hot sore burn of the lactic acid in her body seeping its way into her rib cage and saturated the tissues around her sternum. Everything was painful and the seconds between steps increased. Five seconds. Eight seconds. Existence had become entirely about transporting weight as she heaved her snow boots forward following the slack line that laid out before her and vanished into the now purpling clouds. Ten seconds a step. The telltale bliss and docility that intoxicates the drowning or the hypothermic was washing over her like an IV drip, when she heard their lead climber calling out from a few hundred feet ahead. Carol found her last joules of energy and within another thirty steps the clouds were dissipating.

Unexpectedly, a glaring light took over her vision. At first Carol thought she had gone snow blind, but soon realized it was the intense reflection of the last moments of sunlight bouncing off a small body of water. She squinted and cocked her head. The light moved out of her eyes giving way to an unbelievable scene. A fertile valley. The two hundred or so acres appeared to be floating. The reflected light had come from flooded rice paddies. Carol could make out tilled fields of vegetables and grains. Oxen. A mill and wood burning ovens. A well. But no electricity. No complex machines of any kind. Total analog reality. Overlooking the small kingdom an imposing, almost Brutalist structure dominated the foreground.

The sky was quickly going black, and the otherworldly vista was fading behind the veil of night. Two hundred yards ahead of her, Carol could make out men in long animal skin coats lighting the torches outside the building. Neal Walcott was the first of the six to cross the stone bridge leading to the massive archway into the ancient citadel. The structures had no ornamentation of any kind. The wind was picking up and carried all the still unanswered questions out of Carol's mind as the familiar sense of relief at arriving began to wash over her. Her exhausted body began to calm. She could feel her primitive mental and physical survival instincts receding back into the background of her psyche.

Neal was already concluding the huddled introductions with the keepers of the settlement when Carol reached the group. In the torchlight she could clearly see the group of men from the house had genetic and ethnic lineage coming from every far-flung region of the continent. Carol had always had an excellent ear for languages. Systems of communication. And she had already spent her fair share of time in Asia, but these were the dialects and accents of the people living on the tallest mountains in the world. The group from the house were speaking Dzongkha, Nepali, even Lepcha - a derivative aural form of Nepali used by the nomadic Ro'ng tribe. An almost impenetrable cluster of "ha-as" and "tee-bees" kept her from making a single connection; and yet Neal was becoming more fluent by the phrase as if he had spoken them before.

In the minutes that followed, before everything had been verified to their satisfaction, Carol studied the faces of her co-travelers. Each looking to Neal. Interpreting and speaking through Neal. He was transcending his identity as an academic luminary now. His holistic approach to the coming digital revolution, pushing its boundaries, prophesizing its future and meaning. He was becoming something more. But isn't that what the truly brilliant do? thought Carol. They transcend.

The travelers were taken into the building and across a large interior courtyard to a dormitory. This place couldn't be further from what we're researching, thought Carol. She opened the ancient wooden door she had been guided towards and stepped into a room only big enough to hold the simplest of straw beds, a pitcher of water, and a small plate of rice. The moon beamed hard and bright through her single small circular window. The last thing Carol remembered was wrapping herself in the amply thick blankets at the foot of the bed. As she began the slow proper process of falling into a deep sleep, Carol began to fantasize about the life she was away from back in California and how she, a mathematics professor, had come to be on top of a mountain in the Himalayas.

The group slept almost five days. Waking only long enough to drink water and eat the fresh steamed vegetables and grain being left at their bedsides. Carol only left her room to reach the outhouse. The first two days she saw no one else in her party up or about, but on the third day she walked into the great central room to find Neal surrounded by the monks and countless self-conscripted servants. They all faced three of the most senior monks that Neal had engaged in debate—something these holy men had never allowed of an outsider in any of their lifetimes. Neal's head was bowed. His eyes to the floor in respect for the monks' wisdom in all matters. Neal was speaking Dzongkha, but a Tibetic derivation which gave Carol's linguistic skills the smallest foothold.

The rights of the sun or the wind….? What rights does the sun or wind have?

Before Carol could hear more, two men appeared at the massive half open doors where she had been standing. It took her a moment before she recognized them as their Bhutanese guides. There was no warmth in their dark almond shaped eyes. And even to her groggy mind the message they were sending was clear: No women allowed. Had it been any other day. Any other moment in the rest of Carol's life up until this point she would have let the righteous indignation fly. Let it ignite her prodigious intellect and shoved their patriarchal bullshit straight down their throats… in passible Dzongkha no less. But she was practically sleepwalking, physically exhausted, and relieving her bladder was about her only conscious thought. The two men closed the doors without a word, and Carol filed "male bullshit exists here also" somewhere deep on her mental to-do list of things I will fix before I die.

The next day Carol left her bedroom again and crossed into the great room. Only Neal and one of the monks stayed. They were not speaking. Neal was flat on his stomach in reverence, the monk in deep contemplation sat on a simple comfortable chair in front of him. Carol could tell that part of this detente had already concluded. The once in a generation question, the unprecedented rebuttal, and soon the verdict. She passed through a corner of the hall but both men seemed too lost in their silent deliberations to hear or see anything around them.

It was moonrise on the fifth day when Neal came to Carol's room. She woke slowly to find him at the side of her bed. There was a clarity in his expression. This was no longer her PhD advisor turned research partner. This wasn't the scientist and engineer with whom she shared an R&D lab at the university. That man was a once in a generation impresario of the bleeding edges of where advanced mathematics and networked computer systems meet. He'd won a Nobel prize. But this isn't him, thought Carol. The man in front of me believes in something now. To Carol, the transformation was slightly unsettling. A scientist of his grand merit being certain of anything… but it was an inescapably miraculous countenance.

He handed her a bowl of water, and Carol savored the clear revitalizing minerality. The flavor was true and cold, and Carol could feel the water's glacial origins.

"We are going to be leaving in eight hours. Eat. Stretch. Drink as much water as you can, but you need to be alert in two hours."

He walked to the simple wooden door.

"It's time to wake up now, Carol," Neal said.

And with that he left her room to go wake the others.

Carol instinctively placed her hand on the ground as she had trained herself to do every morning. Over the years as Neal had mentioned aspects of Aryuveda in passing, it had intrigued Carol, and she had quietly adopted certain practices around awareness and sacred rhythms. Her hand touches the ground before her feet to connect the entire person to the earth and to remind her that the planet is not something we simply stomp around on and harvest, it is something we live in. Next, eight breaths eyes closed for the reclamation of her body and subconscious from sleep. Then to reboot the waking self, eight more breaths eyes open. Rise. Stretch. Water to rinse and spit. A scrape of the tongue. Rinse and spit. Water to the face. To the eyes. Water to drink. And then she would begin yoga. First a deep pigeon pose to loosen the hips. Child's pose to soften the back. And then into downward dog to awaken the full body and integrate her mind. The noticeable improvement in her own inner peace and outward performance after she adopted these practices was one of the drivers in her decision to join Neal's expedition.

Carol laid out her gear and repacked her backpack with precision. She put on her watch and noted she had another forty minutes to be ready. Arthur had suggested an Omega timepiece which he would have gladly bought for her, but instead she had bought a watch herself. Just a simple cheap black Timex with a cloth strap that she had got as a traveling watch. Something versatile and strong, but inexpensive. Expendable if necessary. It had been rained on. Snowed on. Stepped on twice. She had expected the watch to break or fail, but the watch had never failed in its duties to Carol. Like a doghearted old soldier the second hand moved briskly to each mark, struck it true, and then continued. It had seen her through so much she had become sentimental. The watch was now a friend.

She applied her base and midlayers and scanned how she was feeling. She was rested. She was in good physical condition. She strapped and tied her boots and left her room for the outhouse. The other scientists were awake and completing their final preparations. Their doors were open, and the setting moon followed Carol behind the windows of her companions' rooms.

Almost over, she thought. I'll be home. Soon.

Carol was the first to arrive in the great central room, and one by one the others appeared. A small simple table and two chairs had been placed at the center of the room. But there were no monks. No servants. No Taeng Chairasit or Neal Walcott, just the uninitiated waiting for their next instructions. From what Carol could read of her fellow travelers' expressions, they also had questions about the remarkably different man who woke them.

Forty-five minutes after they had been told to gather, the four co-operators were still sitting in silence and patience watching the light in the sky imperceptibly brighten until at last Neal and the senior monk appeared before them. Carol recognized the green suitcase in Neal's right hand. It struck Carol as distinctly out of place.

"You are going to have a thousand questions," Neal said. "I understand that. There will be time to ask me questions. All the time you need, but there is no time for that until we are back in the U.S. Right now, we need to focus on the task at hand. Give a deep bow to Rimpoche Loug, and do not move."

Carol and the others did as they were instructed and after a long moment of judgment the monk left the room.

Neal wasted no time. He opened the suitcase which was empty and pulled two hidden tabs. The top of the case lifted and in another moment Neal had produced a prototype IBM RS/6000 N40 laptop, a Nokia 8810 cell phone which Carol knew had no chance of securing a signal, and the smallest satellite modem Carol had ever seen, which Neal placed on the table next to the other equipment. The computer turned on.

Terminal-IBM: ~ Burnbearmachine: Connected

Neal had an open Terminal. He was already running three separate protocols when the fan and disk hard drive inside the laptop whirred. Carol imagined it was the first machine noise ever inside the high chamber walls of the room and the glow of the artificial light of the screen made her eyes palpably sore. The small computer was being leveraged to its full capacity. Satisfied with that setup, Neal pulled a thin aluminum portfolio case from the long side pocket of the suitcase. And from that a large crisp sheet of red construction paper.

"We are all going to meet someone now," he said as he began to fold and refold the paper in precise fashion.

"And they are coming home with us. Everyone will leave from different cities. All the arrangements have already been made. You will receive what you need as you need it. I must head to the AsiaEast conference. When you get home, pick up exactly where your lives left off and we will reconvene once the fall semester has started."

The origami technique being applied to the red construction paper was recognizable now. A complex form to be sure, but Neal executed its steps with total clarity.

The monk appeared once more from the exterior chamber, and in his arms was a tiny girl child who couldn't have been more than two years old. Neal walked to the monk with a deep compassionate warmth for the child. He held out the finished red paper in the form of a flower. The girl's tiny fingers reached out and took the curiosity. The monk gave an acknowledgment and handed Neal the girl before vanishing.

Neal turned to his stunned accomplices with the child who stared out at them with calm recognition.

"Make her feel loved," Neal said.

2

Metal Birds/2016

"Standing on the moon. With nothing else to do. A lovely view of heaven. But I'd rather be with you."

— The Grateful Dead

Telegraph Hill, San Francisco California
October 26, 2016

Judith Almont-Conners pulled into her driveway from the SFO airport. Her husband Raul already had their townhouse secured and the windows boarded. Raul was an excellent prepper. It was one of Judith's favorite things about him, and sure enough by the time she arrived home, everything they needed was already packed and loaded into the family car and they were ready to leave. Raul was not someone who would stay in the path of a hurricane if he could help it. He'd spent his childhood on the island of Cuba watching the shanties ripped away by tropical storms. It had driven him to become an architect.

In the back of their vintage '86 Land Cruiser were two well behaved little girls with two clean dogs licking and wiggling for attention. The mass of bags and coolers now blocking the rearview mirror from seeing out the tall back window was filled with everything they needed to wait out the storm from the safety and comfort of their summer house on the eastern shore of Lake Tahoe.

Everything was done. They were going to be fine.

Judith realized how tightly she was holding the steering wheel. The last few weeks she had been in Seattle as lead associate council in a high-profile domestic terrorism conspiracy trial. It had been a case requiring dozens of presentations involving complex motivations of coordinated events over nearly thirty years. She had completed her briefs almost five days ago and had grown increasingly preoccupied with the storm forming in the Pacific. There was every sign it was going to hit the coast of California extremely hard. She wasn't sure why something felt different to her. Something about the hurricane and the trial and being away from her family ate at Judith, and she had begun to feel like the rest of the legal team was relying on her to hold their hands and show them how to win. It was a feeling she resented from associates their firm was paying several million dollars a year to have on staff.

Judith had been down to the last flight she could take to get home before the storm when she turned to her colleagues in the board room of the offices they were renting and said she was mandating an indefinite paid leave of absence for herself from the firm, effective immediately. It was a provision of her employment contract she had insisted upon but never used, and an hour later she had boarded a plane home.

Pulling into the driveway Judith knew she had made the right choice. She parked and got out of her car and waved to her two daughters who waved back and called out but stayed buckled in. The dogs whined and drummed against the leather with their wagging tails at the sight of her. The girls rolled down the window of the Land Cruiser and the two dogs shook with excitement as Judith bent into the cabin to kiss her children and tussle and squeeze her favorite dog faces.

"Hi Mommy! We missed you!"

"Hi girls. Goodness, I missed you. Hi Meatball. Hi Monster. Everybody ready for our trip?"

The girls and dogs shook in the affirmative.

"Great. Where's daddy?"

"I'm here."

Raul had popped the trunk and was already loading her bag.

"Thanks love." Judith walked to her husband and put her arms around him.

"I missed you," she said.

"I'm so glad you came home," he said.

She kissed him and a mix of positive state hormones released into her brain. Her tribulations abated.

"I just need to grab a few things and I'll be right back."

Judith stepped into her family's home for the first time in almost six weeks. It smelled like her life and her family. The light throughout the house at five that evening was a dark grey, making Seattle's weather feel cheery by comparison. She walked through the kitchen looking at the life interrupted. The girls' science fair projects sitting on the long kitchen island. The hydroponic herb garden already looked bushy. Raul didn't cook as much when she was away. The plants will be overgrown by the time we get back, she thought as she climbed the stairs to the second floor.

Fifteen minutes later Judith set the security system and stepped off her wide front porch overlooking Telegraph Hill. The trees shook and hissed as the wind began to pick up. The wild parrots hung in the Arbutus and Red Flowering Gum trees, screaming and cawing. Behind their flapping wings and vibrant colors, black and immense on the horizon was Superstorm Megra.

Judith's cell phone rang. The ringtone let her know it was one of the co-founders of her firm and urgent. Talking Heads *This Must Be The Place*. She answered.

"Hi Michael," Judith said casually. "How are you and Annie holding up?"

She didn't know why he was calling, but it wasn't unusual for Michael Maxel to touch base with her, and they hadn't spoken since she mandated her leave of absence that morning.

"Judith, the BurnBear retainer was just reactivated."

Judith's heart sank. It was the one thing she couldn't walk away from. His voice was hoarse.

"Why?" she said. "What changed?"

"Some kind of digital WMD has been detected inside Neal Walcott's mind. It's been hiding dormant since the raid on BurnBear Ranch, but no one found it, not in all the years since he's been rotting in Fort Leavenworth. OMNIStack presented evidence in a FISA court this morning and there was a clear and present danger declared."

"What's the real-world impact of the declaration?" Judith asked. She could hear Michael struggling under the weight of the answer.

"They expedited Neal Walcott's execution. Professor Walcott will be executed forty-eight hours from now. Day after tomorrow morning at 8:00 a.m."

She thought for a moment. "And BurnBear found out?"

"Right. If anyone knows how the order leaked, they aren't saying, but about thirty minutes ago we received new documents and instructions from BurnBear."

"That means BurnBear is still operational… There's a sleeper cell," Judith said, hoping Michael hadn't caught the quiver in her voice.

"We don't know the answer to that. I've got a car that's going to pick you up in about three minutes," Michael said. "There are instructions inside a sealed case that came in over our encrypted fax. You are the only one cleared to open it. I know your family's headed to Tahoe, and the storm… it's shit timing, but you're gonna have to leave immediately."

They both knew she didn't have a choice. Judith always kept her poise when it came to catastrophe. This was what she did, and chaos was simply part of it, but it was still terrible news. Judith took a slow breath watching the horizon. She reminded herself that one of the reasons she made ten million dollars last year was the BurnBear retainer. It had single handedly paid for Raul to start his architecture firm. Since the BurnBear trial concluded four years ago every known member of the group had either died or been incarcerated. Since the conspirators' convictions, the retainer had been a matter of general advocacy and administratia she had never expected it to be activated again.

"Ok. I'm ready. Thank you for the heads up, Michael."

She could already see one of the company's cars coming up the hill. She turned back to her family and steeled herself to deliver the bad news.

Judith was a master at delivering bad news.

3

NASAdena/1991

"All mankind can do is move things… whether whispering a syllable or felling a forest."

— Sir Charles Sherrington,
Nobel Prize Winner in Physiology 1932

Border of Nepal and Kingdom of Bhutan, Northeast Asia
June 28, 1991

The group had separated the same morning in Nepal. Carol watched Taeng Charasit swaddle the baby expertly, securing the delicate thing with concentration and care, but while Carol could feel the maternal part of her begin to melt at the very sight of the baby, Taeng looked as if she were working with a piece of equipment. The small girl had been fixed with a heart and respiration monitor, and an infant's oxygen mask was placed gently over the child's face. Taeng strapped the tiny girl to the front of her body before zipping up her outer shell jacket and slung the diagnostic monitor over her shoulder.

They hiked down the mountain most of the morning and by midday they were back to where the climbing had begun a week ago. The drivers were just finishing packing up base camp into the rovers. The group loaded into the other Land Rover and took their same places on the bench seats. The engines started and the now seven, travelers sat in the cacophony of their collective silence. It was evening before anyone spoke. Carol had been quietly boiling. Every person in their group had been put in terrible risk of having their lives destroyed. They all had careers, obligations, and people depending on them. It was unconscionable that Neal and Taeng would shackle them to whatever their plan was.

"Why did you come back to CalTech?" Carol asked, submitting to her need to communicate with Neal. "You told me you were never coming back."

The other members of the group perked up to listen. He gave the question a moment's real thought.

"If I told you right now, you wouldn't believe me."

"Is that what you want from us? To believe you?" asked Carol.

"Technology doesn't require anyone's belief." The way he said the words held a subtle metallic aftertaste.

Carol turned and looked out her window. They were still above the tree line, all snow and ice.

Neal brought his hand to his beard and ran his fingers under his chin before he spoke.

"By the time in human history when I was born, so much of the basic source code of material reality had already been identified and proven. It was just laying around for me to pick up and read. Biochemistry. Genetics. The microchip. We were just handed them. Like Prometheus."

Neal had a soft-focus stare as he unscrewed the cap on a canteen and took a sip of water before passing it.

"We have walked through the most sophisticated labs on this planet," Neal said. "At least one of you has been with me for most of those tours. I've spoken to the greatest living minds on nearly every subject imaginable. Industrialized civilization and I have given each other what we have to offer and I'm far less impressed with it than it is with me."

Carol nodded slowly.

"Ok. What does the baby have to do with any of this? What are we doing smuggling a child? We don't transcend the law. We could all end up infamous. Penniless and locked away."

"That's the idea. Because we are high-profile and leading lives of privilege, we are above suspicion. Because we all have lives and loved ones that we know we would never see again, we can be trusted to keep my secrets."

"Now… our secrets," said Ang.

"The less I say right now the better. It's for your safety and security. Until we are all home."

Carol closed her eyes. She felt the Rover rapidly descending the mountain. They said nothing the entire rest of the day and that night Carol was dropped off at a small train station and handed an itinerary and first-class tickets on the train that night to New Delhi.

"Inherent in all structures lay Utopian ideals," Neal had once said in one of his lectures on Architecture as a manifestation of human belief. "We build things because we need to believe in the illusion of permanence. After all, there is no such thing as inside."

As she walked through the station, Carol could feel the underlying programming and code of civilization. The impermanent assumptions, constructs, and systems surrounding her and creating the illusion. A billion years of organic hardware development to create the human body and less than a million of software development to create the mind, all built atop the framework of a highly intelligent tribal primate.

New Delhi to Abu Dhabi. Abu Dhabi to Istanbul. A train from Istanbul to Amsterdam. With every hour that passed as she retraced the globe back toward her home and husband Arthur, Carol began to feel the still analog eastern world giving way to the first springtime buds of the coming twenty-first century's global networked surveillance state. Security cameras slowly began to appear in her conscious periphery. Paperwork and verification became more sophisticated. The practice of bribes, which granted access and passage in the wilder eastern parts of their journey, now would result in the direct opposite - incarceration and detainment.

Amsterdam to Heathrow. London to New York JFK. Carol thought about the baby as she handed over her passport to the dour man from US Customs. She already knew that someone in the group had successfully hacked the US passport database and added the child. She had seen the protocols running on Neal's computer.

Last chance to blow the lid off this thing, she thought. You could let the agent know right now. But then what?

"Welcome home," the customs agent said as he stamped and racked her passport and customs forms on his desk before handing them back to Carol. She smiled and said thank you. The agent grunted benignly, his hand already in the air waving forward the next person in line.

For her flight from New York into Bob Hope Burbank Airport, Carol ordered two bloody marys and slept until the plane landed and jolted her awake. She compartmentalized everything that had happened, something she was excellent at, and exited baggage claim stepping out into the radiant September California sun. It was so bright she closed her eyes for a moment and could only see the red blood inside her eyelids backlit by the warm light.

She reached for the sunglasses in her jacket pocket. Sunglasses are to Californians what scarves are to the French, she mused to herself. A small smile broke across her face. It had been so long since she had smiled the expression felt foreign. Jokes. Smiles. These were the pleasures of a civilian life in a stable democracy. She hailed a taxicab and put on her sunglasses with relish. She was deeply grateful to be home, and she allowed herself to begin shedding the journey like a snake from its skin.

Cabs!! she thought. God fucking bless taxi cabs.

Carol could hear the mariachi music playing inside the yellow cab before it pulled up. A short doughy man with a classic Mexican handlebar mustache and warm smile hopped out of the driver's seat to pop the trunk.

"Buenas Dias, Senora. Where are we headed this morning?"

"Buenas Dias," Carol said. "Dirijo a hogar."

He lifted her bags into the trunk of the cab and closed the lid.

"Home," he said. "The best destination of all I think."

He opened the back passenger door and Carol got in. He was an independent taxi driver who took immaculate care of his machine. The old caramel leather of the bench seat was soft and well cared for. She rolled down the window and let the breeze envelop her face as the taxi drove away from the airport.

For the first time in two months, the adrenaline in Carol's system was dropping. The muscle fibers in her body were beginning to relax. She took a deep breath. The air filling her lungs was full of the familiar particulates of an everyday life she had once taken completely for granted. The sun and leather and the kind old man conjured a memory of sitting on her grandfather's knee on the porch of the family farm back in North Carolina. She had been lucky enough to do that hundreds of times in her youth. Her grandfather was an excellent farmer. They usually talked about baseball or plants, but a specific moment bubbled to the top of Carol's composite of memories.

She had been about four years old, and that day her grandfather had a small wooden box next to his rocking chair on the porch overlooking the flourishing harvest. He'd called to her from across the yard where Carol had been examining the flowers. She walked to his side, and he lifted her up and brought her into the crook of his arm where she had fit so perfectly. She had snuggled down, her dirty bare feet hanging out over her grandfather's knee. She remembered him teasing her about growing potatoes between her toes, which would make her giggle uncontrollably. Clear as a bell Carol recalled the sound of her own childhood laugh. It was full of an innocence and joy she did not remember jettisoning. For the first time in her life, she was conscious that it had been replaced by a calculating survivalism.

"Lamb. Do you know what the word sacrifice means?" her grandfather said as he rubbed the short beard on his chin back and forth across the top of Carol's head and rocked them both while the breeze pushed the shadows of the clouds across the fields.

"Sacrifice fly," Carol had said.

"That's right! Goodness you're smart. What does it mean in base-ball to make a sacrifice play?"

"You do it so someone else on your team can get to the next base, but it means you're out."

"Yes darling. Exactly."

He reached for the box on the table.

"I want to tell you about some very special people. Wonderful people who had to make the sacrifice play when your Papaw was in the war, so that I could be here with you today. And I want you to know how grateful I am to be here and to know you because they didn't get to meet their grandchildren. In fact, some of them were never born. It's not a fun story, but I want you to know that under-neath… it was about love."

Carol remembered feeling the hot tears dripping onto the top of her head as the old man she loved cried silently before he began tell-ing her his story.

Carol still had that shadow box of medals. Arthur had hung them by their front door. Arthur had called it "a gesture toward the grand meditation of heroism and sacrifice." They were the last thing she saw each day before leaving the house. He was unusually poetic for a pilot and engineer.

The taxi came over the hill and down onto the Colorado Street bridge to Pasadena. It was the mental marker she always used to know she was five minutes from home. But instead of the usual sense of relief and comfort, a quick rush of fear and anxiety rippled through her body. It had been two months since Carol had been home. She was returning to her professorship, her husband, and the life she had worked so hard to have. But it was all in jeopardy now and suddenly the thought of going home filled her body with apprehension.

"Excuse me," Carol said to the driver who was softly humming along to the radio with what seemed like not a care in the world. "I know this is an odd request but could drop me off by the track around The Rose Bowl and take my bags to my home? It's been quite a while since I've been home, and I wanted to watch the sun set."

"It's no problemo Senora," he grinned as he handed her a business card without taking his eyes off the road. "I take your bags right to the door. You enjoy the sunset, and next time you need a ride, you call Bic-Tor Helado, eh?

"Bic-Tor Ice Cream," he said winking into the rearview mirror and laughing to himself for the one millionth time.

"It's very kind of you," Carol replied.

The taxi found a large pull off and came to a stop. Carol tipped the driver extravagantly and watched her bags head home. She found a bench high on the edge of the Arroyo and sat to watch the runners and mothers with prams circling the track around Rose Bowl stadium. She was like a soldier who had seen real combat, back home for the first time. The town around her seemed so miraculous and fragile as to be overwhelming. This construct she lived in, of freedom and self-determination, had sharp edges and boundaries she had never been aware of before. Rules. Systems. It was unevenly distributed. Taken from some and given to others. Lied about until a new collective delusion was called the truth.

Carol loved everything about the fields of science and technology. It was a world that shown her the depth and breadth of her own gifts and intellect, and it had led her to the institutions throughout her life ready to create space and amplification for her. The progress of science and preserved knowledge had been the positive through line of global humankind. It felt meritorious. A clear heritage of progress. Towards… a new age. By choosing to associate herself and her research with Neal's, her life had entered an orbit she now realized it may already be too late to escape from. The collective power of their technical research was already quietly having a major influence. If anyone learned Neal Walcott's lab team had abducted a child and smuggled her into the US, it would make international headlines and worse. She had been intrigued when Neal revealed his plans for a covert research lab hidden inside the practically unlimited budgets of a dozen research programs. He had sold her on the idea of a pure scientific prerogative with unlimited resources and no outside observation. But what the team had brought home threatened to go off like a bomb and Neal still had not explained why they had done it. Some of the greatest scientific minds on the planet had acted for Neal on blind faith and now they simply had to trust him. There was no other choice.

As the sun hid behind the foothills and the sky turned orange, Carol watched the evening arrive. The breeze picked up and brought a chill through the arroyo. The cold made her want to be near Arthur, and she put her shoes back on and started the walk home.

Home, she thought.

Carol was coming back to Arthur and her life a different person.

From their first date, Arthur Nyken had unwaveringly presented Carol with trust, safety, and adoration; and despite a core need in Carol for absolute freedom and self-sufficiency, she had fallen deeply in love. Throughout their courtship he had been neither jealous nor aloof. He adored her while being equally ambitious. He was in such high demand bouncing around NASA's flight tests and engineering teams from project to project, that it had earned him the call sign "Nomad." When he was in the air, he was a pilot who lived to push the envelope, and he had walked away from two crashes that would have killed pilots of lesser skill. The insights gleaned from the crashes had yielded significant technical breakthroughs. In fact, Carol had first met him only a few weeks after the second plane had malfunctioned.

With the sun setting deeper behind the hillside, the sky caught the same shade of purple as the evening she had met Arthur, and for a few minutes Carol reminisced about a time when her life had been much simpler.

It was 1986. Carol's first year on faculty at CalTech with some of the best mathematicians and scientists in the world. She shared the university's dreams of a world where everyone had a computer and they were all connected, and together they were designing and building that world - willing it into existence. The one thing Neal had been clear about to all interested parties was the one thing they were not going to be researching or building- weapons. No military involvement would be tolerated. Neal was especially hostile whenever someone from DARPA or the Pentagon came around, and that day Carol had returned to Neal Walcott's research lab from teaching her lecture class on Conceptual Information Architecture. From outside the lab Carol could hear Neal starting to raise his voice, and she came in to find seven men standing over a deeply annoyed Neal Walcott who sat at the small desk he kept on their laboratory floor.

His "No's" echoed through the mostly darkened lab where he worked during the day and left notes, encoded in his unique shorthand, for the work to be done that night by the lab associates and TAs. One of the benefits of being on faculty had been no longer having to work nights processing Neal's proofs and expounding mathematics. It was exhilarating to transcribe Neal's research, but those nights, filled with cigarette breaks, pizza and coffee were not healthy for Carol. She had done her time and made it to the other side. At twenty-four years old she was already at the center of the foundational computational mathematics research CalTech had invested so heavily in. The university believed that Neal would bring about a quantum leap in large scale data.

As Carol approached, Neal saw her. Clearly, he had had enough of whoever was standing around his desk.

"I'll tell you what gentlemen," Neal said. "If the Pentagon is simply bored hearing "no" from me, go ahead and ask Professor Almont. professor, these gentlemen are from JPL."

"What happened?" asked Carol Almont.

The man in the periphery leaning against the high research table spoke up. Immediately Carol could see his presence in the room was a calming force. He introduced himself as Lt. Colonel Arthur Nyken. He had a kind face and a soldier's posture. He was covered in bruises with his right arm in a sling, but he didn't have the effect of being injured.

It turned out that during a flying dynamics test the left pitch-axis thrust vectoring nozzle of the X-31 test bed aircraft Arthur was piloting malfunctioned, and plane and pilot were sent teakettling through the sky. Arthur had done everything he could to save the plane. But spinning at 10Gs he had to eject or lose consciousness, and two billion dollars had crashed into the Nevada desert.

"And so…" Neal interrupted, "they would like us to make the most dominant fighter jet in history… for them… because they can't seem to pull it off on their own. Do you have any interest in that?"

"I don't know anything about avionics," said Carol.

"Me neither!!" yelled Neal. "Or thrust. Or weapons systems. Or hostile theater analysis. But I'll tell you what gentlemen…. How about I drop my life's work, and Carol's life's work and the rest of the Cybernetics department so that we can go ahead and fix the problems with the thing that your team just finds too tough."

Carol watched a portly man wearing glasses winding up for his rebuttal.

"Settle down, Neal."

Neal stood up and turned to Carol.

"Prof. Almont, would you please tell these men and their nice pilot friend what we do here? They don't ever seem to want to hear it from me. Perhaps they'll finally be persuaded to fuck off forever if you explain."

"We're an information architecture lab focused on linked the human brain to computer systems."

"Great. Done. I'm going home."

Neal put his hands in his pockets and stopped next to the man who had told him to settle as he passed. He held his stare and whispered. "Odie, if you ever tell me how to behave again… I'll rip your head off."

Neal stood there, inches from the man who did nothing but stare back. Neal nodded with authority. He then walked to Carol and his demeanor completely changed. He softened and warmed and whispered to her.

"Your instinct is going to be to say 'no,' but I think you should say yes to him."

Carol was completely confused by the remark, but with that the lanky professor had crossed the lab and left without looking back.

The men from DARPA mumbled their defeated exits, and Carol turned to find the battered pilot standing in front of her. Most of the flight jocks she had met were adrenaline junkies with only three speeds - fast, faster, and fastest. It was a mentality that had never impressed Carol. But there was something steady and honest about Arthur from the first moment. On some primal frequency she felt calmed by him. He asked her to dinner at a little oyster bar just a few blocks away. And with Neal's words suddenly making sense, Carol decided to say yes.

It was the best date Carol had ever been on. The juxtaposition between Arthur Nyken's candidness, prowess, and his obviously gentle personal nature disarmed her.

"Every fighter pilot is different," Arthur said while pouring her another glass of prosecco from the chilled bottle on ice. The beaded sweat rolled down the neck of the bottle as the clear golden liquid fizzed into her glass, and Carol slurped another dressed oyster on the half shell. The shaved horseradish and mignonette swirled on her tongue with the sweet creamy meat of the mollusk. Carol felt her face blush.

"Pilots are a much more diverse species than we're given credit for. Personalities, backgrounds, and underlying skill sets. If you can pass every test the Navy throws at you, you can be a fighter pilot. Tall, short, fat, skinny, black, white. Really different types of people, but the Navy is looking for an intangible common denominator: Intelligence, physical, psychological, and ethical. After that, if you've passed, a certain general meritorious individual tends to be left that becomes the American fighter pilot. But the test pilot guys have something else that makes us a little crazier."

"That's quite a description. Sounds like you might have a death wish," Carol said.

"No. The reason I'm a test pilot, and a lot of other things, is that I have a life wish."

The sentiment made sense to Carol, and over the seven years they had been together Arthur had proven he truly meant it. The thing that made him a great pilot was the same thing that made him a good person- he was truly settled. When crisis struck, he was steady and calm. Arthur put his heart into everything he did, and it made him an exceptional life partner. He had never asked for anything more than her heart, but he had been clear with Carol that someday he wanted children, and she had promised him a family. There were quiet reservations in the back of Carol's mind, but she loved Arthur and decided the doubts would settle with time.

The memory concluded and left Carol's mind as she crossed the last wide boulevard of oak lined craftsman homes. Arthur's car was in the driveway of the tidy yellow bungalow. The sight of their cozy inviting house filled Carol with a palpable desire to abandon Walcott's lab and her professional ambitions and just live some long happy Yuppie life surrounded by celebrations and babies and Arthur. The life he had been building around her all along. In an instant Carol made her plan. She would not tell Arthur about the smuggled child, and she would tell Neal if he could promise the girl would be safe and unharmed, she would keep the secret, but she was retiring. Completely. To start a family.

Carol walked up the wide flower-lined path to the front door and pressed the familiar thumb latch. The door was unlocked, and her bags were just inside the vestibule under her grandfather's medals.

"Arthur...?"

"Welcome home," came his voice from somewhere in the back of the house. "I'm in the kitchen."

Carol could smell something cooking. She took another whiff as she walked to the back of the house. It was the distinct smell of sweet potatoes boiling. It seemed an odd welcome home dinner.

Carol walked into the kitchen. Arthur was at the stove with his back to her.

"Hi honey. What are you making?" Carol said.

"Baby food," he said.

Arthur turned around and there she was. Carol's stunned expression met the familiar dark almond eyes of Neal's child.

"Neal and Taeng adopted a child?" Arthur asked.

"I was as surprised to hear about it as I am to see her in our house," Carol heard herself say.

"Taeng Chairasit stopped by looking for you about the same time your luggage got dropped off. Neal's got the flu, and she asked us to watch her for a few days."

"Yes. She mentioned it to me a couple of days ago on the phone," Carol lied.

It was the first time she had ever lied to Arthur.

Arthur took a tiny spoonful of mashed sweet potato and blew on it.

"I need you to come into the den and tell me what's going on," Arthur said as he fed the little girl cradled in his arms.

Sitting in the den was the DARPA man Neal had threatened years ago at the lab. Across the room in Carol's grandfather's rocking chair was a young woman of about twenty in nursing scrubs.

Carol looked to Arthur.

"Odie Carmichael, this is Prof. Carol Nyken, my wife."

"Dr. Nyken," said the ever-rounding black man of about fifty.

"I remember you Mr. Carmichael," said Carol as she set her things down and walked into the living room.

"Honey, Odie has a consulting law firm now. He deals mostly with government contracts with experimental and emerging technology companies."

"I'd like the three of us to chat this evening Dr. Nyken," said Odie. "This is Samantha, my daughter." He gestured to the young woman in the rocker who smiled and said hello.

"She is a third-year nursing student and she's here to watch the child while I take you and Arthur to dinner. Nothing fancy. There's a little Mexican place just down the road and it's one of my favorites. I hope that all works for you?"

"I've known Odie a long time," Arthur said. "He represents a lot of tech developers and keeps the people and their proprietary IP safe…"

"And very well resourced," Odie interjected. "I also keep high level scientists safe and alive. And out of jail," he said with a genuine smile and knowing look. "I'd like you and Arthur to retain my legal services immediately; right this moment in this room, and then I will take you two to a place with the best steak fajitas you've ever put in your mouth, and we'll talk. If you hear me out and you don't think I can help you and the baby and even Prof. Walcott, then we'll call it a night, and I'll leave all of it alone. "

"Sure," Carol agreed.

The wind swirled around Carol as she watched the glowing red taillights of Odie's Mercedes 300 SEL from the passenger seat of Arthur's '62 Corvette. It had been his dream car ever since Alan Shepard was gifted one after becoming the first American in space. The official picture Shepard had taken with the car had been the north star of Arthur's early life. It exemplified everything Arthur aspired to become. It had hung in his bedroom and his locker from the time he was ten until he returned from his second tour on the aircraft carrier USS Enterprise and bought one with his active-duty bonus.

He'd had the car for almost twenty years now. He did all the work on it himself except for the paint and it was as Arthur liked to say with a little bit of rock n'roll in his voice a "pristine machine."

They pulled into the gravel parking lot of the simple brightly colored shack of a restaurant and soon they were deep in conversation and combination platters.

"… honestly, we don't know what Neal Walcott is doing," said Odie as he dipped a tortilla chip into the salsa on the table, salted it heavily and took a bite. "Since your team returned from the DATAEAST Conference all we know is what he's said publicly. He's starting a new company that he believes, in thirty years will make the personal computer and cell phones obsolescent technologies- Which is a wild thing to say into a microphone at all, let alone three decades ahead of time," Odie said before taking another bite, this time of a hot tortilla stuffed with fajita goodness. His table manners were more feral than Carol had expected. Odie noticed and adjusted. He took a sip of his margarita and wiped his mouth with his napkin.

"And now because Arthur clued us into the… potential criminal liability of Dr. Walcott and Dr. Chairasit's new child… you have a tremendous amount of leverage, Dr. Nyken. DARPA wants Neal Walcott's new company on its roster. Neal Walcott wants to keep his child. Which now puts you at the indispensable center of both. That makes you extremely valuable, Carol."

Odie loaded another warm tortilla with steak.

"It's time to start thinking about what you want it to say on your golden ticket, Professor Nyken."

4

It's All In The Mind/1991

"Give me a fulcrum and I will change the world."

—*Archimedes*

Pasadena California
August 26, 1991

The sound of Carol's shoes echoed as she walked through the structures and spaces held in the unique stillness of a university campus during summer vacation. During the semester, the corridors of the buildings were abuzz with the ephemera of familiar faces, pleasantries, and news of the day; but in the summer a teacher is alone, and the beautiful pantheon of education seemed just for her.

In the nine years Carol had known Neal Walcott, he had made a tremendous impact on her life, but she never felt like she actually knew the man. Back in the beginning of their association Neal was still teaching, still working with the design team directly. The small and intimate facilities were still on campus then. Carol was his PhD candidate in the beginning and every year since had gotten stranger by two percent. Carol had chosen CalTech because no one in the world knew more about cybernetic design than Professor Neal Walcott. And it was not just her career and education that Neal had shaped. She had met her husband Arthur because of him as well.

Carol started on the initial algorithmic design team before their theories had begun to fuse with the then nascent robotics lab. Although Neal had worked just two hundred feet from her, he had been perpetually occluded behind the hum of grad students, server farms and monitors. The first five had all trained directly under Neal. Carol's world had been five massive zero-dust dry erase boards and a rolling ladder she climbed seven days a week and reorganized the equations and theories to suit Neal's notes and latest thinking on a subject. Neal insisted on up-to-date boards. "I can see everything from across the room. Saves time. Saves attention. Directs group focus. Trains the personnel." She had stood on the ladder for two years taking dictation and staying late into the night reorganizing and rewriting the boards before she had been allowed to train her replacement, a brilliant young man on loan from the Air Force Academy named Ryu Murakami.

From the seat a top that ladder, Carol's entire life transformed. The lab techs were always in the room for the passionate discussions Neal would have with visiting luminaries and the CalTech faculty. She had been able to learn the state of global cybernetics in its totality and had gained her own deep insights into the future of blending organic human intelligence with robotics. Those years Carol had felt not only integral to the success of lab, but like she belonged. She had been high up on the ladder reorganizing the underlying Decision Support Systems when Neal came to the mathematical understanding that won him the Nobel Prize. She remembered the exact night he completed his proofs proving the concepts of knowledge degradation and disappearance as they apply to predictability in chaotic events. Knowledge decays constantly, being replaced by new knowledge. Truth was fixed but ever changing. Neal had called it "The Math of New Truth." Things quickly started to change after that. New Truth had proved to be a real breakthrough in Professor Walcott's research and within a few weeks Neal had a startlingly sound mathematical proof that free will does exist, but it is only about three percent of everything a person does in their life.

"To be able to make a choice is a precious finite resource," Neal had concluded.

This idea of mathematical structures inherent in "choice" became the foundation of Carol's PhD dissertation - she began to reframe "choice" as the human ability to augment reality. Her paper Choice and Decision Engines as it relates to the Augmentation of Dominant Realities was hailed as a breakthrough thesis and Neal saw to it Carol was brought on faculty at CalTech to continue her development of a mathematics centered around the malleability of the fabric of reality.

Neal and Carol's breakthrough mathematical proofs in the field of Chaos had almost single handedly banished concepts of randomness once again from science. They received global press attention, but an evolving deterministic reality was more than a lot of people could bear, and while the mathematical and scientific communities heralded the work, the cultural blowback had been significant. The professors had chosen not to respond or engage at all. After a scattering of protesters began periodically finding their way to the campus looking for publicity, Professor Walcott left the grounds of the university almost completely, spending most of his time on his ranch or hiking the ridge lines and trails of Angeles National Forest.

Their work, which Carol had one of twelve supportive authorship credits on, won Neal the Nobel Prize in mathematics. The professor did not have a phone and came to campus especially to hear from the committee. Carol had watched the professor celebrate the news with no more pomp or circumstance than sitting on a bench outside by himself before getting on his bicycle and leaving without a word to anyone. Neal skipped the Nobel ceremony and afterward the entire advanced mathematics department watched helplessly as he spiraled into what the university feared was a terrible depression that threatened to consume the scientist entirely. For four years after the prize, he produced nothing. No formulas. No theories. No practical technologies. He stopped lecturing or giving any input into the department's curriculum. Eventually Professor Walcott stopped coming to work entirely, and after a week of no shows and reports of a closed and locked front gate at the professor's ranch, Caltech had sent investigators to trespass onto the property and break into the house, if necessary, but Neal was nowhere to be found. The research team did; however, discover a new item in the lab. Among the millions of dollars of experimental computer hardware was the professor's unassuming oak wood desk, and on the desktop where there had been nothing, there was now a small statue of Galileo Galilei. Carol recognized it. The original was in the Loggiato at the Uffizi in Florence along with statues commemorating the other great learned men of Europe during the Renaissance. The statue depicted Galileo, arms crossed, protecting his scrolls of scientific insight from those that would destroy them or use their power to oppress humanity. And at the foot of the statue, cloaked beneath his robes, hides a globe of the planet Earth and the world's first book of astrophysics.

The tiny icon heralded the beginning of a more rebellious lab.

Eventually a call came into the university from The Esalen Institute in Big Sur. The professor had gone on a "walkabout" to meet Stanislov Grof and Gregory Bateson, both luminaries in the more subtle emerging sciences of consciousness and material reality. The professor was not to be contacted or disturbed and would not be corresponding with the university any further. CalTech never had any intention to take "no" for an answer and eventually the board of directors coerced Carol to pay a personal visit to the institute.

She still had such a clear memory of taking PCH 1 up the coast of Southern California on a misty Sunday morning about nine months after Neal's declarations. She had braced herself to be barked at by his intimidatingly tall and thin frame and told to leave him alone, turn around and go home. But that was not the man who came out to the front drive to greet her. Even from a hundred yards away Carol could instantly see a difference. Neal looked…. Great. Healthy and vibrant with a peace to him Carol had never seen. His entire aura had changed. He walked right up to Carol's driver side window and asked if she'd like to have lunch with him. He seemed transformed into a deeply present and sensitive person.

Somehow, he had heard she was coming and the staff had already set up tea service. Carol spent the afternoon with Grof, Bateson, and Neal; listening to them describe Neal's intense lurch towards what he kept calling "awareness," and bearing witness to the drastic changes in his nutritional and exercise regimes. He had taken up kundalini yoga and then ayurveda. Transcendental Meditation as taught by Maharishi Maheesh Yogi. Non-dualist Vedanta. And how it all dovetailed into Prof. Grof's work in the sciences of consciousness and something Bateson was pursuing called "warm data." But other than a lot of high-level conceptual discussion, Neal had offered no insight into how any of these intriguing inquiries related to cybernetics or technical computer science and as Carol left, Neal restated he had no plans to ever return to academia.

Carol had totally believed the professor when he said he was never returning to the university, and she told the administrators so. Then quietly one day in the spring semester of the following year, a grad student found a simple flyer posted to the community board in the Advanced Mathematics building that sparked a firestorm of curiosity far beyond the walls of the university. Neal Walcott had announced a lecture series on the campus of CalTech.

The first talks Neal gave were at odd hours in packed lecture halls or in the basement of the Advanced Mathematics building at the university. The topics were bold and sexy and far outside the scope of his previous work. The History of Debt. Cybernetic evolution. Genetic Design.

"Genetics are code. Does that mean people are code too?" Neal had asked his audience.

"You can do a lot of things with code. By definition it's highly malleable and does what it is programmed to do. Now, say you're one of the code writers of this reality-script. What would that source code look like? What does the terminal look like? What is the interface to operate the machine? Belief? Culture, religion, capitalism? What form would it take? If you take the overlays of physics and time, carbon based biological life, chemistry, instinct, indoctrination... morality, macro and micro tribalism, debt... you take all of that... and don't we basically see programming...? Where is free will for the individual? Probably locked away. Trapped within the promise of a self-actualized human species."

"Set the conditions for humanity's functions to be executed. The human machine downloads its programming through attaching an emotional response to stimuli. Fear, lack, the potential for resources, the potential for sex, violence, ostracization, excommunication, incarceration. These ARE the subliminal foundations of control. The question we now face is are they being programmed with malicious intent?"

"By my best estimate you, modern humankind, have 3% free will. Everything else is destiny, psychology, biology. Or..." he paused thoughtfully. "It is being imposed on you. Often through systems of control it's almost impossible to prove are there."

The lectures had seemed provocative in a mostly academic sense. The consensus among the attendees had been that Neal was demonstrating the power of dangerous questions and bringing them into the sandbox of a lecture series where he played both sides of a thorny nuanced scientific discussion. The man discussed wine and beauty and propaganda and revolution. Everyone hung on his every word like he was a prophet, and the energy of the events had always held a positive charge. But now in Carol's memory the scene held a different tone. Her recollection of the morning after Neal's final lecture was vivid. She could see the campus of CalTech awash in red paper. Printed on each was a quote.

"What is this global neo-liberal world order except a massive mining expedition that could only ever end in total destruction? And if that preposition is true, what happens the morning after the inevitable fall of Western Capitalism?"

— Prof. Neal Forrest Walcott, March 3, 1989

The question threatened and buzzed in Carol's face like an angry wasp.

"… the inevitable fall of Western Capitalism…"

Inevitable, Carol had thought at the time. Inevitable is about predicting the future. That word reveals belief and fatalism lurking inside Neal. What is the prerogative of an enlightened fatalist? The child, this new company we've been informed of all these scientists Neal's collecting. He's already executing a plan which begs the question- When did he formulate it? How long has he been orchestrating all this?

Someone in the audience had been recording the lectures without permission and a collection of recordings of the professor's speeches circulated around campus. The bootleg cassette tapes were an underground hit. All of this thrilled the administration who felt their multi-decade investment in the mercurial Neal Walcott was still justified and continuing to pay dividends. They approached Neal with a new contract and shortly there after, he was given a massive endowment to start a new research lab with his namesake

- Walcott Labs. Once he had the money, he was just as iconoclastic and unpredictable. The professor spent a fortune to lure expert scientists and leading mathematicians away from top institutions. They came from different fields of study, mostly medicine and biology, but Neal would give no indication to the university what he was pursuing while cutting deals that had CalTech paying Neal's team ten times their previous salaries. When the administration asked, he would just say he didn't know, and the more the school pushed, the further he retreated.

The first two hires were Dr. Taeng Chairasit, a high-profile universally respected neurosurgeon Neal had been quietly romantically involved with for some time, and Dr. Gregory Langstone, a much younger bio-informationist who had become disenchanted with his positions at University of Liverpool and Stanford, and had been convinced by Walcott Lab's ocean of money and prestige. Another eight months went by, and Neal announced two more personnel additions. Dr. Ang Zhao, a cybernetics and brain research professor from Arizona State, and Dr. Mikhael Shandalow, the radical geneticist (bordering on anarchist), fine artist and embryonic researcher who had just been fired from Brown University after the school had been put on notice that Dr. Shandalow was a "significant person of interest" in the investigation of sharply increasing rates of dwarfism in multiple American livestock pig populations. The Department of Justice prosecutors currently compiling research on the case had quietly put Brown on notice they were considering a terrorism charge which threatened to engulf the school in a conspiracy they wanted nothing to do with and immediately terminated Dr. Shandalow's employment. Neal, on the other hand, either didn't care about the investigation or was intrigued by it and submitted his untouchable hiring request at the hefty price tag of fifteen million dollars a year.

The president of CalTech openly fought Shandalow's hire, calling him "not just a provocatuer, but a true radical" and saying his "destructive sensibilities and theatrics had no place in the fields of genetics." The president had demanded an explanation from Prof. Walcott right there in the board room to which Neal had simply risen and walked out. As he did the president of CalTech had yelled after the professor saying that all they had gotten out of their billion-dollar lab investment was a roster as expensive as the Dodgers and what he dubbed Prof. Walcott's "Bohemian Rhapsody," a comment that irked Neal considerably.

Shortly after that, Neal announced a final public lecture. CalTech had tried to mend its relationship with Walcott and offered to make a prestige gala evening of it with him on stage at the concert hall, but the professor did not reply, and Facilities Management received a booking request for a small unremarkable classroom. The night of his lecture, the hall was so crammed with attendees everyone was sweating. The CalTech AV club had petitioned Prof. Walcott to be allowed to have cameras and microphones to record the lecture and for it to be broadcast live on Pasadena's KPAS UHF station. He had agreed. The line to get into the event stretched hopelessly out and around the building. Large speakers and some small television carts were brought out onto the quad and the people who had failed to get into the building gathered around them like campfires.

The next morning someone had printed thousands of red paper flyers printed with Prof. Walcott's last public remarks and scattered them across the university. When the Santa Ana winds picked up that morning, Prof. Walcott's words were unavoidable as the flyers blew all over campus. Many suspected the mess was by design and groused about the gesture being non-ecologically sound and deeply disrespectful to the custodial crews that were going to be picking it all up.

"The problems of this and the coming century are simple stupid problems focused on soil, food, water, and health. Why are they all such massive failures?"

A few weeks later Neal stopped by the lab on campus. He spoke for a few moments to the techs before he sought Carol out and asked her to attend a series of private talks he was going to give. Carol had said yes but the later lectures didn't happen for a year, given to a group of just six at the professor's farm above the Pasadena Arroyo where he lived alone and had built every structure on the fifteen acres.

The ritual each time was the same.

As the sun went down over the foothills the few attendees would slowly begin arriving on Neal's ranch and making their way to his vegetable garden where they would help harvest their meal from the rich black soil. The evenings always started with innocuous patter, a discussion of the conversation between Buckminster Fuller and Maharishi or the poly-rhythmic musical structures of Asia, but inevitably the conversation would begin to tilt towards graver topics, burning and smoking like a cigar while Neal only listened. Operation Desert Storm. The impacts of failures and corruptions of the allied world order after World War 2. The global programming and staging of war theater. Global ethno-facism's uncomfortable ties to global capitalism.

It always reminded Carol of the great schools of philosophy in the ancient world, how at dusk Neal Walcott would begin stacking seasoned dry wood for a hearth in the large fire pit beside the wooden tables. The night would begin to take over the sky as they dined.

Neal made beautiful fires.

The group talked about everything including themselves, and over time Carol had learned a great deal more about the other attendees than she knew about Neal. They all seemed to have shades of true brilliance, cynicism and skepticism mixed with technology, travel, and government.

The gifted surgeon Taeng Chairasit had a far eastern appearance and spoke many languages, but she had been raised in Southern California after her father took their family and fled from Bhurma to Cuba where Taeng was born. Nine months later, her father had bought a dilapidated gas station in the United States, and they all immigrated to Bakersfield California. The station was on a long quiet stretch of road that got busy about four hours a day with farmers and ag-tech employees making their commutes. There was a cottage at the back of the property, a one stall auto repair garage next to a small cashiers' window, and enough space to build something else.

The cottage was in worse shape than her father had thought, and the family spent their first Christmas sleeping in the auto-garage. Her parents were both wizards with their hands. Most of Taeng's earliest memories were of watching her parents build things together and listening to the shorthand Bhurmese slang they chatted to each other in while they assembled or disassembled some project together.

First, they fixed the signage, installed new pumps, repaved the drive and painted the shop. Business picked up. Her dad designed a logo, had uniforms for the station attendants made, and started handing out matches and gum with the brand emblazoned across it. It all struck a chord with the community and the oddly named Chair Gasoline was born. Eventually Taeng's parents contracted to have a collection of cottages around a central courtyard built on the property and over the next thirty years they paid for and facilitated the immigration of dozens of relatives from all over the world. Taeng had become her father's English interpreter at about eight years old, and her family diaspora had required her to travel with him extensively. Seeing firsthand how corrupt the world order is at such an early age had made a cynical impact on Taeng that had stayed with her. She had a foul mouth when she drank, which was just bordering on too often. She liked to swear in English and tell dirty jokes. When she spoke, Taeng liked to talk with her hands and stare above as if there was some enormous white board with her thoughts scrawled across it. Carol could hear her disillusionment with the American culture and political system.

Prof. Ang Zhao spoke little English and during conversations Taeng would echo the gist in Cantonese to include the petite fierce woman who would reply, and Taeng would tell the group in English. Carol had learned that for six years as a grad student in the halls of Arizona State, she had defined the mathematics of bipedal musculo-skeletal motion which earned her a doctorate and a professorship. The next great summit of her research came within her first decade on the research faculty designing and engineering robotic replicas of the individual parts and systems of the human body, and interpreting the firing patterns of the brain resulting in kinetic movement and writing an interface program to simulate the patterns between a computer and the synthetic muscles. When she had defected from Arizona State she was on the brink of transforming the entire field of both human cybernetic prosthetics and autonomous humanoid robotics.

Although the man tried to keep a fairly low profile, Carol had heard of Dr. Gregory Langstone when he had popped up on the international scientific community's radar for being dragged in front of the WHO International Genetic Data Commission after he helped two UK high school students create a frog cloning lab in their parent's garage using little more than excellent protocols, razorblades, and microscopes. Eventually he was drafted onto what would become the Human Genome Project where he first met Neal Walcott. He had bounced from U of Liverpool to Stanford before landing at Walcott Labs. Carol had never heard him espouse any personal opinion or belief. He was affable and almost obsessive in the way he pursued all manner of adventure activities- sky diving, white water rafting, spelunking, hang gliding. Eventually he had become the western head of the U.S. Orienteering Association, designing and devising competition courses across the pacific coast.

Doctor Shandalow was fifteen years younger than any of the other scientists in Neal's orbit. He was thin and dark, with deep set black eyes and a thick Russian accent. When they would gather in the garden Shandalow would say little and help less, preferring to sit on the side steps of the ranch house smoking cigarettes and watching the sky slowly darken.

The person Carol knew the least about was the protean Nancy Yarpas, an older woman with short white hair who was obviously a horticulturist of rare talents and insights bordering on a spiritual gift. It was clear she had walked away from modern existence. Carol got the impression the woman either had a formal Phd or at some point had read the full contents of the American public libraries. She had the eyes of a wild thing and made odd genuine noises while she listened but said little except to correct the group's poor technique as they gardened.

After dinner they would pour a second glass of water, the only beverage Neal had ever served and join the professor in the makeshift amphitheater. But the night a year ago when he had finally revealed his conclusions had been something different. Carol had been the first to arrive only to find the garden gate closed and Neal already building a hearth. He had three bottles of wine, a decanter, and six exquisite crystal glasses sitting on a rough old tablecloth.

"What's with the wine Neal?" she said as she picked up a bottle.

It had a rough woodblock print of a bird and in calligraphic letters it read Screaming Eagle 1982. When she approached Neal, he turned. His expression was blank, but his eyes were so clear the color of his irises had seemed to change from his usually green to a deep blue and yellow.

"Are we celebrating something?" Carol asked.

"Could you decant two of the bottles please… and just keep everyone quiet while they arrive."

"Of course," Carol said.

She did as he had asked and quietly corralled the others as they arrived. Carol poured the first glasses while Neal lit the hearth and tended it until dusk while everyone sat watching the intense colors of the sunset wrap the arroyo.

"About four years ago," Neal began, "After intense personal deliberation, I opened my heart and mind to the new truths. Evolving truths. It has changed my personally held views and beliefs… drastically. And privately, I began to act."

The group had no idea what he was talking about. But every single one of them was listening intently knowing that what Neal chose to focus on mattered to humanity. He was a once in a century intellect, who seemed destined to bend history. Carol had never seen a man who could wield reality like Neal Walcott. It was otherworldly how gracefully and dynamically the man could evolve, and the ferocity and speed with which he could build working technologies.

"After the… prize," Neal said, "DARPA offered me a billion-dollar lab. In my own office. It… it… stank. Horribly. It was visceral. I could smell it. And before I could suppress it, I threw up. There in my office.

I'm not completely without social grace, and I look up to apologize to these two men from DARPA and their faces didn't register a thing. Just two puppet people propped up, ready to pump all the money in the world at me, whether I wanted it or not. They were only offering me the illusion of choice because the military industrial complex is coming for my work, your work, and to swallow the rest of science too. I don't think anyone anywhere is going to stop it. I find the consequences of this… new truth… unbearable."

It was a serious thing for Neal to say. He took a long slow breath. There was an electricity in the atmosphere that night that made Carol's heart race.

"Through some eras of human history, the scientists shaping our reality chose to keep transformational technological breakthroughs secret. I've decided we are at the dawning of one of those eras, the last one in fact, and I want to know if you agree with me."

He took a long gaze into the roaring fire.

"Do we live in a system of benign neglect? Or a system with actual malicious intent? What does science serve? Who do we serve? And what happens if we fail to protect Science?"

Neal tended to the hearth and took a first sip of his wine. It was the most complex thing he had ever tasted.

"I started something, years ago, that I've decided I'm not going to share with them. Ever. In fact, … I don't want them to even know it exists. Which is why I can't tell any of you what we'd be working on yet, but I can't do this alone. There is a choice facing me. An unavoidable choice with the gravity of a black hole that I must make, and I searched the world for the right people to help me."

The thoughtful group sat in silence.

"Please go home tonight and consider our era in the larger context of human history and the history of life on this planet. Consider the technology that we know will arrive in the next thirty to fifty years, and where the power and the money in this world are."

It all seemed like several lifetimes ago.

Carol had become acutely aware of how the expedition with the Walcott Labs team had affected her. Since then, she had lost almost twenty pounds, and her clothes hung loose on her svelte frame. Her sense of taste had changed. Back in the U.S. the food had all been too sweet or too salty. She was sure she could taste the industrialized processes themselves. Alcohol was too astringent. Coffee too acrid. Red meat smelt and tasted only of the iron saturating the bloody flesh. And even when she changed course and collected fresh vegetables and whole grain wild-yeasted sourdough bread from the Pasadena farmers market just south of her house, and the vitamin rich food tasted sweet and nourishing, even then, she still felt a new resentment toward her body being tied to these biological cycles and drives. Eat, sleep, defecate, procreate, exercise, think. Self perpetuation and maintenance. Death. But the weight of that existential machinery dissipated when she went home each evening. At home, she was happy.

The abducted girl had stayed at the Nyken's house for almost four weeks. The first few nights, Carol and Arthur had been on high alert, nervous they were only moments from arrest and infamy. But there had been no knocks at the door. No authorities. And eventually they had concluded that the Walcott group had indeed successfully smuggled the girl across the world without detection and at some point, soon would make their plan for the child known. Whether from fatigue or not she couldn't tell, but eventually Carol relaxed and began to prepare for the fall semester while tending to the small, sweet child with the constant help of Arthur. All this clandestine childcare had been assisted by the time difference between Western Asia and the US Pacific Coast. The girl was already pre-programmed to sleep during the day and be up at night. It wreaked havoc with Carol and Arthur's circadian rhythms. It was obvious the girl possessed a highly intelligent mind, awaiting her physical development. The Nykens could tell she had also never encountered the modern world. She had never seen a screen of any kind. Never tasted sugar. Never heard recorded music or artificial sounds. She was a true tabla rasa, as if she had been dropped from nothingness with all the prized adaptive human faculties and none of the anchors. She beamed with anonymous human potential.

Three weeks into caregiving, the circuit breaker for the house blew out for inexplicable reasons during a slight heat wave, and with the power off, Carol opened the windows throughout the bungalow. While they waited a few days for the repairs, candlelight and a constant subtle breeze filled their world with calm and tranquility as the couple cooked everything in danger of spoiling from their refrigerator, hand pureed all their fruits and vegetables to make baby food, and played with the little girl on the redwood floor. The child's focus was uncanny. As Carol and Arthur performed the tasks of daily life, the little being would watch intently. If it was something novel to her, she would lock in with an unblinking stare. Both Carol and Arthur swore they had actually felt her drawing the information and experience toward herself to absorb it, as if her curiosity contained some kind of psychic undertow.

The secret and circumstances of the child made her existence a singular experience. For Carol, there had been no pain and no pregnancy. It meant no doctors or cooing acquaintances, and no governmental or institutional contact. Inside this artificial construct Carol began feeling a blooming completeness to her life. She was conscious of a growing paradoxical vulnerability making her weaker and magnitudes stronger at the same time. This life happening in secret was a surprise attack on Carol's guarded heart. She watched the joy radiating from Arthur as he played with the child. Even though Carol knew intellectually the entire situation was temporary, she allowed herself to let in a deep sense of contentment, watching over the tiny sleeping being totally submerged in an ocean of soft natural blankets they had curled and fluffed into a nest for the baby. The Nykens had fallen in love with the child. She was miraculous.

The next morning Carol heard unfamiliar tires pulling into the driveway and looked through the expansive front picture window to see Nancy Yarpas, the feral horticulturist from Neal's ranch, and Dr. Taeng Chairasit stepping out of a red minivan. Carol's first instinct was to take the girl out the back, but she knew it would be futile. There was a firm knock at the front door. When Carol answered she was greeted with no pleasantries.

"I'm sorry we weren't able to be in contact," Taeng said. "There were complications with the preparations being made. We couldn't risk exposure. I know you understand."

Carol's eyes grew wide with indignation. "I'm far from under-standing all this."

"We are ready to receive the child," Taeng said flatly, ignoring the snipe. "We need you and the child to come with us as soon as you can be ready. Walcott Labs new corporate campus is operational. Your understanding is there waiting for you."

Carol told the two stone faced women the girl was sleeping and to give her a few minutes. She ascended the stairs into the master bedroom where the child was still nestled happily in the center of the sprawling bed like she had been every night since her arrival into their home. Carol felt a tremendous double bind of wanting to keep the child and knowing it was impossible. She took a quick shower. In her closet she found that Arthur had cleaned, pressed, and hung her laundry before he had left for JPL that morning. Carol put on fresh clothes, packed a day bag with food and diapers, and left Arthur a note on the counter that she would see him tonight. She swaddled the still sleeping baby and came downstairs. The two women hadn't moved from the foyer. They said nothing and opened the front door into the bright morning sunlight. Taeng popped the handle to the side door of the van and slid it open making sure Carol and the baby were safely buckled before closing it. Carol's thoughts were a tempest as they backed out the driveway and her happy yellow house receded.

Why would such a prominent scientific mind do something like this? Neal was at the pinnacle of every aspect of modern life. When he began this new journey of considering machine learning's connection to objective truth, ecology, and the human species' ultimate destiny he seemed full of curiosity and life. His dower countenance had evaporated like the pooled rain in the humid jungles they had traversed together. Everything they had each earned over the last two decades was in jeopardy because of this secret plan. What could be important enough to jeopardize all of this? Carol felt betrayed, but at the same time she acknowledged to herself that she had chosen to say yes to Neal's plans because she had trusted his judgment. She had allowed herself to become involved because she believed that Neal held some grand philosopher's stone to mankind's future.

Carol hadn't spoken to Neal since the abduction. Not once. All they were told was to sit tight, return to their normal lives, and await instructions which would arrive before the Fall. Carol had been watching the calendar. There were only a few days left of summer before the university would ramp up for fall semester, and she hadn't heard a whisper of what was coming next. Carol guessed the girl had been placed with her and Arthur initially because it was less suspicious. The world of academia was too small, and Neal Walcott was too high-profile.

"Please roll down the windows. I need some fresh air," Carol said trying to hide her distress.

Nancy rolled down the windows from the front passenger seat and a fragrant air billowed into the van. Carol let the unusually chilly breeze enter her nostrils and fill her lungs to calm her slight nausea. The wind smelled of roses, rosemary, and palm. The scent was something she had never been conscious of until she came home from the expedition, and now all of Pasadena smelled of this perfumed garden. She knew it had always been there, but she had been unaware. This new awareness of aromatics also had the converse effect of making the noxious olfactory elements more offending. She smelled the petroleum in the engine and the tires and the road all around her combusting and rotting in the sun, crowding the air.

Carol instinctively checked the tiny knit cap of the girl wrapped like a happy little burrito in her arms. They drove out into the base of the foothills and past the family ranches scattered into the quiet crescent. Carol looked out her window and down into the thousands of palm trees living in the Los Angeles valley. The misty pastel view sparked the memory of something Neal had once said to her.

Humanity is a momentary, chaotic, and transient species that is either ending or just beginning. When we're inside our civilization… living it… it seems so durable. Some trick of the mind makes it truly feel like providence. But that providence is an illusion - always. Everything we create is to subvert the true nature of our existence.

After all, there is no such thing as inside. It's all in the mind.

When Neal Walcott had forged Carol's academic career with his golden tenured and global foundation-endowed hand, the offer that changed her life had been a flippant, "There are six spots. Five are taken. And I don't particularly like any of the other candidates." After those short uninspired utterances Carol became magnetized to millions of dollars in grant money and access to every info architecture and cybernetics research lab in the world. Neal had fundamentally altered the trajectory of her life, and more than the money or accolade, the research was finally paying off. The proofs of how digital data and intelligence could be blended were going to be the bedrock A.I. to organic intelligence structural theory. Cybernetic science was continuing the augmentation of the human species. It will create a profound new harmony between humanity and its technology. That plan had all made such beautiful sense to her, and now it was filled with paradoxes and contradictions. Once she was back in her life, she hadn't been able to shake the nagging fragile realities of the institutions of civilization. She had also concluded that she had been anemic in utilizing her position at CalTech. It was a tremendous platform. She could affect real change. Lend her voice to solving mankind's problems. She could build upon their lab's tremendous progress. The infrastructure and technology would arrive early in her lifetime to organize and choreograph human operations on Earth. It could lift billions of people out of abject poverty all over the world. And all this potential was in tremendous jeopardy because of Neal and a darling child.

Her head began to swim as she thought about how far her instinctual attraction to raw scientific power had taken her. No one had coerced or forced her to do any of this. She had entertained offers from a dozen top universities' advanced math labs, but she had chosen CalTech because of Neal, precisely because he was willing to cross lines others wouldn't. Was any of this that much of a departure? He was basically still who he had always been. A true radical pioneer.

The van pulled down a long unpaved road and stopped in front of a twelve-foot perimeter fence. Carol was surprised to discover that she knew where they were headed. Out in the middle of an expansive field of grass the immense shell of an old airplane manufacturing hanger blocked the rising sun. CalTech had purchased the facility for ballistics testing originally, but nothing had ever come of the land. All the boards and directors had been out to tour this place five or six times, but nobody had ever come up with a use worth the investment. Neal had used it a couple of times over the years on projects Carol didn't have anything to do with, but it wasn't the clandestine location she was expecting. CalTech would obviously be aware they were all here, which meant DARPA and the Pentagon knew too. Taeng handed Nancy a lanyard which Nancy swiped, and they drove onto the property. The road was in terrible shape. The van bounced and jostled as they drove across the long grass breaking through the vast tarmac in front of the building. A few specks in front of the immense structure became five or six other cars. The whole thing seemed overly casual.

Nancy parked next to the other vehicles, and exited they van. Carol followed Nancy and Taeng up to the building with the sleeping girl in her arms. Taeng swiped her lanyard with the dull concentration of routine.

I'm last to be brought here, Carol thought.

"How long has the team been coming here?" Carol asked.

"Neal should be the one to tell you about everything," Taeng answered as they entered the building.

The front section of the building had been partitioned into an unassuming makeshift reception and offices. There were no demarcations of any kind other than a sign printed on reamed printer paper pinned to the cheap partition that read:

"Welcome to ReGenOS. Make yourself… at home."

"ReGenOS," Carol asked. "Is that the new research corporation?"

"Yes," Taeng replied. "One of the engineers put the slogan up as a joke, but a few of us think we should consider using it."

"What are the core competencies?"

Carol could see Teang considered brushing her off but then recalculated for some reason and answered the question.

"We'll we're still getting our sea legs, but I'd say, at least for the foreseeable future, we're focused mostly on genetic sequencing, surgical instrument design, and the data associated with the brain."

Carol decided to press.

"How many people are working here?" she asked.

"At this facility, all together about forty. But we're outsourcing to other firms all over the world. This is the new public facing side of Neal's research, but his name is not official on it anywhere and the programs are compartmentalized so none of the teams have access to all the information except Neal's team. The black box project team, which you would be a part of Carol, that's significantly smaller. It's just Dr. Langstone, Dr. Zhao, Dr. Shandalow, and myself. But even then, none of us knows everything that we're doing… except Neal. This way please."

Carol was suspicious of Taeng being so compliant.

Nancy walked to a side door and turned a simple levered handle. Once past the nondescript entrance, the rest of the facility was a sprawling labyrinth. They loaded onto a small electric cart and began briskly down the long wide hall and turned the corner. The next corridor had huge bay windows down the left wall. As they drove past, on the other side of the thick safety glass Carol recognized a large decontamination booth and clean room filled with zero dust clothing, gloves, and helmets where several technicians were preparing to enter the inner, much larger, chamber. The tram zoomed down the hall until

Carol could see what was in the second room- an expansive space filled with rows of black glass cabinets that stood out to Carol as if they were made of solid gold— they were a set of networked Paragon machines. In the world of computer science at Caltech, The Paragon was famous. The parallel supercomputer Intel had built at Caltech was about to be named fastest supercomputer in the world. They each ran more than two thousand Intel i860 processors and were at least six million dollars a piece.

There must be two hundred million dollars worth of computational equipment in that room, thought Carol.

The tram continued past the next partition where there was a second large lab. It looked brand new, as if no one had entered yet. Dozens of large steel safety cabinets lined the walls. There was a row of protective suits, but not the clean suits for working with microchips and computer systems. These were hazmat suits of some kind. There were centrifuges and incubators that were easy enough to recognize, but she couldn't identify all the equipment. Some kind of specialized microscopes and a few pieces that were completely foreign to her. Overall, it looked like a molecular biology lab. Between the paragon network and this, the facility seemed poised to become some kind of grand biological data processing operation, but Carol had only gotten a flashing glance as the tram continued along and stopped in front of the final door which read NEUROPOD 1. Taeng exited the cart, walked to the security lock, and swiped her lanyard. The light went green.

"Neal's running a few minutes behind his schedule today," said Dr. Chairasit. "We're still getting this place on its feet, but he will meet you inside shortly."

"Why all the way in here? What difference does it make? What's inside?" Carol asked, holding the child tightly.

"It will be easier to show you than to describe. Please Carol. He'll only be another minute, I promise."

Carol stepped off the tram and walked past Taeng into the room. The door closed behind her. Inside, Carol and the baby were surrounded by the specialized equipment of a large operating room. There were four patient operating tables, each the focus of their own smaller dedicated space - demarcated, color-coded, and numbered. Each space had duplicate equipment and then certain unique instruments tailored to the specific station's focus. All four of the tables were still wrapped in the sterilized vacuform coverings they had been shipped in. Carol crossed the room. Neal had added an element to his research Carol hadn't anticipated- medicine.

A complex set of automated arms kept several muti-lensed cameras elevated high over the table. Massive domed surgical lights all pointed to the Mayfield vice clamp at the head position of the operating table. About twenty feet away on the periphery of the room was a wide metal research counter covered in equipment and monitors. Banks of smaller screens and diagnostic equipment were on three portable workstations on casters.

Carol heard a soft beep at the door and the long frame of Neal Walcott entered.

"Carol," he said with what registered to her as genuine human empathy.

He crossed the room with the same "hurried by time itself" stride he'd always had, graceful for such a lanky man.

"Because the girl has been with you, we've been unable to include you in these preparations the last few weeks, but I want to say thank you personally. For everything you've done, and for what you've helped me accomplish. I don't think any of this would have survived… without you. So, thank you."

Carol didn't know what to make of Neal's comments. There was something a little stilted in his speech like he was having a bit of trouble forming the words. Whatever righteous spin Neal was trying to put on it now, in the eyes of dozens of international law enforcement bodies they were nothing better than human traffickers.

"Tell me why we've smuggled this child around the world? We've committed multiple crimes. How does all this fit together?" Carol asked.

"I'm… not im-impressed by your new routine as my scientific and moral wet blanket, Professor Nyken. I find it… dull, and I never used to find you so dull," Neal snapped back with an acid tongue. Carol could see he was genuinely angry and that she had begun this meeting with a closed mind. She had not taken him seriously which was a mistake, but just as quickly as he had been overtaken by indignation it evaporated away. Neal composed himself and brought the rolling chair next to the operating table in front of Carol and the baby. He spoke with a relaxed soft voice.

"Do you think I did these… things… flippantly? That I didn't under-stand… the gravity of what I had pulled everyone into?"

"I'm sure of one thing Neal," Carol said adjusting her tone. "That you didn't do any of this without a tremendous amount of consideration and prep… but you have created a series of events here with an inescapable gravity to them. I can feel my life being pulled into it. All our lives. And you still haven't told me why. What are we all doing here? What are you doing here?"

"Alright," he said as his body and face relaxed in the chair, and he leaned back against the rolling steel medical cabinets just behind him. "The practical function of ReGenOS is to develop the patents and proprietary manufacturing infrastructure to merge genetics and data processing with human performance mind, body, and any other more subtle forms that may emerge outside the current definitions of self. The development of the intellectual property alone is enough to fund the project for several decades but eventually we will be the company that brings cybernetic implants to the public."

"You sound sure," Carol said.

"Oh, I'm certain of it," said Neal with clairvoyant resolve.

"Where does the genetics component fit in?" Carol inquired with genuine interest.

"Cybernetics is only a bridge to the real quantum genetic technology breakthroughs that will arrive in our lifetimes. As soon as there is a social advantage, cybernetic implants will become as prevalent as cell phones. The first time the world sees someone who couldn't play the piano ten minutes ago playing Rachmaninoff's Prelude in G minor because they have a brain implant, billions of people will get them. But even that is an era of tech ReGenOS we will also make obsolete."

"How?" Carol inquired.

"Well," Neal said pensively as he ran his fingers through his short tidy beard. "In the course of my research I've come… to the… conclusion that humanity is fundamentally maladapted to cybernetics at a genetic level. We can make powerful implants, but humanity needs to be debugged at an evolutionary level to take the next step."

"What next step?" Carol asked.

"Humanity now possesses technology that can selectively reprogram not just the genes of organisms, but the very molecules that make up the genetic information," Neal mused. "We are making life from non-life every day in this new era. But can complex artificial life exist, reproduce, and evolve on its own? We don't know yet. If so, is it possible for this synthetic life to achieve true consciousness? These are still unanswered questions."

Carol thought about what Neal was driving at.

"The most bleeding edge synthetic biological experiments are only capable of producing bacteria and microbes," Carol replied. "The science you're talking about will take fifty years or more, and that's if it ever materializes at all."

He took a moment.

"What?" Carol was having difficulty hiding her frustration, but Neal seemed not to notice.

"In order to perpetuate our species," Neal postulated, "We would need to stabilize on this planet, and then colonize and terraform the entire solar system. We need to become a unified cybernetic and artificially enhanced humanity journeying into deep space. Do you think it's likely the current human race makes it that far before committing global Hari Kari?"

"No," Carol admitted.

"The only chance for the long-term survival of the human genome is rapid artificial evolution. We must become something else in our lifetime, or we will go extinct. I have not given up on us, Carol. But we are locked, and the world as we know it, is our tomb."

Neal brushed the crown of the sleeping child's head, and his voice contracted to a whisper.

"Try to see this moment in human history more clearly. Organic biology is already over. For the first time on this planet our species has technology that puts us out in front of natural evolution, redesigning the genetic code of the natural world has already begun. Humanity has no reverence for the natural world in the face of such power. Absolutely none. There is no going back. It's inevitable and it will reinvent everything. We see every day where our species drives this planet. The force of our knowledge is too great, and technology is too widely distributed. We are going over the waterfall and the species will take full control over its own genetic manufacturing."

Carol changed her tactic. "I'm sure you're right, Neal," she said after some thought. "Tell me about the company. What exactly is ReGenOS designed to do about all of this?"

"We are recoding nature's operating system," he said bluntly. "Now, that alone is not terribly remarkable. There are labs all over making that their business, and synthetic life is already here on this planet, but as you said it is microbial." He paused. "Except here where we are light years ahead of the rest of the industry."

"Ahead of the industry by how much?"

"You already know by how much," Neal said warmly as he looked down at the little girl.

"You engineered her? Why?" Carol asked.

"All babies are engineered. We just had more control."

Carol followed Neal's gaze as he examined the room. It was a surprisingly makeshift and ad-hoc production. A real experiment. All hand built and special-designed equipment. Custom software solutions and proprietary tech. Ready to begin.

"Genomic engineering is going to become far more common, less expensive, and a great deal more radical," Neal said soberly as he looked around the room. "There's not a lab in the world within multiple major breakthroughs of what we're doing because they either lack the expertise, the money, the machinery, or the clearances under international law. We're the only group with all four. Most teams don't even have two."

"You're still performing illegal experiments," Carol countered.

"Do you believe they'd do it now if they could?" he asked.

Carol answered honestly. "Yes."

Carol understood. She settled her thoughts before she spoke.

"Once you knew how far out ahead of the rest of the global genetics field you and Taeng were, you engineered her in the east where you knew it was possible to hide what you were doing."

"Yes," Neal nodded. "In the West we could hide behind an ocean of money and the prestige and tenure of the institutions. We had dozens of companies that didn't know what they were working on," he said as he pulled a Polaroid picture from his shirt pocket and handed it to Carol. The image on the plastic sheet was faded and overexposed. Carol first thought she saw an image of flowers wrapped to take home and put in some water. But in a moment the correct interpretation, that of a tiny baby came through. Her umbilical cord still attached and fallen out the bottom of the cloth she had been wrapped in. Scrawled in thin blue ink was the date in Chinese.

"There was a surrogate mother," Neal offered. "She thought she was carrying for a Chinese couple having trouble conceiving. She was paid well, had the baby in an excellent black-market hospital in Mongolia; Taeng and I were both there, we delivered the baby, and the woman never had any idea of our plans."

"She's actually your daughter?"

"Yes," he said. "She's not a clone, or some artificial organism. She's a regular human baby that's been engineered to have advantages and aptitudes that make her healthier, stronger, even kinder, and more empathetic. And not just an emotional empath, she's an electrical empath, the first ever."

"What does that mean?" Carol asked.

"She has a special adaptation that allows her to interface with complex raw electrical signals through touch alone. With training, it should allow her to interface directly with digital data sets. Full comprehension and coherence for input and output are possible. She's miraculous, but she's only the first human with the natural potential for a digital consciousness. After her will come millions of others like her, and when they arrive, humanity becomes something else entirely."

"Which could make her..." said Carol finally understanding how the child fit in.

Neal smiled.

"What if the Singularity wasn't some far off computer with an artificial intelligence that achieved consciousness? What if instead, human consciousness achieved artificial intelligence?"

"That was your breakthrough concept, wasn't it?" Carol asked. "The first powerful artificial intelligence, the first self aware computer, could be human."

"Yes."

"She couldn't have been your first attempt. How many experimental embryos didn't survive?"

"Sixty-three," Neal said casually. "But there were hundreds born. She was the only one that showed any aptitude at all. We don't have the control to engineer a single child yet. But we were able to increase the odds to the point that one with abilities was almost sure to be born. We monitored hundreds of fetuses."

"How could you keep that many pregnancies secret?"

"Most of them were in remote and tribal lands. Places without medicine. It was the only way to keep the project clandestine."

"How many women died?"

"Zero," he said with more than slight indignity. "They all knew the risks. The surrogates all survived their miscarriages."

"All the other women miscarried?" Carol asked.

"Yes," he replied. "Once we knew a fetus lacked the adaptations we were seeking, the pregnancy was terminated. It was a serious choice. The world is a serious place. None of those women will ever have to worry about money again."

"You intentionally placed the girl in the orphanage?"

"She had to be a total secret until she was old enough and strong enough to transport. While she was in their care the monks sensed something special in her and the way that she arrived. They believed this child was a Kami, for lack of a better word, and got very protective. It was quite difficult and expensive to make sure she made her way to the monastery."

"I'm sorry. A commie?" Carol asked.

Neal chuckled. How could he laugh about any of this? Carol thought.

"No, a Ka-mi. An elemental force of the universe. A buddha. Eventually they agreed that she wouldn't be safe in the monastery."

Carol felt the weight of the girl in her arms. She was getting heavier.

"Do you think she's a buddha, Neal…?"

"No," he said. "I think she's a little girl who didn't ask to be born… just like the rest of us."

"She didn't ask to be at the heart of this company's research either. If you think I'm going to allow you to use any of this facility to reverse engineer this child, you're insane."

"Carol," Neal said. "These operating tables and all this equipment aren't for her. They're for me. I already t-told you she is the bridge, but I'm the one who's walking across it."

He reached to his temple and pressed his fingertips under his hairline. There was a slight pop, like the sound of a snap button. He lifted his hair off his head and placed the surgical wig on the metal countertop. He felt further back, and Carol heard a second pop before he lifted away a small perfectly circular piece of the back of his head and placed the disk next to his hair. Neal turned slowly on his stool until Carol could see. Underneath, wrapped in tight post-surgical dressings were two small sets of fiber optic cables protruding from the antiseptic and sterile hole in Neal's skull, still hot pink from recent surgery.

Carol felt a flush of stress and danger chemicals sweep through the systems inside her body, but she stared with an almost blank expression on her face.

"We're ahead of schedule with the installation," Neal said facing away from her.

"Installation of what?"

"The Brain Computer Interface. I've already achieved Output so we can calibrate the instruments and begin recording… Input will take more time."

Carol's mind was quickly assimilating the information. The disparate specialties of the of lab's project leaders were racking into focus.

"In this building," Neal said as he collected his head, "we're poised to own the next two brain technology revolutions back-to-back. First cybernetics. Then genetic engineering. If we had let our secret breakthroughs leak, we would have given away a once in all of history opportunity to tip the balance. That's why she's here. To be the first digital-native human mind. And it wasn't going to happen unless we committed to keeping her a protected secret. No one in the entire world knows she exists except us."

He thought for a moment before adding, "Until we want them to know."

Carol sensed a depth of awe she had never felt coming from him before. There was reverence and wonder, these were states of being unassociated with the stoic and aloof professor.

"Each time a person dies, everything they ever knew or learned dies with them. We can write books and make documents and photos and film, but the "knowing" is gone. The answer to solving this problem is speed. We must speed up knowing. Dominant life on this planet is all about speed and human science and technology are advancing to the point where it is no longer a radical thought, at least to me, to see a time when instinct, intelligence and adaptation collapse into themselves, and we are hurtling toward a great single exponential organism bound by nothing… ever again," said Neal.

"With her in the world the species has a chance," Neal mused as he beamed with a father's pride at his daughter. "I have given the planet and the species my absolute best. Either we thrive, or the human genome goes extinct. It's one or the other. This gives us all a chance."

"A chance to what?" asked Carol.

"To evolve."

Carol needed just another second to complete the plan she had been formulating in her head.

"If this is ever going to work you need my cooperation… and my silence."

Neal looked up to meet Carol's gaze.

"The combination is going to be tremendously expensive for you," she said.

He barely batted an eye.

"That cost is already built in," he assured her. "Everything is prepared."

The door beeped and opened, and Odie Carmichael stepped inside.

"Hello, Carol. I've prepared your agreement with ReGenOS. Like I said at dinner, it's your golden ticket."

═══════

That night Arthur Nyken sat in a corner booth at Green Street Bistro sipping ice water, attempting to decompress. He enjoyed people watching and took in the scene of the restaurant. Arthur had been in the air three times that week testing a new vectoring package, but his focus had continued to drift since Carol had arrived home. The test flights had taken all his concentration, but he had struggled.

Professionally and personally his once solid stable life now had the same sensation as an experimental jet malfunctioning. He could try to hang on to his test pilot job a little longer, but he felt like his era, the era of aviation centered around the human pilot, was ending. At JPL, deep space exploration and drones continued becoming a larger portion of the aeronautics testing.

He looked and felt older. And his relationship with Carol seemed to be getting more complicated too. Carol had been with him for almost nine years now. He was still every bit as completely enthralled by her as he was after their first date. She was fascinating and brilliant, emotionally steady but spontaneous… well, spontaneous was the loving way he framed what others might call highly unpredictable. But it was a chaos that excited Arthur because he knew she genuinely loved him. And they were both so capable and dynamic, it gave the impression there was nothing they couldn't accomplish together.

On the street outside a familiar form walked past the large front restaurant window. Arthur saw there was no baby in her arms. He knew their next conversation would be one of the most important of their lives together. This meal would mean something significant. He politely got the waiter's attention and ordered a bottle of Roederer and two escargots just before Carol arrived at the table.

"Hi Handsome," she said and kissed Arthur hard on the cheek.

She looked radiant. Unburdened. Sure.

"Hi beautiful. You look great."

"I'm feeling pretty great," she said as he stood and pulled out her chair just before the champagne arrived. She gave him a hard kiss and breathed him in.

"I'm famished and we have a lot to talk about," Carol said.

"There's food on the way darling. Don't bury the headline," Arthur said with a loving smile shining in his eyes. They toasted each other and took their first sip.

"It's… a lot. Ready?"

Arthur nodded and took a sip of wine into his mouth.

"Neal is leaving the faculty at CalTech, he's going fully into the private sector and to focus on his… new family, and as of about forty minutes ago I've formally been named as his successor."

"Wow," said Arthur, genuinely stunned.

"It's going to be my Advanced Math department now," Carol beamed and took a deep sip of champagne. "I've also been put on the board of Neal's new company."

"Jeez, that is a lot. What are they doing?"

Carol savored the wine before she swallowed. "Brain mapping mostly. They've made some quantum leaps in non-invasive high fidelity brain scanning. Eventually they'll own the algorithms and interface that can interpret raw human thought. They're building a platform of hardware and software to integrate it all."

"That's incredible," said Arthur. He lowered his voice. "And DARPA and the child?"

"The federal government offered Neal total immunity and a smooth adoption and citizenship for the girl in exchange for his military cooperation."

"I knew it," said Arthur with personal satisfaction as Carol continued.

"Neal agreed. I'm the DARPA liaison for the girl. I get full access. We can continue to see the baby. I have the seat on the board, CalTech, and DARPA. So now I will now be collecting three seven figure paychecks a year."

Carol slowed when she saw the look on Arthur's face was not excitement.

"That sounds like a tremendous time commitment, Carol."

"Actually, I told them I would only commit to the deal if I had a full-time personal staff and was obligated to a zero minimum and no more than fifty hours a week. I've been thinking a lot about time lately. How precious it is."

Their waiter presented their escargot to the table and refilled their champagne glasses which were both already empty. Arthur broke the end off the loaf of bread between them and skewered a snail from the sizzling iron escargot plate in front of him. The morsel was so hot it almost burned his mouth, just how he liked them. He placed the second bite of bread into the bubbling garlic-soaked olive oil.

"I want you to stop test piloting," Carol said.

"And do what?" Arthur asked.

"Start a family with me," Carol said.

5

Did You Ever Read Infinite Jest?/2016

"The real problem of humanity is the following: We have Paleolithic emotions, medieval institutions and godlike technology."

—— E. O.Wilson

San Francisco, California
October 26, 2016

Judith Almont sat in the back of her company's discreetly modified Chevrolet suburban security transport. Part of how they had made the firm successful was their ability to assure safe transport of some of the most hated people alive. It was no small or inexpensive thing. Her firm Maxel, Conners, & Alonso had all their cars made in Canada at INCAN Armored Vehicles, a specialty vehicle dealer. The vehicle was an MRAV class transport. The paneling and windows were bulletproof. The entire body had been fitted with armor plating. The vehicle could take a mortar or a direct landmine blast and still run. She had watched the demonstration herself at INCAN's western Toronto headquarters.

Judith read what they had received from BurnBear and placed it back in the case. The digital locks whirred tight, and she immediately called Michael Maxel.

"Hi Judy. Go ahead."

"I want a security detail for my family. I'll have a location pin in a minute, but they're on the 50 East somewhere outside of Concord. I need our lake house swept before they arrive."

"OK," he said. "I'll dispatch that right away. Are you or they under immediate threat?"

"I don't know," she said. "The instructions BurnBear gave were odd. I'm headed to Burbank airport. Agent Murakami has been reassigned to Aurora. I'm to meet him on the tarmac."

"And then what?" Michael said.

"I assume something else will happen once we're both there. Michael, if there is something inside Neal Walcott's mind valuable enough to BurnBear to expose a sleeper cell, we have to assume another attack is probable. Even if the execution is delayed."

Michael took a moment to think before he spoke. She could hear the chatter of keyboards at the office. Michael was already in the firm's situation room. He had four associates and assistants carrying out every word he said. Judith knew the scene well.

"I'll file a request for stay of execution for Neal Forest Walcott within the hour and contact DOD and Leavenworth directly," Michael said. "It's all going to be denied, but we need to demonstrate the firm did absolutely everything it could to pursue Professor Walcott's rights and prerogatives. BurnBear, they're obviously surveilling everything even if we don't know how. I'll let the flight crew know they're headed to Bob Hope. You can be wheels up in twenty minutes. I'll file for the stay immediately."

She hung up and called Raul. Her husband's familiar voice came on the line.

OCT. 26, 2016
Architech Headquarters
Pasadena, California

The atmospheric pressure continued to drop.

Agent Ryu Murakami checked the time on his phone. He was already late arriving on Architech's immense corporate campus tucked up into the still wild and open edges of the foothills above Pasadena California. His Department of Defense Citation X had crossed the Rocky Mountains headed west while the entire Pacific coast was preparing for the landfall of Superstorm Megra a little after five o'clock the next morning. The flight from Andrews AFB into Burbank Airport had been rough, and the strong headwinds had forced a refueling stop at Offutt AFB in Omaha, which meant they had landed almost two hours later than scheduled.

The agent had woken up this morning in his bed in Georgetown. His direct involvement with Carol Nyken and Aurora had all been years into his past. Just before lunch as he was walking to the commissary at the Pentagon, Agent Murakami had been approached by his commanding officer in the atrium and escorted to a briefing with the heads of intelligence. They informed Ryu that Neal Walcott's execution had been expedited four years because some kind of sentient digital weapon inside Neal's mind had turned on and started counting down. This had been detected by OMNIStack. OMNI had submitted a brief in a FISA court that morning. Professor Walcott's existence was deemed a clear and present danger to the United States; the change of date was approved and signed off on by the president. Professor Neal Walcott would be executed tomorrow at 08:00:00 which made the next twelve hours extremely dangerous. If there was some part of BurnBear still operational, this would draw them out.

The question of how the information about Walcott's execution leaked was still unclear. The suspicion was a breach in Aurora, and no one in the government knew her better than Ryu Murakami. Now after three years in quiet board rooms and labs, Agent Murakami had been reassigned back to Aurora, and before he could even eat a sandwich he was on a plane back to California encouraging all his psychological scar tissue to split open.

Ryu was on a plane back to California and not to Ft. Leavenworth to witness Walcott's execution because within twenty minutes of the top secret FISA court rulings, Carol Nyken, the CEO of Architech and Aurora & OMNI's covert handler, had submitted official documentation to the state of California to run for governor and announced a joint press conference with retiring governor Jerry Brown at Architech's corporate headquarters for the very same night. The Pentagon was caught completely by surprise and the joint chiefs, among others, had been pissed. But "pissed" was the weakened position the Nykens had put them in by announcing the news to the world and hiding in the global spotlight created when one of the world's richest women, and owner of the quantum leap bio-tech and A.I. company Architech, announced she was now running for office. From the US Government's perspective with Neal Walcott exterminated, and the Nykens operating Architech and OMNIStack in the governor's mansion of the sixth largest economy in the world, Aurora represented a real challenge to the neo-liberal world order.

Architech, the Nykens and even Governor Brown must have been planning for a contingency of Carol running to succeed him for some time, but the Nykens had never discussed any political aspirations with the DOD... ever. They had engineered a scenario where everything that happens now would be in-front of every camera in the world. Ryu knew they had all entered the final phase of this horrible chain reaction Neal Walcott had catalyzed. BurnBear. Architech. Aurora. The Walcotts. The Nykens. They had all made their moves once the weapon turned on inside Neal Walcott's mind.

A harder than expected landing jolted Murakami away from his analysis. The plane came to an abrupt stop and the crew dropped the stairs. A military escort met the plane and rushed Agent Murakami across Los Angeles. Ryu could feel the terrain incline at the beginnings of the San Gabriel Mountains in the far northeastern corner of Pasadena. His driver turned off the public road system onto Emma Nyken Memorial Drive and pulled up to the wide portico checkpoint before the entrance to the campus. The radios and chatter of dozens of interdepartmental agents and law enforcement officers buzzed like hornets as the left side windows of the black Suburban lowered. Agent Murakami and his escort offered their credentials and were quickly waved through.

As his transport drove closer to Architech headquarters, Agent Murakami tried to focus on the job at hand. He hadn't spoken to Mara Walcott, codename Aurora, in almost three years; but he expected to be face to face with her again tonight. Ryu's exposure to the power of Architech and Mara had taken a toll on the agent. He was prepared to do his job, but he truly did not want to see her.

Ryu and Mara had been overly practical about the end of their association. They simply ceased contact. It had been the only romance either of them had ever known, and it happened in the middle of a covert war that started before either of them were born. Neither had any future expectations for love or passion. The world did not seem interested in romance this century.

After the raid of BurnBear, and their conviction, his assignment with Aurora was concluded. Ryu had been recalled back to Washington and given a year's paid medical leave which he had spent sleeping and speaking to practically no one. He was exhausted. Too tired to move or manufacture emotion. For most of the next year he had sat in a quiet room reading a stack of books, drinking tea, and sweating out his nightmares.

Now, Ryu was finally going to see the manifestation of what all the covert violence and death in those years had been for. He was going to see the operational brain of OMNIStack, the official A.I. of the United States and the most sophisticated quantum computer in the world.

But for the almost trillion-dollar investment that was legitimately changing the geo-political balance, the official A.I. of the United States had a secret only the Nykens; POTUS, the Joint Chiefs, BurnBear, and Ryu knew. That Aurora, the core of the dominant digital entity on the planet is still human.

And she's getting tired.

The increasing offshore winds of superstorm Megra blew across the landscape. On either side of the road leading to the center of campus were almost three miles of ecology designed and maintained by OMNI. Ryu could see OMNIStack had mimicked, in part, the drive to CIA Headquarters at Langley. He had driven down both roads dozens of times in the twelve years he had worked for the DOD, but he hadn't seen the Architech campus since it had been finished. The last time he was here, the campus had been nothing except a smooth wide road out to a row of large steel sheds. The raw flesh of the ground fully exposed for miles. Something yet to be, conceived into the side of the steep rock face of the foothill ridge.

The A.I. had selected the trees, designed lakes and shaped the fields, which had all been harvested from a forest planned for demolition in Southern Oregon, and replanted the already fully grown natural ecosystem in patterns designed by OMNIStack to ensure security and secrecy on top of an invisible surveillance network. OMNI oversaw the entire project itself, operated most of the construction machinery and the ecosystem had thrived. Architech's in-house marketing firm had made a major news piece out of OMNIStack finding and making the request to acquire it, like a sculptor asking for clay. Like a god.

The company now called the half a million square foot hanger built directly on top of the old Walcott Labs and housing the quantum inner workings of the computer tasked with transforming the American Republic, The Barn. As Ryu looked out the windshield the massive structure now loomed at the distant end of the road.

The treeline ended and the road opened up as wide as a runway. Beyond were sweeping fields ambiently lit by hidden fixtures. The sides of the road leading to The Barn were choked with cars that had carried a selection of technical elites to the announcement of a grand new initiative for the state of California.

Ryu's driver stopped the Suburban. "If for any reason you need my assistance, just let me know Agent."

Agent Murakami's mind was already inside the building.

The very last time Ryu had seen Mara Walcott they had walked together at the beginning of OMNIStack's installation of the forest. They had both known their relationship would end when his assignment did, and after an intimacy and passion that had transformed both of them in different, almost opposite ways, that day came. They had said little as they walked through the construction site. Ryu remembered vividly how he broke an hours long silence by reciting a poem he had memorized for Mara. It had taken him that long to work up the courage. So old fashioned and of course she could have recited it herself, and every other poem ever published. He knew she remembers everything, but he wanted to be memorable. The poem was the last thing he said to her. And halfway through, she had taken his arm and walked closer with him until her security detail arrived. All that construction was a distant memory hidden beneath the now flawless grounds, and as Ryu walked across the wide ascending platforms to the main entrance at The Barn, he recited the poem silently to himself, "On Stripping Bark from Myself" by Alice Walker.

Entering through the grand doorless mouth of The Barn into the external atrium felt like entering a sleeping leviathan. It all reminded Agent Murakami of being in St. Peter's Basilica in Rome. The rings and layers of grandeur, at magnitude, designed in part to induce the individual into a kind of overwhelming psychic submission to the Catholic god.

It is a space designed to evoke something. Something approaching Awe, thought Ryu.

What is the inverse of Awe? he thought next. The answer came to him before he could catch and kill it.

Horror.

The floor across the expansive opening was made of bamboo. An entire jungle's worth of sustainably cultivated and harvested material swirling and feathering beyond any one line of sight. A wide black stripe ran across the floor and in semi-precious materials and flushly inlaid into the bamboo, a massive sans serif ARCHITECH had been carved too large for any person on the ground level to read. Ryu's gaze drew upward into the grand volume of Architech's cathedral, he had no problem reading the campaign banners hung in the immense envelope of space above the atrium.

An A.I. for every Californian. An A.I. for every American.

Above the banners, about forty feet up, a metal mesh began on the curving and sloping walls. On it, thousands of small octagonal panels silently flicked and flitted like a flock of birds. The panels were changing color while also changing from clear or mirrored too completely opaque. Ryu had read about the architectural flourish and had originally thought it sounded uselessly flamboyant, but walking underneath it the energy and color did evoke some kind of fusion between data and consciousness. It gave Ryu the general impression of a mind. He was processed through a final security screening, issued credentials, and allowed to proceed toward the two massive sets of open blast doors. He could already feel Mara's gravity coming from the next room. Ryu continued to recite the poem to himself.

Ryu entered through the hanger bay doors and stepped onto the massive Master System Control Platform elevated eighty feet above the true floor. He counted fifty-six A.I. operational personnel officers currently interfacing with the computer about internal diagnostics and data architecture. Most of the communication with OMNI was a combination of highly tailored digital holographic workstations and verbal interface. They had petitioned the FDA to allow them to begin cybernetic interfacing implants of employees working directly with OMNIStack, but that was still illegal.

The technicians' holographic augmented reality systems were the only thing filling the empty space. The techs were clearly annoyed by the thousand or so guests wandering through their workspace dressed in every manner of attire and standing in matriculating clumps listening to the retiring California Governor Jerry Brown give his initial remarks. Poised comfortably in chairs off to the side of the center podium were Carol and Arthur Nyken. It had been a long time since he had seen them.

They look transformed, thought Ryu.

Long gone were the brassy dazzling technical ingenues, the grieving parents, the newly minted global data czars. Now they had the same look of weary resolve Agent Murakami saw on the faces of the career spooks and soldiers. Ryu could see the Nykens' complete commitment. They were no longer afraid to install a new reality. One with the promise of thriving digital humane democracy and American superiority. One with Carol becoming leader of the free world.

Ryu soft-analyzed the crowd as he walked toward an empty pocket on the left side of the podium only half listening to the governor's speech. Some attendees stood looking self-conscious and overdone, more like they thought they were headed to a movie premiere. Others, Ryu mostly pegged as rich VC Silicon Valley geeks who looked like they had been roused from between a bender and a hangover. But a core group dressed in the modest unassuming attire of serious engineers and computer scientists stood still, focused intently on the governor.

There was no sign of Mara.

"The ark of human potential is here. Is in California," the Governor said with a classic barky snarl. In content and tone, it struck Ryu as the retail political brand Jerry Brown had been successfully selling to California for decades. But Ryu also knew the governor experienced a deep and profound reckoning with his conscience in recent years. Privately, Brown sees a real global revolution as the inevitable consequence of economic inequality meeting global climate disasters. The only question is whose revolution will it be and what kind.

Real power has never been ceded without violence, Ryu thought. He hoped that wasn't true, but he couldn't think of a counter example.

Murakami reached the far end of the platform and looked out over the railing to the vast lower decks of The Barn. Below was a city-sized network of forms and structures undeniably reminiscent of a brain. An infinite-thinking topiary maze. Throughout the labyrinthian channels Ryu could see technical engineers deep inside their insect-like cycles of endless maintenance, optimization, and development. Every moment OMNIStack was evolving and keeping the Americans dominant.

"California is the beating heart of innovation, technology, and cultural achievement," the governor asserted. "This place has reimagined itself repeatedly. California is an American jewel of global export. Pioneering social justice with robust democratic institutions. We are a top ten global economy taking the international lead in climate change." The governor paused. "None of it… has made a difference in the overall fate of our nation or the world."

That was a hard left turn, thought Ryu.

"We have done our best and it has not been nearly enough," the governor continued. If you need proof of our failure, just look off the Pacific coast tonight. Superstorm Megra will make landfall in about nine hours from now and it will cost the state billions at the least."

The internal frustration and anger were visible on the governor's face.

"Our state burns out of control. Much of the so called "green" technology turns out to still have a devastating petro-chemical and environmental footprint. We already do not have enough water for both the fires and our food. I see no future for the people on this planet."

Ryu could feel the audience becoming more present and still. They had heard Californians speak like this, but never the governor.

"And even if we meet those challenges, it will still not be enough for what is coming. A foundational change like nothing the world has ever seen is here. The planet is becoming a much harsher place for humanity, and I see very little real leadership anywhere in the world, except here. Right here in California."

Godammit that Jerry Brown is good at what he does, Ryu thought waiting for the governor's lift.

"I do not submit to a lesser future," the governor declared into the microphone.

There it is.

"With Carol Nyken and OMNIStack, democracy and the American dream flourish in the twenty-first century and guide the rest of the country and the world toward a sustainable democratic future on this planet for the human race."

That's the pitch. Nyken equals a sustainable democratic human future.

"With all that in mind, please let me bring the future governor of California to the podium, Carol Nyken. Carol."

The crowd generated a circadian round of applause. Ryu hadn't seen Carol in several years except in the media. She looked impeccable in her now iconic long yellow jacket and tailored linen and silk jumpsuit. Carol knew how to embody the Jungian archetype of the sage techno shaman. She had learned from the best, after all. Ryu saw there was also something unreachable in her eyes that hadn't been there when she was younger. The countenance of a great watching being who's transcended into another realm of space-time. Before she stood, she pressed down on a cane in her left hand. It was not the rise of a broken body or of an old body. It was the rise of a strong injured body. Her walk to the podium radiated a humble dignity. The tone of her voice had deepened. She was truly someone else now.

"In just three years," Carol said. "OMNIStack has been a revolution for the U.S. Federal Government. The government can talk to itself like never before because everyone has the same trillion-dollar partner. It is fluid, fully transparent, impenetrably secure, and creates the ultimate liaison between the people and our resources and capital."

No one could deny the project had been a nominal success. Since the Supreme Court had ruled it was legal to turn OMNIStack on, and after the BurnBear sedition which put Walcott and his followers in Ft. Leveanworth or in the ground, by metrics and anecdotal reviews

OMNIStack was revolutionizing the dynamics of government and defense. Connected and resourceful, OMNIStack was a single government entity everyone worked with simultaneously.

For a moment Carol turned to look behind her and out into the vast interior space for a moment before continuing to address the crowd.

"That's the thing about OMNI," Carol said. "At its core OMNIStack demands transparency and accountability of itself. Building the official A.I. of the United States of America took all the collective knowledge, insight, and talent available to us. And then we were still only halfway there."

She continued.

"But it is here now. It's done. And every consideration and its machinations are audited by the US Department of Artificial Entities - a check and balance first suggested by OMNIStack itself. Because democracy matters to it."

As Carol spoke, her eyes discovered Agent Murakami in the crowd. Her expression didn't change. She just held Ryu's stare for a moment; silently acknowledging his presence and continued.

"The previous half-century of American foreign policy has made us less safe. We live in a world of amplified threats and authoritarians across the globe are actively installing their own global agendas. OMNIStack's interface between the Department of Defense and the State Department is responsible for dramatic improvements in many of the most unstable theaters of conflict in the world."

That's true, thought Ryu. The results were indisputable. OMNI was the transformational technology on the planet. The atomic bomb of its moment There wasn't a country on Earth within 25 years of building this kind of central operational intelligence. With OMNIStack the Americans were tilting the balance of power away from Asia back to the United States.

"But this is not a speech for the world," Carol said. "This is a speech for California. The best chance the future has, is if the next American century starts with us right here in the Golden State. Because my fellow Californians we have an opportunity, but so does everyone else. Someone is going to install a new version of reality. Here in California and everywhere else. You can see it happening all around you every day. And now, right now, is the best chance we will ever have for a twenty-first century democracy that's potent, ethical, transparent, and instant. Predictive. Supportive. OMNI connects problems we couldn't even see because of their scale and complexities, and submits prescriptive policy, briefs, and budgets. Then it's up to the people of this country to make their own choices. If it can do all of that for the most powerful nation on earth, what could it do for our state? For your local and regional communities? Or for you and your family?"

Carol continued.

"And in the absence of all other options, I say we have an obligation. California must lead this new version of American reality. We have been left no other choice. American life offering real parity, real equity, real policy. Real justice. Abundance while producing far less waste. Energy collection and consumption. Every facet of our lives must be reimagined, brought to industrialized scale, and distributed. And then... it has to work. Because technology is by definition a technology when it works whether you believe in it or not."

"When I am elected governor, I will integrate OMNIStack into California and into our lives. I will be on ballot, but OMNI will be in the room with me, and you, every day. Thank you."

The crowd stayed still as Carol walked to Arthur who stood and reached out his hand. There was no music. It wasn't a pageant. He smiled at her, and they began to walk to the edge of the podium. Carol's rhetoric echoing inside The Barn had been a compelling vision.

Well that officially changed things, thought Ryu.

Architech had just put the world on notice, but Agent Murakami knew they were far from the only global systems player attempting to bend the future. Do they think they have a once in a thousand lifetime chance to run the table on global world order?

Ryu felt the magnetic field of his body shift and flutter. He closed his eyes.

"Did you read Infinite Jest?" an instantly recognizable voice behind him asked.

He took a moment for himself before answering. "I did," he said without turning around.

"And...?"

He opened his eyes and turned to meet the welcoming eyes of a woman he instantly realized he was still intensely in love with. Some of the softness in her round dark features had hardened along with her general countenance, but she didn't look haggard. She looked healthy and thriving. Ryu knew he did not.

"It gave me the screaming fantods," he said.

A genuine smile warmed across her face. Whether she had missed him or not, she seemed present with him now.

"I've been reassigned to Aurora this morning. There is supposed to be a firewall between OMNI and the military, Mara. The change of date on Neal Walcott's execution. You're inside the intelligence and military systems."

She nodded. "Yes."

"Why isn't OMNI reporting the breach?"

"Because it doesn't remember it."

"OMNIStack catches a weapon turning on in Neal Walcott's head and the same day Architech basically becomes a global political party… and you are inside the FISA court system, and you told the Nykens? These are serious federal crimes, Mara…"

"Well, I suppose they could arrest me or shoot me. But they would have to be prepared for Aurora to become public knowledge and then the whole world would know there's a wizard behind OMNIStack's curtain."

It wasn't that Agent Murakami was unimpressed by the play, but he feared being dragged back underneath, into the Nyken and Walcott black ops ground game which he knew was an arena of real violence.

"If you and The Nykens make a play for the White House, it could be constituted a threat to the republic."

Mara reached for his arm which Ryu hadn't expected.

"It's gotta start somewhere. Why wouldn't it be California?"

"What has to start somewhere?" Ryu asked.

"I just wanted to confirm what you already knew," she said. "I hope someday we talk together about Infinite Jest. Good luck with your assignment."

Ryu watched her cross back through the crowd. She was collected by her security detail and fell in behind the Nyken contingent. As they exited through a nondescript door at the far side of the platform he could feel the effect of her distortion field dissipating. Once she had gone, he made his way back past the gawkers and schmoozers. Even though he was in the nerve center of the most powerful computer in history with a thousand people, the room felt emptied. He stepped out into the night and down the stairs to his transport.

As his driver headed for the Burbank regional airport, Ryu watched the Nyken's Eurocopter EC135 flying overhead towards the Architech private airfield. For the next half hour his stomach gnawed at him as his car crossed Los Angeles.

Ryu leaned forward from the backseat toward his driver.

"We need to make a quick stop before we get back to the plane. I need to get something to eat."

"I'm sorry Agent Murakami I have strict orders. No stops. For any reason. You are headed straight back to D.C."

Ryu knew the type of agent he was speaking to. There would be no deviation. A few minutes later, after passing several glowing golden shrines of fast food, they were back on the tarmac at Bob Hope Airport. At the end of the runway another corporate jet was just touching down and began taxiing towards his waiting plane. Ryu caught the logo. Across the tail in large gold and red letters - MCA. Emblazoned on the fuselage - Maxel, Conners, & Alonso. Ryu's transport came to a halt on the tarmac in front of the Defense Department jet as the second plane was parking alongside.

He exited the Suburban and collected his bags from the back as the gangplank lowered on the MCA jet. A four-person security detail exited first, followed by Judith Almont-Conners.

Ryu tried to swallow but his mouth was arid.

"Agent Murakami…" Judith called out.

Ryu's escort was now standing about three feet away. The expression on his face was quite serious. "You are to board the DoD jet immediately and return to Washington for debriefing."

Ryu wasn't intimidated. He tossed his brown leather duffle over his shoulder and began walking towards the planes and the rapidly approaching Conners envoy.

Judith called out. "Agent Murakami, I need to speak with you! Immediately!"

"Agent I will report any deviation directly to the...," Ryu's escort barked.

Ryu interrupted him. "Agent... Please. For yourself and your country... Shut up."

Judith's security detail gave her some space as she approached Ryu.

"Agent Murakami."

"Ms. Conners," Ryu said.

The high blasting halogen lights cast wide deep shadows across the space.

"I know you hoped to never see me again, Agent and I am sorry I have to land on top of you so to speak. But I have very explicit instructions from BurnBear."

Ryu felt a rushing drop in his guts.

"How can there be new instructions from BurnBear?"

"I was hoping you could tell me. Perhaps we both have half an answer."

Judith's cell phone rang. She pulled it out of her pocket. Across the screen - Michael Maxel. She answered.

Agent Murakami watched the color drain from Judith's face as she listened and then hung up the phone.

"Agent Murakami, you are not returning to D.C. tonight. You are headed to the San Francisco FBI building where you will shelter and wait out the Superstorm Megra."

"I don't understand," Ryu said.

"The Nyken's plane is missing, and the storm is making landfall."

He had just seen Mara less than an hour ago. She had been standing right in front of him. He could have asked her to walk out of there with him. Judith's voice felt far away.

"Carol and Arthur Nyken, Odie Carmichael, and Aurora were all confirmed passengers. There was also a news crew. And their plane just vanished off the radar screen. There is going to be a tactical stryker team launching from the San Francisco FBI building after the storm. They want you there. They say it's the only chance you ever see Aurora again."

It's all happening again, thought Ryu. Somehow Neal Walcott and Burnbear are back.

"We need to go now and get ahead of the storm, Agent."

The wind shifted direction as Ryu followed Judith to the MCA jet. He could smell Judith's onboard chef had already begun preparing them a meal, but now he had no appetite.

6

A Little Woodworking Studio On The Water/2016

"Only those who will risk going too far can possibly
find out how far one can go."

—*T.S. Eliot, The Hollow Men 1925*

USCG Air Station San Francisco
October 27, 2016

Captain Emily Hankerson hadn't slept well since her stryker team was deployed. She was six hundred miles from her home and the glaring amber light of the high-pressure sodium security lamps blazing across the base had finally succeeded in giving the captain full blown insomnia. She was the only one awake in the stillness of the barracks when the orange light outside her bunk window flickered as a shadow crossed it in the earliest hours of the morning. She sat up and watched from her second story window as the black silhouettes of two jeeps with their headlights off approached on the road. They could have been going anywhere on the base but somehow Emily knew they were coming to rouse her.

The captain and her crew weren't usually stationed in the bay. Her stryker team had been activated from Kingsley Field in southern Oregon last night at 21:00:00; along with two other Stryker IFV crews and shuttled to the Coast Guard base in San Francisco. The teams were trained to be highly adaptable but hadn't received orders. Originally Emily assumed they were part of the anticipated response to Superstorm Megra whose landfall was due this morning. In the last forty-eight hours the profile of the storm had grown to stretch from Central Mexico to Washington State. But they had received no explicit mission parameters, and what real difference would three tactical teams make with a storm two thousand miles wide? The longer they didn't receive instructions, the more Emily became convinced the strykers had been activated for something else.

Captain Hankerson climbed down off her top bunk and walked across the cold unfamiliar linoleum floor and past the eleven other soldiers still in their beds. Emily missed her bedroom back in Portland. She missed Dante. She splashed some water on her face and let herself fantasize for a moment that she was home, and Dante was just climbing the stairs to her apartment. Emily's boyfriend of four years was a cop and the gentlest man she'd ever met- just one of a dozen of Dante's surprising contradictions. It had taken Emily a long time to see how dynamic he really was. Now he seemed limitless to her. Someone sure of his talents with a deep capacity for empathy. Although he was years ahead of schedule to make Lieutenant, the badge had begun to chafe, and he was explicitly preparing to make the transition from law enforcement to government. But Dante was going to be on the force four more years regardless. He'd have benefits and pension for life. Emily would discharge in two years. They both loved her flat and the plan was to lay in bed eating pizza and watching muppet movies until their family sprouted up around them like clover. It was a beautiful simple future, but something about the storm deep on the horizon making its landfall just before dawn, had popped the stitching of that dream.

Emily usually had positive emotions about storms. A soldier knows a hard rain keeps the world from fighting. To Emily, a city with everyone inside, all blanketed in the white noise of water landing across the whole thing, was the sound of peace. It meant she could relax. It's part of why she loved Portland. Those stormy days and nights when Dante arrived at her apartment with hot soup. He had always showered, shaved, and changed into his civies before he came over. The soup was always just what Emily had been craving and somehow still too hot to eat. Always from yet another great unknown little window. Curling up with Dante in her bedroom listening to the rain and eating soup, those had been the times she had felt safest and most content in her entire life. Emily prided herself on being an excellent soldier with a stellar career ahead of her. She also loved her life in Portland. For a time, she thought she could manage both, but in the last year "both" had made it harder to be either Emily or Capt. Hankerson. And she had begun to wonder if she was going to have to choose.

The sound of the base jeeps parking in front of the building woke most of the other soldiers and a few moments later two men silently walked into the dormitory. It was the base commander and his attache. They turned on no lights, roused all three on call Stryker teams, and told them to be suited up and on the tarmac by 04:00:00.

Ten minutes later Captain Hankerson was the first to exit the barracks. She double-timed across campus toward the open hangar where her vehicle was being prepped. The wind had begun to pick up. Visibility was already almost zero. A floating rain hung in transparent atmospheric curtains, and the thick mist was moving from behind the buildings and across the common yards like a stalking predator prowling the base. Beyond the hangar, the air station ground crew worked the tarmac with enormous fans and blowtorches. Huge billowing plumes of cloud and steam glowed and roared from the landing strip in the middling darkness of pre-dawn.

As she went through final checks with her maintenance crew she had quietly leaned in to her mechanic and asked…

"I thought the field was closed."

"It is."

"So, who's landing?"

"That's above my pay grade, captain. But your Stryker is ready to go. Watch yourself out there in all this."

After all three vehicles were checked and loaded, the teams sat in the dark awaiting further instructions. All the teams could do was drink water and watch the distant flickering of the offshore lightning. The hurricane was coming; but for now, everything on the base was still. Captain Hankerson's phone danced and glowed for her attention. It was Dante. She sent the call to voicemail, shut off her phone and stowed it.

The wind was already cresting sixty miles per hour as ground crews finished preparations. Emily recognized the roaring engines of a C-17 about six hundred yards out and saw the crew's collective gaze fix at the far end of the runway. The huge plane broke through the fog like a killer whale, lingered in the air for another five seconds, then landed hard on the tarmac. The back gate was already coming down.

Two humvees and two black suburbans with government tags were pulling up at the back of the plane about a thousand yards away. A man dressed in full tactical rain gear with a metal hard case locked to his wrist and a four Marine personal escort exited the back of the plane. Inside the C-17, Captain Hankerson could see full sky hospital modifications had already been installed in the hull.

The first real lightning they had seen within five miles popped inside a low black wall of cloud on the horizon at the western perimeter of the base. Two Marines opened the back door of the second humvee and the man got in. The convoy started towards the hangar.

Emily's navigator leaned forward in the seat next to her.

"This is some Mission Impossible shit if I've ever seen it."

The comline in Captain Hankerson's helmet kicked on.

"Stryker Convoy, Stryker Convoy. You are now operational. Be advised this storm will make landfall in the next thirty minutes. On shore winds will be cresting one hundred and thirty miles an hour by 04:37:00. This is now a one-way trip convoy. Get to FBI-SFO and go with your asset inside. You will take shelter at that facility and receive further instructions."

The captain watched as her NAV display downloaded the mission parameters. FBI building - San Francisco 450 Golden Gate Ave, San Francisco, CA 94102.

The humvee arrived inside the hanger and the man with the case never broke stride as he lifted himself up into the eight-wheel armored Stryker.

"Captain Hankerson," the man said.

The captain turned in her driver seat. "Sir."

"I am Lt. Col. Harold Rutledge. This convoy is under my direct command. Here is your hard copy mission parameter."

The captain recognized Rutledge. He was the JAG corp rep they sent into hot situations. His reputation as a truly fearless tactical oversight manager had begun to precede him.

The captain took the binder handed to her.

"We are in a more fluid tactical situation than you have been briefed on, Captain Hankerson."

"We haven't been briefed at all, Sir."

The colonel took no pause.

"You have a single objective. Deliver me to the FBI building in San Francisco within the next twenty-five minutes. If I am K.I.A. or incapacitated before I reach my objective, this case locked to my wrist is to be delivered to DoD Agent Ryu Murakami who is currently sheltered in that building. His fingerprints and retinal scan will unlock the case. I can't give you any more information than that. Understood?"

"Yes sir."

These are the convoy's exact instructions. I want us off base in thirty seconds."

"Yes sir."

The captain cleared her mind and focused.

<hr>

Thirteen miles north of the Stryker convoy Agent Murakami felt a void in his gut. In the crowded basement rooms and hallways of the FBI building, he couldn't even be alone. For a man of Ryu's immense skills and sensitivity, sitting in the basement inside the FBI San Francisco field office was an interminable personal hell, but the only thing he could do was wait. His mind raced with just the few fragments of information he had. Moment by moment he could feel the foundations of all the psychiatric and emotional work he had done to move past his PTSD being pressure tested. He was aware of a mental feedback loop slowly increasing in volume; and waiting for the storm of the century to hit and pass before he could take any action. It had put his psyche's functionality in danger.

The fluorescent lit hallways full of skilled people without answers evoked Ryu's most traumatic memories as the stairwells below festered and echoed with all the quiet impotent frustrations of hundreds of US federal agents, employees, and military personnel. The storm was going to open and swallow everything. SATCOM internet and communications had already begun to fail yesterday morning. And all flight operations west of the Rocky Mountains had been halted before the superstorm's landfall on the North American Pacific Coast.

Ryu wandered into the crowded mess hall where he was handed water and a protein bar and watched the large analog Cent-Con command clock turn over its numbers. Estimated time until wheels up on any new flight operations in Northern California was currently set for 05:53:00 tomorrow morning.

The agent could sense a growing fear needling its way into everyone's brain. A contagious thought, spreading like a virus from mind to mind. Exchanged looks and overheard discussions. The struggle was returning to survival. This storm. These bunkers. An endless panoply of asymmetric threats. Ryu had caught the thought.

This is what living on this planet is now.

Agent Murakami closed his eyes and focused on slowing his breath. He meditated on the fundamentally disturbing thoughts and plucked them from his mind by the root like a weed from a garden, before incinerating them. Just as his father had taught him. Ryu filled his lungs again and let his memories come.

Ryu's father had been sixty-four years old when Ryu was born, almost forty years his mother's senior. The age difference always raised eyebrows but the romance between them was deep and real. Nori Murakami had been a respected woodworker and furniture maker from Tokyo who had started as a lumberjack at fifteen and eventually built and sold a small furniture manufacturing factory and consumer brand for almost fifteen million dollars in 1979 and retired to Laguna Beach California to open a small handmade furniture gallery just off the water. He met Rhonda Sukamoto when her family was vacationing from San Francisco. Rhonda had been a senior in college and had wandered into Nori's gallery out of a general attraction to the lines and weight of the objects and furniture in the front window.

Nori had been married once "when I was a kid" he would say, but they hadn't had any children. He had been alone as a child, orphaned, and then living in the lumber camps. Then married. And then alone for almost five decades. Not unhappy, and not uninvolved for periods, just alone.

To Nori having control, and not ceding it to anyone, had been the thing he was convinced had kept him alive and safe since he was a teenager. He had been born with keen intuition and pluck. No one had ever suggested he learn the craft of woodwork or start his own company. He had immigrated to California even though he didn't know a soul or speak English all those years ago and set up his workshop and gallery on the beach. All those choices he had made by instinct.

Ryu's father had learned how to conduct business in English by watching The Price Is Right religiously each day and imitating Bob Barker and Ed McMahon. His Price Is Right imitations through his thick Japanese accent killed for decades with the Americans and tourists who were drawn into his gallery by his innovation and craftsmanship, and to whom he sold beautiful things and what he called "a story." For almost fifty years he had control, right down to deciding to take the first bite of the good ham sandwich that he had prepared for his lunch, until he heard the front door to the gallery open and looked up. The rest of the man's life Ryu's dad swore that when he saw Ryu's mother for the first time entering his shop, all he saw entering was the spirit of a rabbit. This adorable wonderful curious brilliant rabbit living inside a beautiful young woman. Not just any rabbit, his rabbit. The rabbit that needed him. Ryu's father had told him and his siblings about that first impression many times. To Nori, the story was meant to instill in his children proof that the miraculous was possible.

He had watched the rabbit instinctively sit down at Nori's favorite piece in the shop, a gorgeous ultra-simple tiger oak desk which separated into three pieces and collapsed flat for transport. All hidden joinery. He watched the beautiful young woman run her hands across the desk examining the feel of sitting behind it for a moment, before turning to Nori and saying, "I think this is the most beautiful thing I've ever seen. Did you make this?"

He surrendered.

Ryu's grandfather had demanded a full audit of Nori's finances and personal affairs before he would allow anything as scandalous as an association between his blooming young college-educated daughter and some old beach bum furniture maker, and Rhoda's father and uncle, and their accountant, had discovered that while Nori lived simply, he was worth well over eighteen million dollars, had no debt, and was an artist and craftsman of public stature in Japan although he had not been back to the islands in nearly three decades.

The two men reframed Rhoda's instant infatuation as perhaps something more special, and they decided to take Nori out for dinner. By the end of the meal, the entire Sukamoto family had been completely charmed. Nori and Rhoda had four children in five years, and she died giving birth to the youngest of the four - Ryu.

Most of Ryu's memories of his father were of the workshop behind that gallery. Their family home just up the hill up the long wooden staircase. He could recall being fed gummy worms as a small child by a joyful kind old man in denim pull-overs with the sleeves tied around his waist, who missed his wife very much. KCVI 890, the local rock n' roll station would be on the beautiful stereo system across the back wall late into the night. Ryu and his siblings would lay across everything like a pack of hounds and listen to the sound of their father running a planer and the waves coming into the beach through the open bay windows and feel the night sea breezes that somehow smelled like the moon. By instinct, his father would stop working twice a day, turn off the radio, light a candle and incense in front of a picture of Ryu's mother and meditate. Nori had given Ryu a great many progenical gifts, one being a unique sharpness of mind.

Ryu calmed the swirl of nostalgia and finished his water before leaving the mess hall. He walked the corridors of bureaus and offices looking for enough space to lay down on the floor and stretch, but people were everywhere. The subterranean levels of the building were starting to take on the uncomfortable atmospherics of a hot house. The psychic residue of too many people bunkered, thinking about all the other reasons they may have to live like this.

Ryu chose to go down as many levels as he could. After ten minutes of discovering staircases and access halls, the agent found enough space under the basement staircase in the deepest level of a service stairway to lay down. It was cool and dry and quiet, and Ryu dropped into half pigeon pose and took a deep slow even breath. This was the kind of night where if you let yourself, existence could become an unrelenting blanket of needle pricks tearing at every raw and hot nerve fiber. The agent breathed into his stretch and silenced his thinking mind.

Stay limber. Keep your bio-systems in harmony. Rest your mind and stretch your muscles. Worrying burns energy you're going to need. No thoughts. Attain presence.

═══

On the other side of the bay the fog and wind were quickly intensifying. The tide crawling up the embankment of the I-101 near the Presidio was beginning to show its teeth as the convoy rushed north at top speed. Lt. Col. Rutledge sat quietly keeping an unblinkingly stoic expression and watching the countdown on the heads up nav display. Although the Bayshore Freeway was the fastest route by twenty-seven minutes it was a calculated risk to take the narrow exposed gash of land, flanked on either side by water and already half-submerged.

Eighteen minutes until arrival. Then find Murakami and make the com-link. Every minute matters, thought Rutledge. Once the storm hits, we all lose communication. It will be out for hours.

Lt. Col. Rutledge allowed himself a single glance out the window at the old city. He was a native Northern Californian, representative of a streak of career JAG Corps lawyers the University of California had been producing since the school's founding in 1868. The familiar view of the tall, gnarled cypress trees along the shore of the San Francisco Bay now had the appearance of something loose and impermanent to him. The city was an old wooden ship about to take the storm's thrashing. In college, Harold's ROTC platoon had studied the Presidio and the military history of the bay. The project had made a deep lasting impact on the man. The timeline they had covered began when the native peoples had crossed into California from the Alaskan land bridge some fifteen thousand years ago. An entire civilization of forty native nations living up and down the coast. Through that class it struck him how mutable and impermanent human civilization is, and he had never been able to stop thinking about it since. No matter how dominant a species or a civilization… it ends. No matter how long it endures… it is destroyed. The Ohlone Tribe had been one of the most sophisticated American cultures ever. They had created profound music, art, cuisine, diplomacy, religion, commerce and trade, philosophy, and an intense understanding of how to be a balanced part of their ecosystem. Some would call that collective understanding a form of highly developed technology. And for ten thousand years that had been the dominant human life in California. It must have seemed unquestioningly right and eternal.

And then the Spaniards land, he thought.

By 1776 the Spanish have an army occupying the Pacific coast with a large fort on the bay, and Ohlone have all but gone extinct. Under the pretense of Christian assimilation their way of life is destroyed and their world exploited and exported. Ten thousand years, and then cacophonous violence, and then it was like they had never existed. In 1846 President James Polk hears rumors the Spanish are shipping mining equipment into the Presidio and quickly deploys the federal army to annex the bay. Less than two years later the American Gold Rush is on.

Ten thousand years. And then a gold rush. Two hundred years and then this storm.

The convoy exited the freeway and moved into the Mission District of the evacuated city. The predawn was silent and insulated by fog and rain. A gust of wind landed against the side of the convoy and pushed the Stryker to the middle of the four-lane road. Visibility was dropping fast.

Convoy. Convoy. Bring up AR overlays onto your HUD.

Col. Rutledge watched Captain Hankerson engaged the radar based augmented reality heads up display, never taking her eyes off the field of view. Her swift competence and control put Rutledge slightly more at ease.

Captain Hankerson switched on the com. "ETA 4 Minutes."

A hard wave of water and wind came rushing down the cross street. The AR overlay errored out for just a moment and the Styker took a hard skid laterally. A leaf-filled oak tree snapped, shearing the signages off two businesses as it crashed into the right lane. The convoy swerved but never slowed. The vehicles snarled and bullied their way across the abandoned flooding streets. The huge washes of rain followed the transports over street crests and down the other side in steep sheets. The water moved like it was hunting. The Strykers barreled across Lower Pacific Heights and down the steep hillsides into Chinatown. On the opposite corner the convoy at last spotted the FBI building.

"One Minute! One Minute!" Captain Hankerson called into the com as she hit the console's hot mode preset button. Two short siren blasts and the environment filled with red light and adrenaline.

Col. Rutledge spoke up on the com.

"I need access into that building immediately, captain. California will lose all SAT-COM as Megra makes landfall. Ryu Murakami must make that COM-LINK."

"Yes sir," she called back.

Emily revved the lead stryker over the curb and up the sprawling concrete stairs that occupied both sides of the building's street frontage. The convoy came to a halt inside the brutalist concrete spires dominating the first six stories of the FBI's major west coast tactical response hub. The interior lights were out. The abandoned lobby looked like the ruins of a grand tomb from some ancient forgotten civilization. The entire building had been braced and reinforced for the storm. Eight Marines cleared the second and third transports and set to securing the perimeter with their guns drawn.

———

Ryu had just stilled his mind when he began to hear some commotion from the floors above. People were yelling. Lots of people. And they all seemed to be saying the same thing, but he couldn't make out anything other than the general round barking of the syllables. A large metal doorway to the stairwell echoed loudly as someone opened the door.

"AGENT RYU MURAKAMI!!! RYU MURAKAMI!!! ANYONE HERE?!?"

Ryu stepped out from under the stairs and looked up several floors to see a red-faced female captain in full tactical gear.

"Are you Murakami!?!"

At the end of the hall two Marines stood on either side of the door to the secured room. The colonel ushered Ryu into the room and closed the door.

The room was a SCIF. Small and without any comforts, but totally secure.

Colonel Rutledge unlocked the metal case from his wrist and placed it on the table in the middle of the room. The screen lit up and instantaneously Ryu recognized the figure looking at him from the other side of the link. It was President Obama. His deadly serious countenance was a far cry from the jovial and measured statesman the country usually saw. A small countdown clock was running behind the president in the corner of the screen. 45 seconds left till the com would cut out.

The storm hit exactly twenty-four hours before Neal Walcott's scheduled execution.

7

Eppur Si Muove/2001

"Man exists only in so far as he is separated from his
surroundings."

—*Vladimir Nabokov*

Pasadena, California
August 13, 2001

Neal Walcott rose at three a.m. like he had done six days a week for ten years now. He had escaped the gravity of that sycophantic world of acolytes and tenure, the hard Darwinian tooth and nail scramble for resources and personnel. His professorial life was a distant memory he no longer visited. He had transcended and could now stay in the atmosphere above the systems.

He got out of the bed he shared with Dr. Taeng Chairasit to begin his morning meditation. He lit the candle on the thin disc of glazed pottery that lived in the exact center of the long tiger oak chest at the foot of their bed. Neal had built nearly every stick of furniture in the room and every piece was filled with meaning and memory for him. He collected his blanket and unfolded it before taking a seat on the floor and beginning his mantra.

A little after four a.m. Neal checked on his sleeping daughter, then walked down the wide planks of old growth redwood he had made into the ranch house staircase by salvaging a grove of trees in Angeles National Park from being destroyed by wildfire, technically a felony, and milling them in his wood shop on the property. Every morning as his bare feet touched the wood he thought about that fire.

Neal walked into the kitchen and passed the large hearth oven. The surface was still hot from the blood orange marmalade Taeng,

Mara, and Nancy had cooked and canned the night before. He put a kettle of filtrated well water on the wood fire stove. While the water heated, Neal walked to the pantry on the far side of the kitchen and opened the double doors. The smell of the jars and vacuum-sealed bulk ingredients filled his nostrils. He reached to the far-left side of the shelves anticipating the pleasant weight of the hidden pocket door latch which moved smoothly to reveal a digital diagnostic station where for the last decade he had logged his initial output onto a duplicate networked Paragon his team had secretly installed at the ranch.

The kettle whistled and Neal pulled a jar of lapsang souchong tea from the pantry shelf. Tea was one of Neal's last pleasures. He checked the temperature and carefully poured the remainder of the kettle water over the tea pot and cup to bring them to the correct temperature. The dio-terminal filled the kitchen with a soft green glow and the cursor on the screen of the main monitor blinked with anticipation as Neal steeped a strong dark brew. He lifted his hand to his bare head and located the snap, popping a coin of surgical steel attached to his skull and swirling his finger into the sterile plastic casing to hook a four-wire fiber optic output cable which disappeared into his head. Neal attached his cable to the dio-station input and recorded his baseline readings.

Before his lab achieved Output, Neal had felt locked inside of time, like trying to move through liquid glass that had been poured on, slowing him down. He had resented the limitations of it, but Time thankfully was relative, and now he was only a few hours away from having all the time he could ever need. Neal took his first small sip of hot tea and closed his eyes beginning to focus on the functions of his Pons and Medulla. His consciousness softened. The machine properly calibrated and initiated the night's data processing. There was a definite sensation of evacuation.

The dark little deal Neal had made for what the Pentagon was now calling Aurora was simple and elegant. The Pentagon knew about Mara's potential and how Neal created and trafficked her and all evidence had been expunged forever. In exchange Walcott Labs and ReGenOS would become pillars of this new CalTech-DARPA cartel. The power of this new circuit had been tremendous, but it was well understood that Carol Nyken was a little red button that could destroy Aurora and blow the whistle on them all. It's why Neal had put her there and made sure she was installed as DARPA's liaison to Aurora, a consultant with full access and a high seven figure salary. It had proved an enduring arrangement. While other labs were writing grant proposals, Neal had quietly moved into the apex predator position when it came to multiple fields of emerging technology. The bedrock of this new empire is the university. The engine is Mara. The fuel is the Department of Defense and DARPA's endless blackbox budget.

The vision had been Neal's from the beginning.

The technology they were building was incomprehensibly complex, but the plan to birth it had been simple. With enough computational power, focused like a beam on just one mind, they had created a technology capable of recording and digitizing the Neal's consciousness. A fast enough computer, connected to and created for just one mind, could identify and decode even the most complex patterns in the brain. A programming language for the human brain and machines to communicate, a robust brain computer interface, with comprehensive Input/Output would mean the birth of a cybernetic network like no form of communications network ever known to mankind. An evolutionary leap beyond everything that came before it. Neal would possess the ability to interact with reality and communicate without muscle, just brain. It would be the expansion of the human nervous system to include a world outside the self. The decay of the analog industrial world and the bloom of new truth.

A new dominant reality.

By the time Neal had achieved his goals their partners would get the rights to the technology and would be free to proliferate their research any way they want. Like seeds in a garden, eventually the global cybernetics industry would bloom. Underneath that garden, ReGenOS would be the soil. Inside his black box, Neal built an ever-growing networked paragon machine, cybernetic equipment and procedures, and studied Mara. Walcott Labs was developing the next two major technology breakthroughs simultaneously. Just controlling the cybernetic technological revolution would have been enough to be ubiquitous, invisible, and dominant well into the 21st century. Gene tech opened up possible futures that were still too distant to comprehend. At the same time, he was covertly using the facilities to begin unsupervised human Brain Computer Interface trials on himself. Prof. Neal Forrest Walcott was poised to become the first digital consciousness on the planet.

The economics of a computer that large for a single mind were astronomical. The answer was why he came back to CalTech from his walkabout. He needed an enormous endowment. It would be over half a billion dollars to create the machine and regardless you'd never get it built without the Military Industrial Complex confiscating it. So, first CalTech had signed the new lab endowment deal, and he had assembled his team with a massive war chest leftover. Then, he had come to negotiations with DARPA. Neal saw in the eyes of Odie Carmichael, and every other DARPA official that had slithered into his offices, visions of a future where the United States commanded a neurally linked military. He had no intention of handing that future to the Pentagon.

After years of training Neal had developed sensitivity to his own brain activity. It had become relatively simple for him to take control of his heartbeat and brainwave patterns. He could feel the storm of cells firing in their natural quantum language and could distinguish clearly between the simultaneous and overlapping chemicals and electrical patterns of sensory stimulation, thoughts, and kinetics. But he was only fully conscious of a fraction of his actual overall neural production. He was still chasing after the raw electrical gale. Neal knew the trillions of synapses were there to be harnessed. The electrical chemical current connecting a hundred billion neurons. The quantum experience of self and awareness. The persistent illusion of reality and autonomy of the individual. Millions of action potentials firing every micro-second mystically transmuting into consciousness and form. He was the intrepid cartographer of his own inner space, but he wanted more than a map. He wanted control over its full potential. And his team had devoted their lives to securing him that power. After today he would no longer be human. He would be something else.

Neal emptied his teapot and took a last deep sip. He disengaged himself from his dio-station, pushed the terminal back behind the pantry wall and closed the doors. He stepped outside into the brisk pre-dawn atmosphere and loped casually around the wide porch of the large wooden ranch. The world was quiet and still, and Neal took a long look out across the property. He loved the place. He put on his gum boots and walked across the dark field to the livestock barn and began feeding his sheep.

===

Carol had been lying to Arthur for nearly ten years, and they had never been happier.

She had never told him about Mara's true origins, or Neal's surgical experiments, or that his business partner Odie Carmichael was lying to him too. It wasn't worth it. Her deal with DARPA and ReGenOS had gone off without a hitch and ushered in a completely new era in their lives. She was installed as a multi-million dollar a year consultant with both organizations and took over the advanced mathematics department at CalTech. She had been making seven million dollars a year as her star was rose across the world, and Arthur's consulting company Architech Areospace had become a booming business.

Even with all the success, they had stayed in their little yellow craftsman bungalow, and chatting with her daughter in the first minutes of the morning as she drove Emma to school was Carol's favorite moment of her day. She always made sure there was something wholesome and hot in Emma's hands and she never forgot the thermos of one of Emma's favorite beverages in the center console. Emma had received her mother's pure dynamic intelligence, but Carol's favorite parts of her daughter, she got from her father. Emma had developed tremendous pluck and emotional equilibrium for such a young person. The child was bright bordering on brilliant, curious and open, and was in an exceptionally good mood nearly all the time. No matter what turmoil or injustice or pain, the little girl bravely cried, loved, mourned, and inevitably started smiling again.

On this morning, just like most mornings, Carol and Emma Nyken drove to Neal and Taeng's ranch to pick up Mara. The property looked great. Over the years the Walcotts had invested in turning the sprawling foothill ranch into a true family home. It was well manicured and bright. The house and the barn and the miles-long wooden perimeter fence were all in excellent repair and the couple was always tinkering and doing something to make the place just a little more beautiful, sustainable, or productive.

Systems management on the ranch had been taken over several years ago by Neal's horticulturist Nancy Yarpas whose presence there had become a fixture. The squat bulldog of a woman always had dirt under her fingernails and sometimes in her teeth and had practically no patience or attunement to people. Nancy was there this morning, standing out in the pasture with her dog Maurice, the two of them almost hidden in the milky veil of thick mist, spending time with the plants and turning the amending soil and smelling it. Her hand rose above the mist, and she gave a neutral wave to the car as it drove to the house. Carol and Emma waved back and smiled.

Carol never knew the whole story, but somehow Neal found Nancy in a small tidy cabin out deep in the wilderness of Angeles National Forest, and had coaxed her back into civilization enough to convince her to re-imagine the systems of the Walcott Family ranch. Nancy had softened a little over time, and was every bit as gifted a systems designer as a botanist. Together with the Walcotts she had produced proof of concept for a number of sustainability experiments. Nancy had begun by amending the soil to prepare it for planting. All twenty-two acres of it with a group of CalTech grad students over about four years. Some of the students went on to other projects, but some continued apprenticing for Nancy at the ranch. Together they built a small water tower and several wells. The water system fed into a stunning multi-level hydroponic green house as big as most barns. None these truly miraculous feats had any personal decoration. Form had completely followed function.

Mara Walcott and Emma Nyken both played on their academy tennis team, and practice for tennis started at six thirty a.m. whether you were eighteen or eight. Mara was already stretching in her academy warm up sweats on the front porch of Neal's house as they pulled up. The unusually tall ten-year-old was ranked number 8 in

California's CSTA under 12 division. Her ability and sophisticated style of play had provoked international attention in the world of youth tennis. The Walcotts had rejected any and all scouting attention with extreme prejudice while still supporting Mara's right to play.

Few days went by without Carol, Arthur, Neal, and Taeng getting the chance to watch Emma and Mara play tennis. Most of her matches she was precise and dominant, but occasionally she would catch an opponent she couldn't beat. That was when the girl really shined on the court. Mara would lose, but she would be completely focused on her opponent. Game by game she would assimilate the style of her opponent. The effect of this smaller younger girl losing three straight games and then taking the match deep into the fifth or sixth set by mimicking her competitor had been enough for Mara to put the whammy on more than one girl. But even the ones she lost to she would begin the match truly outclassed and by the end of the second set she had mastered their style and was throwing it back across the net.

Mara did not know about her origins. All she had ever been told was that she was Neal and Taeng's daughter, and that she had an exceptional mind. This "exceptional mind" was why Carol, or one of her parents, picked Mara up early from school on days she didn't have a tennis match. Half the time they headed to her father's lab and played WonderGame and half the time she went with them and did something totally surprising and new she had never experienced before. White water rafting down the Kern River. Plein air painting in Big Sur. Spelunking the lava tube caves in Lava Beds National Monument. They went on real adventures. Sometimes Emma or Emma's Dad came too.

Mara was happy.

They had begun diagnostic tests on Mara before the ink on the deal between Walcott and the Pentagon was dry. Blood tests, tissue swabs, brain scans, and cognitive and physical tests. They were complicated sophisticated tasks and challenges, but to Mara it wasn't a clinical experience, it was all presented to her as "the wonderful game," which over the years had shortened to WonderGame. WonderGame began with colored blocks; and plunger buttons and lights in the first year, all while Mara was being brain scanned, and all vitals recorded. It had developed into an experiential adventure. All the while Neal was continuing his personal development and training.

Carol had been explicit she wanted there to be no visible surveillance or security around the girls. Ever. And that outside of the Walcott Labs data collection and personal development of Mara, there would be no additional disruptions to either Emma Nyken or Mara Walcott's development. Both girls would be safe and allowed to grow up like normal children. Carol made sure everyone knew she would always put the girls first before anything else. She would never have to endure any surgery that wasn't medically necessary, and both Mara and Carol would need to directly authorize any invasive procedure. The girl would be given every opportunity. Her fascinating genetic advantages and natural properties would be patiently nurtured, but she would never see anything other than a life-saving procedure. Or Carol would blow the whistle.

======

Dr. Taeng Chairasit heard Neal rise out of bed. She had been dreaming of cinnamon buns dripping with warm cream cheese icing and strong dark coffee. The dream had been so vivid she could still smell it. After today's procedure is a success, tomorrow morning I am going to just sleep till I wake up… and then eat a cinnamon bun as big as my face, she thought as she flipped her pillow over and laid her head back down on the cool natural linen pillowcase. The next time she stirred it was nearly eight am. The house was silent. Taeng washed her face and walked downstairs into the commissary kitchen.

Everyone was gone. She made herself a cup of coffee, a single cup had never affected her performance as a surgeon, and she proved it to herself testing her steady hands as she sliced open one of the grapefruit she had picked from the citrus grove yesterday. She put the slices in her favorite smooth clay bowl and opened the wide bay doors to the courtyard. Taeng walked the covered path to the tall simple wooden building behind the house. The lights were already on inside. She placed her hand on the familiar form of her residential lab's doorknob and entered the spacious personal office. The building was a single room, tidy but full, with a high ceiling. Along the exterior wall there was a wrap-around worktable with two rows of tall shelves filled with manuals, monitors, scopes, and prototypes of all kinds. Spools of wire and thick blocks of clay sat in stacks next to work lamps, magnifying glasses, and microscopes. The abundant windows filled the space with morning sunshine that splashed and pooled across Taeng's research which covered every available surface. It was a manifest externalization of the surgeon's conscious mindscape which for many years now had been focused on the intersection between neuroscience and cybernetics. Taeng felt ready.

The doctor took a first bite of grapefruit as she locked her home office door and collected her completed procedural binder and flipped open a light switch panel revealing a hidden keypad. She typed her personal 6 digits and the immense lab table in the center of the room made a whirring noise and pivoted forty-five degrees revealing a long ramp down to their underground facility.

Neal had cut the deal with DARPA and Carol Nyken, but they didn't know about the ranch neurolab.

The cover of a conventional marriage made everything they did simpler, but Taeng also played her roles as wife and mother with reverence for both Neal and Mara. There had been times she thought she was truly in love with Neal and there had been a moment in their collective past where she thought he was truly in love with her. But all of that was inconsequential to why they had come together. They needed each other. It was a true opportunity to change history forever, and in Taeng's secret heart she believed humanity would ether rapidly evolve, or the entire planet would go extinct. She had said "yes," given it her all, and neither Neal nor Taeng had misplaced their trust. They had never met anyone who could work as hard as themselves and the synergy had been exponential. If they executed their plans successfully, they would knit the fabric of a future reality. They would be fundamental.

The Walcott Labs neuro-surgical research and development team had been moving at an astounding pace, but there were only a handful of people on earth capable of developing these technologies and no amount of money or support could move them any faster. It was bespoke hardware and software from soup to nuts totaling over a billion dollars, everything tailored to Neal down to the genetic level. Together they had been able to develop a robust, almost exhaustive set of data on him. She had studied Neal Walcott's body and brain as closely as any scientist or wife could and had contributed to several key design features of the devices she would be using on him.

When the project began it was just Taeng and Neal. The group at the university had no real idea how Neal intended to apply their work, they just knew it was an exciting rich vein of research. Once Walcott had full funding, they had expanded by securing partnerships with companies and labs in biology and biomechanics, organic and synthetic chemistry, physics, electrical engineers and neurologists, and medical experts of all kinds. At the peak of the research phase, what started as an idea in Neal's mind had grown to almost three hundred individuals in dozens of labs all over the world. The work had been carefully compartmentalized and the labs siloed from each other by thorough security protocols and ironclad non-disclosure agreements.

It was a risk to build the devices at all, but that wasn't Dr. Chairasit's concern. She wasn't in charge of the software or array designs or their fabrication. Or project secrecy. She oversaw the installation. Today she would peel back her husband's scalp, open his skull, and install three banks of permanent electrode censors and micro data-relays on either hemisphere and an internal CPU to manage the kit, all forever inside the organ of Neal Walcott's brain.

Once the decoded stream is uploaded back into the mind, theoretically you would have near total comprehension of your conscious and subconscious. It also seemed probable that new information could eventually be added directly to a mind.

Once the Paragon system at ReGenOS had adequately decoded Neal's neural patterns, that data had to be converted into mathematical information and stored. So first the data had to be emptied from Neal's head and output onto a vast storage system-The Paragon. Then Neal would have an Input relay and an internal CPU containing a set of neural algorithms surgically installed in his brain. Once those were optimal, next thing would be to upload the digitized neural-stream from the Paragon back into Neal's mind. This would achieve Input. And those installations were happening in about six hours.

When Taeng came down into the operating room, there was just Neal sitting pensive in her grandfather's barber chair. His right hand curled and rested on his face, knuckles pressed against his lips, an unblinking stare. Taeng knew her husband was keeping quiet on the real potentials of successful installation that even he could only speculate about. A brain linked to a computer as powerful as the Paragon would be a cognitive apparatus thinking in dimensions far outside the current realm of digital and biological systems. Long held almost sacred concepts of Self, Identity and Body were all poised to be atomized in the new world of networked digital human consciousness no longer confined to expressing itself through muscle, movement, and words. External and remote tools absorbed into the body. Now, thought alone would be enough activate the outside world. He would be able to move through the vast tides of digital knowledge, data, and news in a completely different temporal reality in the native quantum bio-electrical cadences of computers and brains. A space of near infinite time and limitless mental capacity where Neal would be able to bypass every currently held law of interaction with the physical world. He would be able to communicate without sound or muscle. To operate machines with nothing more than his mind, and how many devices or operations he would be able to perform simultaneously was still anybody's guess. After the installation Neal would be reborn a new thing, and like most new things, he would be helpless until his form and capacities matured.

Taeng had inherited the chair from her grandfather who had been a proud barber with a thriving shop next to the family gas station once he arrived in America from Bhurma. He had the same steadiness of hand. Same dexterity and precision and grace. He taught Taeng how to shave beards when she was around six years old. Her grandfather had noticed she liked to watch him shave his customers when she was in the barbershop, so he started telling her what he was doing while she watched. Then one day after the shop closed and with her parents looking on amused and proud her grandpa paid her twenty dollars for a shave, instructing her how to hold the straight razor differently on different parts of the face and promising her she wasn't going to hurt him. The little girl did an immaculate job and when she was finished her grandfather turned to her parents and said just one word: "surgeon." She barbered after school and on weekends nearly every day, putting all the money into a savings account, until she left for college.

Taeng walked to her barber's tools, stopping for a moment to place her hand on Neal's back. She wiped down his neck and then covered him in her grandfather's barber cape. Neal's toupee was gone, and the subcutaneous magnetic surgical snaps in his scalp looked like stones pressed into mud.

"Would you say You and I have a complex relationship?" Taeng asked with a smile in her eyes.

Neal smiled back. "I would."

"It changes completely after today."

"Yes," said Neal.

Taeng thought for a long time.

"I'll miss you," she said.

"I'll be gone," he said.

8

Think Twice/2001

"No tree, it is said, can grow to heaven unless its roots
reach down to hell."

— Carl Jung 1951

Pasadena, California
August 26, 2001

"On my mark. Three, two, one."

The surgical team moved an unconscious Neal Walcott from the gurney to the operating table and rolled him onto his left side. Dr. Langstone operated the foot pedal to adjust the height of the table and Dr. Zhao and Dr. Shandalow monitored his anesthesia while wrapping the circumference of his cranium in sterile foam pads before they brought the multi-appendage domed surgical lights in close, hovering over the operating table and positioned the multi-lens cameras at various angles before wheeling in portable workstations populated with monitors. The team would be locked into their stations for the entirety of the procedure.

The installation had five components. A set of three arrays on both sides of the cerebrum connected to wires that would wrap around his cerebellum like a headband of platinum, gold and glass laurels inside his skull connecting wirelessly to his data relay CPU. Underneath each of those arrays were twin deep tissue input/output transmitters. They were puffs of small sharp metal hairs spiking in every direction, capable of both receiving the complex firing patterns of the neural networks of the brain and generating them. They would be the hardware fusing into Neal's consciousness and experience of reality. Third would come the wireless CPU. The small digital relay transmitter was a smooth metal dot which simply because of the organization of the human brain sat unavoidably conspicuous and mystical, at the center of Neal's forehead squarely at his chakral third eye. It had sparked some interesting metaphysical discussions. The CPU would operate the first set of neural algorithms so the information could be broadcast to a surface transmitter and amplifier. The spew of wires from the back of Neal's head would be gone and he would be able to connect to the Paragon system wirelessly.

The tiny, barbed grids they had developed in secret were a true revolution from the blocky thick grids of electrodes everywhere else in the still latent world of neuro-technology. Other labs were convinced they were at the cutting edge of brain listening technology using electroencephalography (EEG) grids plated on the surface of the scalp, or the more sophisticated ECoG grids dropped onto the outer surface of the cerebral cortex, but they were all several decades from the level of sophisticated technology being inserted into Neal Walcott's mind. The inferior devices of the other labs could begin to listen and paint a soft blurred portrait of the human brain, but they were all being developed and targeted as generic commercial BCIs that would someday be brought to the public at large. On top of that they were working exclusively with patients who were either not human, or people with severe disabilities and trauma. The Walcott Labs team had engineered the exact reverse, designing absolutely every aspect of their stack, processes, and materials to just one individual with a healthy and powerful intellect and none of them were sure who or what he would be afterwards. Their competition also had nothing close to the hardware and software stack of the networked Paragons processing Neal's entire neural stream with as much computing power as had ever been applied to anything.

Taeng repositioned Neal's head, optimizing the position of his skull, making micro adjustments before applying the initial vice of the

Mayfield Clamp. The surgeon set the three steel pins orbiting the vise, stopped to inspect the positions of everything for visibility and instrument trajectory, readjusted the third pin, then drove the steel through Neal's scalp into the Frontal and Parietal bones with sixty pounds of pressure each. There was a tiny puff and cracking noise as the bone was pierced, like a bolt gun set low and shallow against a cow's skull, and Neal's head became unnaturally still. The team locked the rest of their patient's body into place.

Dr. Langstone turned on the stereo and loaded Taeng's eight-hour CD mix into the rotating changer. Taeng had themed and paced the song list to the rhythms and length of the surgery. It was a habit that had carried over from her days picking the music in the family barber shop. The opening cymbal tapping of Dave Brubeck's Quartet off a live recording from Amsterdam in 1964 began to play from the stereo.

"Alright, everyone ready?" Taeng asked.

The team gave a collective affirmative, and the performance of the complex ballet the four-person surgical team had been rehearsing for so long commenced. Dr. Langstone plugged Neal to a dio-station and recorder and began bringing the images up. Among the scopes and speakers was a router connected to four monitors displaying brain vitals. The first three separated activity and topography. The larger fourth monitor synthesized the triptych into a three-dimensional composite that could be turned and oriented with a trackball mouse. The bumping sizzling hum of the raw electrical signals being generated by Neal's brain vibrated and popped from the station's audio monitors. There was no concrete information in the white noise of Neal's neural activity the team listened to, but the sound did offer a certain general cadence timed to the waves and patterns shown on the monitors, that Dr. Chairasit had found subliminally instructive.

Taeng prepped the bipolar, a two-laser scalpel which would make a precise incision and could follow it with a cauterizing second beam. The team washed Neal's head with sterilizing sponges the color of red clay and painted wide around the left hemisphere of the patient's skull with a disinfectant surgical adhesive before dressing him with multiple layers of surgical paper. Widest around the surgical area they laid a blue cover sheet and attached it to the scalp with several staples. The patient had been transformed from a person into an anonymous body of systems.

A first thin line appeared on the composite monitor, Taeng confirmed its position, and the incision point was projected onto Neal's scalp. Dr. Chairasit held the scalpel to the skin, gently squeezed the tool and like magic the tissues parted. High oxygenated blood enthusiastically fell from the site, but the next millisecond the cauterizing laser had sealed the open vessels, and the first smell of hot flesh found its way into the atmosphere. Dr. Shandalow applied small orange tourniquet clamps and peeled back Neal's scalp. Bloody underneath was his skull. The site was cleaned, and a raw pink bone was the only thing between the team and the inner dimension of Neal Walcott's mind.

While Dr. Langstone brought up the next set of coordinates and projected them onto the bone, Taeng brought her instrument station closer. Dr. Chairasit steadied the bipolar over the projection on the skull and followed the points precisely. When she was finished, she gave the piece a tap and a twist with a set of micro-pliers. The skull fragment broke off cleanly with an audible crack, and the surgeon dropped the skull fragment into a medical jar filled with nutrient and oxygen rich gel, which was sealed and placed in a low boy fridge unit under Dr. Zhao's station.

Dr. Chairasit looked closely at the brain's Dura mater. The next part would not be so quick. The tough leathery membrane wrapping the brain held to the organ like a wheat pasted poster. First it would have to be partially dissolved without any solution leaking into the brain's tissue. Next the organ and the membrane would need to be separated, and the Dura mater peeled back.

It was four hours of painstaking precise work but eventually the Dura sheath was peeled away and the raw purple and red of Neal's brain became fully exposed. The first micro mesh array would be installed in the Parietal Lobe. One of two Temporal Lobes, the Parietal is responsible for unifying senses into a coherent experience, language synthesis, and optical coherence and vision. The final device they had designed and manufactured blurred the line between biomechanics and cybernetic SCI sensors further than ever before and here it was in her hands. Inside a compact circular case was a micro-sterilized environment and atop a small foam cushion sat a thin wispy form. At the end of each fine hair the white strand turned bright gold. It looked more like a dandelion caught in part of a spiderweb. Dr. Chairasit's steady hands took confident care of the implant in her tweezers. She placed the implant on top of the brain tissue, checked the alignment of each tendril, got the diagnostic greenlight from Dr. Langstone and pressed the implant into the Neal's brain which yielded with no resistance like a hot needle into warm jello. The surgery was going well enough, but this was only the first device installation. Next would be the implant of the deeper hardware.

"Dr. Zhao, can you give me a little clean up here please. How are his vitals looking?" Taeng said without looking up from her task. She could see a blood vessel had started leaking.

"Everything is nominal doctor. We've got a slight rise in temperature. Point four degrees. Brain patterns, heart rate and breathing are all good."

"Ok. Prep the deeper installs please Dr. Shandalow," Dr. Chairasit said as she reached for a pair of micro-scissors and her bipolar.

Dr. Zhao gently suctioned and dabbed the site clean and Taeng cauterized the vessel closed. It was still early in the procedure, and she was becoming concerned that the brain might begin swelling, but the only way to combat that was to work quickly. She reached across the tray holding her sterile tools for a small set of forceps.

"Deep hardware number one is ready doctor," said Greg Langstone.

Taeng positioned a pair of cup forceps in her hand and checked the dio-station monitors.

"Great. Thank you. Stand by."

She was going much deeper into the organ now. The implants further in would give Neal's BCI both hi-fidelity output and coherent input, but it would require successful installation of all four of them. The entire team knew tunneling so far into multiple sections of the brain risked catastrophic hemorrhaging even after installation was complete. It was expected for the brain to swell slightly, they had cleverly built the response into their designs so that the swelling would press the electrodes snugly into their respective positions, and a hollow glass cap Taeng herself had conceived of gave space for the brain tissue to enter and stop the device from floating or moving in the jellylike mass.

But if the tissue swelled too much and sent the fine wires too deep into the brain's folds, Neal could die from implants they would have no way to access again and there would be nothing they could do but euthanize the scientist. Dr. Chairasit slipped the forceps between two fat wrinkles of the cerebellum and injected the first deep electrode grid array implant with precision. Then she threaded a collection of thin gold and platinum wires back to the surface to be connected to the wireless micro relay sitting on his brain matter. They temporarily closed and protected the site with a molded surgical plate before unlocking the Mayfield clamp and rotating Neal's head to begin the duplicate procedure on the other temporal lobe.

Dr. Chairasit had been inside the left side of Neal's head before for the primary Output installation. This was supposed to be the faster side of the procedure. Three titanium screws were quickly removed, and the small concave disk of surgical steel was lifted revealing the initial four wire output array they were going to replace. The site was not as tidy and clear as the doctor had hoped, and the surgeon quickly informed her team they had hit a snag.

"We are going to fall off pace. There's more scar tissue than the readouts indicated. It's formed around the dura mater from the last surgery and has partially fused to the brain tissue," Taeng said.

Fuck thought Taeng.

"What do we do?" asked Dr. Zhao.

"We settle in," Taeng answered in a calm steady authoritative voice. She was already concentrating on the micro-tweezers and angled metal scalpel in her hands. She lifted the ribbon of old wires and cut them away.

The gifted surgeon worked diligently until sundown, her team anticipating her need for swaps of instruments and communicating updates on Neal's vitals and neural stream recordings. They were running almost three hours behind schedule by the time Taeng had peeled the protective sheath from Neal's other lobe and installed identical implants. Next, she brought the wires to the surface ready to be collected and threaded them to the front of the patient's skull just like she had done before. It had taken a dangerously long time, but the installations could not have been done any faster. They had been perfectly performed. Neal's pieces of bone were retrieved from their nutrient solutions and reattached to his skull and sutured into place. Dr. Chairasit pinched the clamps holding the skin back and unfolded the scalp back over her husband's head securing it into place with staples and waterproof bandaging.

There was a slight change in the crackling static of Neal's brain activity coming over the dio-station speaker. Dr. Langstone had let his mind wander. The procedure had stretched five hours over the initial estimates they had made, but his ear had caught the shift. He checked the triptych of monitors and the the composite image. Something was off in the blood flow of Neal's brain which was now affecting its functioning.

"Doctor Chairasit there's some decreased activity on the Transcranial Dopplar. The blood in his brain is starting to slow. His condition is deteriorating."

"I know," said Taeng without looking up. "But without the CPU the rest of the hardware is useless."

"We could do a second surgery," said Langstone.

"You know we can't. The brain will start mounting an autoimmune response and we'll lose the wires. Look at how much scarring I've had to wade through from the last installation. We have to do it now."

Everyone knew she was right, but this was beyond risky. The final invasive stage was tricky delicate work, but it could be done quickly if everything went smoothly. Dr. Chairasit held the disc bone saw perfectly still and pressed the pedal at her feet. The saw popped a perfect circle from the front of Neal's forehead.

"How we looking on the TCD?" asked Dr. Chairasit.

"Another 6% decline in activity."

"I only need another few minutes."

Dr. Chairasit reached for the final tool, conceived for exactly this moment. The two feathery mildly magnetized antenna of this strange futuristic devining rod were inserted under Neal's skull away from the brain tissue and separated until they collected the wires from each lobe and fished them back to the open hole in Neal's forehead. Once all the wires were accounted for, they were braced and locked in place.

"CPU," Taeng barked.

Dr. Shandalow cut open a sealed clear plastic bag with a large red stripe on one side. Scrawled across the bag in his handwriting were the words, "STERILE CPU INSTALL. DO NOT OPEN." He laid the bag flat on the surgical cart next then sliced the bag down the middle and cleared both flaps with the red stripe away. Inside was a leafy gold and black slightly curled concave strip. The symmetrical veins of the CPU awaited fusing with the lobe array wires.

The volume of the neural sound coming from the speaker, which had started as a sharp popping hiss, was starting to sound like sand pouring through an hourglass and getting noticeably quieter.

"We are at 88% cognitive activity. If we drop another five, he could have permanent damage. Doctors we have to move faster," said Doctor Langstone.

Dr. Zhao had brought her station close to the patient. It was her turn. In her delicate still hands she held a micro-soldering iron and set of tweezers.

"I'm ready Doctor Chairasit," said Dr. Zhao.

Taeng stepped back, moving into a supportive surgical role and positioned their video microscope over the CPU. She brought the image up on Zhao's station monitor.

"Eighty-six percent," said Dr. Langstone.

As Doctor Zhao fused the first three array wires into the CPU she spoke. His voice was quiet and calm.

"Taeng he's going to be fine. I'll be finished and he'll be in post-op before his blood flow gets critical."

She was quick. As each wire was soldered a tiny yellow light on the CPU began to blip.

"CPU is coming online," said Dr. Shandalow. "Hardware and software are all nominal so far."

Dr. Zhao stepped quickly to the other side of the table to begin connecting the wires from the other lobe to the CPU.

"84% of normal brain activity. This is really dangerous Doctors."

"Your commentary does not help," snapped Taeng with genuine venom. "We're almost there. It couldn't have been done any faster."

"Maybe it shouldn't have been done at all," replied Dr. Langstone.

The second three yellow dots lit up.

"CPU is operational. Brain activity is holding at eight-four percent."

"Ok, let's get him closed up."

The disk of bone was painted with a high calcium surgical bio-glue and reinserted into Neal's skull. A thin metal plate was glued and micro-bolted in place, covering the surgical site. Neal was bandaged and moved into post-operative care. By the time Taeng had scrubbed out, Neal's neural activity had rebounded to ninety-two percent. Dr. Shandalow and Dr. Zhao would take the first post-op nurses shifts. Gregory would take over at noon tomorrow. If anything were to happen, Taeng would only be a stone's throw away in the ranch house and she could be at Neal's bedside or back in the operating room in a matter of minutes.

Taeng and Gregory walked back up the ramp and into Taeng's home lab. The morning sunshine was gone. It was now nearly midnight and outside the door, the grounds of the ranch pulsed and chirped with the sounds of organic nocturnal life in late August. Taeng walked to the keypad and typed her code. The table whirred closed like the stone over a tomb. The room felt different now. The world had changed. But the night sounded the same.

"I'm going to have a cigarette before I turn in," said Gregory. "Would you like one?"

"I would," Dr. Chairasit replied.

Taeng hadn't smoked a cigarette in decades, but the three others on the black box team all occasionally smoked fags from a single shared pack of Benson & Hedges Premium Virginia Round 100s that was always laying around.

The cellophane squeaked as Gregory slipped his left hand into his back trouser pocket and produced a new pack. He cut the blue seal on the regal gold foiled packaging with his thumbnail, flipped open the box, popped the sticker on the glowing yellow inner paper. He shook out the first of ten clean white sticks and offered it to Taeng who lifted the cigarette gracefully into her fingers as they walked outside into the cool night air and sat on the side steps of the ranch house porch. Gregory drew his Zippo lighter across his pants and flicked it up toward his mouth. The lighter sparked and his lips stiffened as he drew the hot fire through the cigarette and took a first inhale before holding the flame of the lighter out for Taeng who placed her hand delicately on his wrist and leaned in. The hot smoke filled her lungs and throat. Taeng closed her eyes and leaned back to rest her head on the newel post. She took one more drag, stubbed out the butt into the dirt, and walked back up the wide redwood stairs to the room she would never share with her husband again.

9

No Face/2016

"If you want a picture of the future, imagine a boot stamping on a human face — forever."

— *George Orwell, 1949*

FBI Building San Francisco, California
October 28, 2016

Ryu finished lacing his new boots and followed the stryker team from the locker room. There had been no other word from BurnBear since the stay of execution was rejected. It was only minutes after the stay was denied that Judith Almont had met Agent Murakami on the tarmac at Burbank airport and they discovered together that Architech's corporate plane carrying Aurora had vanished as superstorm Megra hit the Pacific coast making a search and rescue impossible until after the storm passed.

The US Intelligence Services had begun silently considering their tactical options against OMNIStack itself should it come to that, and Ryu didn't expect them to like their choices in that regard. Their best guess was the ruling on Walcott's execution order had leaked, which forced a hiding sleeper cell of BurnBear to expose itself in an attempt to save Neal Walcott and whatever digital WMD was still lurking inside his head. BurnBear's second objective was obviously to reclaim Aurora by any means necessary, and they had accomplished that.

A bomb hidden inside a mind, inside a skull, inside a man, inside a cell, inside a prison. And he's still found a way to do what he promised he would, thought Agent Murakami. I don't know that destroying his brain ends this. Could there possibly still be something at BurnBear Ranch? There's absolutely nothing left of the place. It was destroyed and completely dismantled, piece by piece. Broken down and cataloged to the smallest detail.

Colonel Rutledge was first up the stairwell followed by Captain Hankerson and the rest of the two Stryker teams. The hard soles of all fourteen soldiers clopped and echoed towards the top. Colonel Rutledge shoved the crash bar of the heavy metal rooftop door; there was a loud clack of steel against steel and Agent Murakami stepped out into the first fresh air that had filled his lungs since arriving. It reminded Ryu that at his most basic he was animal on a living planet. The helipad was still being drained and dried, and the ground crews were pulling the tie downs off the helicopters that had been secured and covered to weather the storm. Ryu and Colonel Rutledge had a moment to walk to the corner of the building and look out at the old wooden city by the bay but even though they were eight stories high there was no view. The power was out all over San Francisco and the sky was still a deep shade of night. Just a vast expanse of nothing enveloping them. There was nothing else they needed to say or go over. They had their orders, and they had their plan.

The twin-turbo shaft engines of the two Sikorsky MH 60 Pave Hawks growled to life, and the teams loaded onto the transports. Agent Murakami took Stryker Team two in the nearest chopper with Captain Emily Hankerson and five others. Colonel Rutledge took Team one in the other. Everyone found their spots, locked in, and gave a verbal ready. Com between teams on all radios was good, and they were cleared to go. As soon as they were airborne the two helicopters pulled a hard right-hand bank flying out into the darkness. The chopper pitched so hard Ryu was practically looking straight up at the other side of the helicopter. Strapped in against the other side was Captain Hankerson. She had the presence of a calm seasoned veteran soldier. Ryu had only known the captain for a few hours, and he was already glad Colonel Rutledge had assigned her to Ryu's team after he had been assigned command of Team one by executive order of the president. Agent Murakami didn't want command of the team. He'd told the president and Rutledge so and when neither of them said a word, he accepted his assignment. Now he looked across the red lit cabin and cockpit at the soldiers under his command. They were professional tactical fighters.

Why in god's name would anyone put me in charge of these people? Ryu wondered. I'm the youngest greenest person on this mission.

The pilots' FLIR/NVG goggles were down over their eyes. The world surrounding the two aircraft was still dark, but the sky was beginning to glow from somewhere deep beyond the horizon. The covert operation made a beeline towards the most rural corners of north-eastern California, almost to the border with Nevada. It was their best guess since the hurricane had knocked out all communications and satellite images over the area. They didn't know what had happened to the Nyken's plane, all anyone knew was the Architech corporate jet had dropped off all radar and lost com just before the storm hit, and it had occurred ominously near the previous site of BurnBear Ranch which had been completely destroyed in the raid nearly four years ago. Other than that, nobody knew what was out there waiting for them. There had been no reports of a midair explosion, or sightings of the plane headed toward any non-extradition zones, which made it most likely the jet had suffered a mechanical failure, but a mechanical failure occurring near BurnBear Ranch was no coincidence. The team decided the plane would be most likely to make an emergency landing at Quincy-Gansner-Spanish Creek Municipal Airfield on the far northeastern side of Tahoe National Forest. It was a rural little facility surrounded by tall forest pines that barely had enough runway for a piper or a cub, let alone the massive Architech LearJet Global 6000.

Sitting across from Ryu under the pulse of the thwooping heli-copter blades, Captain Emily Hankerson oversaw a final weapons check of her team. They hadn't had time prior, but it only took her team moments to complete and confirm. Agent Murakami was taking a bit longer. Captain Hankerson could see Ryu knew firearms from the breakdown he was giving the rifle, but he was looking slightly lost when it came to the advanced features as he prepped the next gener-ation smart weapon he'd been issued. He was an excellent shot, but all his training and experience had been with traditional firearms. This gun felt more like learning a new software program.

"New tech for us too," she said easing into advising the agent. "We got these about three months ago. Seen them before?"

"Not really," said Agent Murakami. "I trained on the HK."

"I know," said Captain Hankerson. "I read your personnel file while we were in limbo at FBI-SFO. You're quite a marksman."

Ryu gave a quick nod without really looking up from the weapon. There was a double scope and small touchscreen. Near the trigger were a small red button and next to that a touchpad about the size of his fingertips.

"This rifle is gonna make you better."

"Sure. If I can figure out how to fire it," said Ryu.

She reached out her arms to demonstrate.

"May I?" she asked.

Agent Murakami handed her the rifle. Captain Hankerson flipped and spun the gun with the precision of a drill team member and began her 90 second orientation. Ryu appreciated the captain's help.

"Ok. I know this looks complicated but what we've got here is actually simpler than the HK416 you trained on. This is a custom spe-cial-ops smart rifle with a precision guided firing system and bio-met-ric authentication. The double scope is for shots from a fixed position, but the system will tune into a single eye piece when you're in heavy motion like where we are now. The system has gyros to counter any bouncing and help steady the muzzle."

She pressed a small hidden button on the back of the touchscreen and the screen turned on but did not appear to be emitting any light into the environment.

"Second diffusing layer makes this a no glow screen. You can turn this on, and it won't give away your position. This weapon has been issued to you and will require your face and fingerprints which it already has - loaded from your personnel file. There's a camera on the screen and bio-mets on the grip stock and by the trigger. You gotta green light all four locks before it will fire. Once you green light them the weapon is hot until you lock it. The lock is one touch on the bottom of the grip and a confirmation. On this mission Rutledge has overall control. He can restrict or override any weapon under his command."

She turned the rifle back over to Agent Murakami. Now in the bottom right-hand corner of the screen were four small red lock icons, and a moment later his own face appeared, and the first red lock turned green and opened.

"Ok," said the captain. "Now hands on grip and stock. Feel for the fingertip grooves."

Ryu moved into the familiar position, the butt of the rifle against his shoulder. His hands slid instinctively into place. The second and third locks went green, and the final red lock began to flash.

"Last bio-met is below the safety. One touch and the weapon goes hot. The gun has its own encrypted wi-fi network which is linked to the other rifles and any other opticals in the team's gear. There are recordings being made with the front and rear-facing cameras. What the scope sees is broadcast on the screen or you can show the feed from any other camera in the network. You paint the target with the paint button next to your thumb. Then all that's left to do is shoot. Red button or trigger fires a 50 cal. EXACTO round. That stands for Extreme Accuracy Tasked Ordinance. You fire that bullet and it's got a brain."

"And eyes. And control like a house fly going three thousand feet per second," said Agent Murakami finishing the same thought. "The EXACTO project came across my desk a few years ago."

Captain Hankerson was pleasantly surprised at Agent Murakami's prior knowledge.

"None of us has clearance to fire our weapon, captain. That would be an additional escalation," said Agent Murakami.

"We know. Everyone knows."

It was dawn when the two helicopters reached the northeastern foothills of the Sierra Nevada Mountains. The sky began to glow a soft shade of orange and from half a mile out from their destination, Ryu couldn't see anything but devastation. Most of the airfield had been reduced to rubble, knocked down with impunity by Superstorm Megra. Among the wreckage of corrugated metal siding and cinder blocks, the 40 foot in diameter black tube of the Architech corporate jet's fuselage and the bold white lettering of the company's logo drew the pilot's eyes.

Colonel Rutledge came over the com system. "Stryker Team two. This is Striker Team one. You are landing at the airfield, or what's left of it. We are continuing Northeast. I need as much information as you can give me about what you think happened here and you need to be ready to be wheels up again in twenty minutes. If Aurora or Carol Nyken are down, there you let me know immediately."

Ryu clicked his com on. "Copy Striker Team one."

"Alright, be safe Agent."

The two helicopters split up, and Ryu watched as his transport descended to the demolished airfield as Colonel Rutledge's team continued their current course toward where BurnBear Ranch had been.

Stryker Team two's chopper landed and four of the members dropped out of the helicopter and secured the grounds around the airfield as best they could. In the ruins of the airfield a shooter or explosive could easily be hidden. Agent Murakami scanned the mid-ground in front of him for anything suspicious. After about five minutes the team called all clear. Ryu lowered his rifle and jogged to the wreckage of the Lear Jet. The right wing had been ripped nearly clean off and the jet was leaning completely onto its side. Two of the strike team officers were already stepping out of the half-overturned fuselage.

They met Murakami with just a slight shake of their heads.

"No one's alive in there Agent and somebody got here before us. There are boot prints and the black box is missing," said the closest officer.

"Bodies?" asked Ryu.

"Yeah," the officer said with a tinge of grief.

Ryu hopped over the pool of water surrounding the dented door hanging from its bottom hinge and stepped into the cabin of the plane. The inside of the aircraft was in no better shape than the decimated airfield around it. The interior safety glass had cracked, and spider webbed, and the honey blonde oak wood cabinetry that had so tastefully appointed the cabin was floating in about three inches of standing water in the back half of the plane, broken to the point of nearly shattering from the impact of the landing. The white leather and suede bulkhead was splattered with dark red blood stains and viscera from the multiple bodies that had been thrown like crash test dummies against the walls and corners inside the wreckage. But they all hadn't died in the crash. Two flight attendants both had gunshot wounds. The attendant with two bullet holes in his chest had been running down the aisle when he was shot. The other woman had a single bullet hole in her forehead appeared to have just unbuckled her seat belt. There were the bodies of two people with press credentials still around their necks. All their phones, laptops and cameras were missing. Another confirmed identity was DOD fixer Odie Carmichael, whose body and face had sustained severe trauma. He had been almost broken in half. But there was no sign of Mara Walcott or Carol Nyken, and when Ryu checked the cockpit for the flight crew, which had included Arthur Nyken, they were also missing.

The comlink in Ryu's ear popped on.

"Agent Murakami, we have more casualties outside the plane. You need to come look at this."

Ryu exited the crashed jet and went back outside into the destruction. Multiple members of the striker team spread out across the airfield began holding up their hands and reaching for their com.

"Eighteen."

"Agent, I've got thirty-three. There are bodies all over this airfield. Looks like every one of them has gunshot wounds."

Another soldier checked in on the com.

"Twelve. All gunshots from behind. This was an ambush."

"That's why there's so much destruction on the airfield," said Ryu. "These people were in the middle of securing everything for the storm. Which means they were all dead before the Nykens crashed."

"That would require an insane amount of preparation," said Captain Hankerson.

"Indeed, it would," said Ryu.

It was like Neal Walcott had predicted this day decades ahead of time, and if that was true, they all needed to expect that he had planned for exactly this scenario, thought Agent Murakami.

The com of a distant team member from across the field kicked on.

"Agent Murakami, there was a local law enforcement response before the storm. Two sheriff's deputy cars. Four deputies all high velocity rounds to the head. They were all dead before they got all the way out of their cars."

Ryu opened his com.

"Stryker one. Do you copy?"

Hal Rutledge came over the radio.

"Go ahead Stryker two."

"Colonel, we have a mass casualty event at the airfield. Close to a hundred bodies are here. Looks to be all tactical gunshot wounds except for the crash victims. This was a coordinated attack synced to the plane crash and the storm. They emptied the field before Architech had even taken off. They were waiting for them. After the plane came down sheriff's deputies responded. They didn't know what they were walking into. I'm sure none of them ever even got to their radios."

Colonel Rutledge's com kicked back on.

"Have you located Aurora?"

"Negative. The Nykens and Aurora are missing. Co-pilot is missing too. There were bullets in the flight attendants."

═══════

Edge of Tahoe National Forest
Donner Pass Road Quincy, Ca

Rolly watched the sun begin to peek from behind the ridge line. The peaceful orchards were filled with the small songbirds who were just returning, long hidden from the storm and now cheerfully drinking and bathing in the pools of rainwater and hopping between the debris of the thousands of oranges that had fallen to the ground. He loved this place, and it had all been destroyed. His favorite fly-fishing spot was just down a bypass road through the fruit orchards from where he was standing. A couple miles off the side of the road was the little secluded grove where he and his wife had lost their virginity on a star-filled night over forty years ago. All these peaceful sweet memories swirled up from his heart to his mind as he managed his roadblock crew arriving with barricades and tire spike stripes. Somewhere in the distance of foothills he was starting to hear the thump of helicopter blades.

The sheriff knew Colonel Rutledge. They had met the day OMNIStack had attacked BurnBear Ranch. Keeping Plumas County, the pristine wild rural place it had been before Walcott and the ranch had become a large part of Sheriff Kemp's job since the raid and he had honestly thought after Neal Walcott and BurnBear's trial and conviction, that it was all over. But then he got a call just before the real teeth of the storm took out all communication. He had spoken to a competent concise Colonel Hal Rutledge who had informed him that an Architech corporate jet was presumed to have crashed in his county. He agreed with the colonel, it couldn't have been a coincidence. Rolly Kemp didn't keep up much with business news, but he remembered Carol Nyken from the day at the raid too. He didn't want her or OMNIStack anywhere near his county.

Four of Sheriff Rolly Kemp's deputies were unaccounted for when the storm hit, and everyone was forced to shelter in place. On the call the colonel had been blunt with Rolly, he had two chopper teams ready to try to find his deputies, but his people were most likely dead. And he needed the sheriff to co-ordinate a massive North-South roadblock to bring their killers to justice. The sheriff had been in this part of California a long time now, and he knew there wasn't another way out of this canyon except straight down Donner Pass Road and right into his roadblock. He had Trukee PD on the other side, but somehow, he just knew they were gonna come to him. He was sure of it.

After everything that had happened in the last seventy-two hours, he hated admitting it even to himself, but Sheriff Kemp really wanted a donut. Adrenaline and grief had always made Rolly hungry, and he wished he had a fresh buttermilk old fashioned, and a piping hot cup of black coffee. But he had passed the site where the donut shop used to stand about forty-five minutes ago. The shop didn't exist anymore, and the only donut left was half a six-foot-tall fiberglass sign that had been bolted to the roof on top of the concrete rubble of the only place within forty miles that had been open twenty-four hours.

This country can't take a shit anymore with a computer telling 'em how to do it, thought Sheriff Kemp. What in god's green goodness do I need an A.I. for?

The radio on the sheriff's belt came on.

"Sheriff Kemp come in."

"Go ahead Colonel."

"We found your people. Two cars all four deputies are dead. I'm sorry Sheriff."

Kemp knew those men well.

"It was a tactical assault on the airfield while everyone was securing their planes and hangers. Right now, we have 86 confirmed dead. Somebody's got some very real fire power out there. You let your people know they're playing defense only. You will not fire unless fired upon."

"Copy that, Colonel."

Jesus thought Sheriff Kemp. There aren't six thousand people in the whole county. I must know all of them.

"What's your location?"

"I'm on the south side, but we have both sides of the pass covered. If they're anywhere inside the valley nobody's leaving without us seeing them first."

The yellow tinged beams of a single pair of headlights crested the horizon about two miles away heading down the abandoned road towards the roadblock.

"Funny you should say that sheriff…"

Colonel Rutledge's helicopter flew high over the truck racing down the road and past the roadblock. Sheriff Kemp felt his stomach drop with the vertical descent of the helicopter as it landed behind the barricades. The colonel leapt onto the graveled concrete of the two-lane road and recognized Sheriff Kemp immediately. He was the only person standing still in the bustle of law enforcement behind the roadblock, and it was obvious from 100 yards that the tall leather-faced man in uniform and a green and yellow Oakland A's baseball cap was in charge. Hal walked to where the man of about sixty-five years old was watching the truck speeding towards them. A pulsing pop preceded the sight of the second helicopter by a few moments before they could both see the black Pave Hawk about a mile to the east of the truck. The helicopter's nose was down, and it was quickly gaining on the truck on an intercept path.

"Sheriff," said the Colonel as he approached Rolly Kemp.

The man turned just his head, his eyes behind wire-rimmed glasses and firmly shook the colonel's hand.

"Colonel. I figure we've got about two minutes before that truck gets to us. You wanna give me the reader's digest version on how this is gonna go down?" the sheriff asked in a flat unemotional voice.

The colonel wasted no time.

"We've got that second team in the sky behind them. We need to do absolutely everything possible to take both people in that truck alive. I cannot stress that enough. Every possible effort needs to be made."

"And by both people you mean Carol Nyken and the Walcott's daughter?" asked Sheriff Kemp

"That's classified," Rutledge said.

Rolly returned to watching the road.

"We ain't some trigger happy rough riders if that's what you're gettin' at, Colonel."

"I'm glad to hear it sheriff. This would be the worst day for any of us to get itchy."

They watched as the truck rise over the final hill between the vehicle and the roadblock another four hundred yards away. The vehicle crested the peak and rolled to a stop.

Sheriff Kemp got on his radio. "I want all my men to keep their firearms in guard position. I don't want to see anyone in high ready."

He looked up and down the line to check and saw his officers and deputies with the muzzles of their guns pointed down.

"That's fine. Now we're gonna let Colonel Rutledge here lead. From here on out special ops has command. We take orders from him until this is resolved."

He turned to Hal and handed him the radio. "You're show, Colonel."

Colonel Rutledge open the comlink.

"I don't want to see any drawn weapons from anyone," Rutledge said as he walked in front of the barricades to get a better read on what was happening. The truck was just sitting there. He could see two silhouettes illuminated from behind by the glow of the red brake lights. He lifted his thermal binoculars and set the rangefinder. In the black and white display, he could make out the two individuals. They were saying something to each other. Carol Nyken was behind the wheel. Aurora was across the bench seat from her. Even from this distance he could tell they both looked like hell, but Aurora was clearly in need of immediate medical care, and Carol Nyken was agitated.

The second helicopter team was almost in position. Rutledge calmly opened a direct com-link with Agent Murakami taking care to be outside of earshot of any of the officers at the roadblock. He could hear the background noise of the blades of the helicopter and then the agent's voice came on the line.

"I'm here colonel."

"Agent, we have an increasingly agitated Carol Nyken in the driver's seat of this truck. Aurora looks injured."

"Has anyone made contact with them?"

"Negative, but I'm about to try. I am granting clearance on your rifle."

"Colonel any other member of this team…"

"Negative. No other member of the team aims a gun at that truck. I will not give clearance for their weapon to go hot. They don't know about Aurora. They do not have enough context to make that call. You are the only one with clearance to understand the full situation. Every gun down here is safetied. No other rifle in your ship has clearance. You will be the only gun on her."

══════

"Strike Team two. Strike Team two. We have a confirmed sighting on Aurora. She and Carol Nyken are in a yellow 1976 Ford F-150 doing approximately eighty miles an hour. We've coordinated with local law enforcement who are preparing a roadblock. Aurora and Nyken are headed southwest on Donner Pass Road, and we are deep in Tahoe National Forest. I mean way back in here."

Ryu and the second stryker team were already hopping back into the helicopter and securing their harnesses.

"Sending GPS coordinates now. Our ETA to the roadblock is six minutes."

39.290467, -120.935756

Ryu took the few steps to the cockpit. Through the windscreen of the Sikorsky, he could see the ruby glow of the truck's taillights was only seconds away. He tapped the pilot's shoulder and gave the signal to turn the airship 90 degrees and hover. The pilots nodded. As the helicopter spun in place Agent Murakami returned to the cabin.

"What's the word Agent?" Captain Hankerson asked for the other members of the team who were listening intently.

"Rutledge notified me he's only giving my weapon clearance. We're holding position here while they try to make contact. I'm the only gun on her. That's all I know right now so everyone sit tight."

Ryu secured himself into the gunner's position and leaned back letting the straps across his harness bear his weight and steady him. He raised his rifle and pressed the button on the back of the touchscreen. The first red lock turned green. Next Ryu felt for the bio-metric grooves on the stock and grip. Three green locks. He moved his trigger finger below the safety and and pressed the smooth oval-shaped pad. The weapon was now hot. Ryu could feel the gyros inside the gun optimizing the smoothness of his movement as he lifted the rifle and pointed the gun at the driver's side of the stationary truck down on the road one hundred feet below.

In the screen of the rifle was an infrared display of the top of the truck, but he couldn't see the inside. Agent Murakami reached for his com to Colonel Rutledge.

"Colonel I'm getting a murky picture in my thermal vision from the roof of the vehicle. Can you send me the feed from your binoculars."

"Sending now."

A moment later the screen in front of Ryu changed and he could see the two figures inside the truck with immense clarity and definition. Agent Murakami's thumb moved onto the paint button and a bright red target contracted around Carol. A red targeting dot dropped onto the video feed from the Colonel's binoculars. He could see Carol putting a cell phone to her ear.

Murakami's comlink popped back on. Even though he watched her dial, he hadn't expected Carol Nyken to be on the other end of the com. He recognized the voice immediately.

"Hello Ryu."

"Carol. What are you doing?"

"I need you to listen very carefully. I have been released to deliver a message. BurnBear is willing to offer the DOD a deal and you have to convince them to take it."

Agent Murakami kept his rifle fixed on Carol Nyken. His finger hovered over the trigger.

"I'm listening," he said.

If you don't do what they say, they'll use Aurora."

"Use Aurora to what?"

"Turn OMNIStack from an asset to an enemy."

"That's not possible."

"They've hacked her Ryu. Burnbear hacked Mara. She's a weapon now that they control. Even if you put a bullet through her head, her cognition is so fast they'll still have enough time inside Aurora's mind to do everything they're threatening."

"What do they want?"

"They will allow Neal Walcott to be executed, and you can have Aurora, but Neal must be given the unsupervised internet connection. No less than nine uninterrupted minutes before he is euthanized. If you do this BurnBear promises no attack once Neal is dead, and they will release Aurora. If you don't, they strapped her with a bomb. Anyone comes near the truck, or you don't do what they say, and she dies."

"Do you understand the terms of the deal they are offering Agent Murakami?"

"I do."

"Good."

Carol Nyken had barely completed the monosyllabic word before Ryu's rifle let off a single shot that split the air like thunder. The EXACTO round ripped through the top of the truck as if it were paper. In the same moment, the .50 caliber bullet entered the back left side of Carol's skull and in less than a millisecond exited out the front of her mouth covering the interior of the truck in an explosion of brain, blood, and teeth, through the engine block and into the road.

It couldn't have been more than twenty seconds after the rifle had gone off that the helicopter skids struck the ground. The tracking round fired from the helicopter had blown a hole in the roof of the old truck the size of a softball. Carol slumped over the steering wheel with Mara bound and booby trapped across the bench seat next to her.

By the time Ryu had unlocked his harnesses both Stryker teams had already cleared the Pave Hawk's rotors. He was the last one out of the helicopter. Ryu had never seen a veteran tactical team inserted inside a hot scenario before. Without knowing what kind of explosives were strapped to Mara, four techs had foregone the robot and a drone cam because they didn't know how much time Aurora had left.

They moved so fast, he thought. Like a single lethal and life-saving organism. Like a Yokai, his father would have said. Ryu had always found his father's Shintoism anachronistic, but watching the stryker teams neutralize that scene was indeed watching a violent and powerful Yokai spirit descend from the god realm.

Lethality all happens too fast now, thought Ryu. Everything is moving too fast.

The team cleared both people from the vehicle and Ryu saw Carol's body. Half her head and most of her face were missing. What appeared to be the remains of several wires were coming out from her head.

The bomb techs had swarmed Mara. She was unconscious, half naked and non-responsive, but she was alive. Black duct-tape was wrapped tightly around her mid-section. The pipe-bomb had been a hasty malicious job. Even with her waifish frame the skin at the edges of the tape bulged. Mara's bare breasts and the black of the tape gave the horrible impression of some violent corset. The white of the pipe was barely visible beneath the nails and bolts rolled in layer after layer of hot glue. The raw nails had been wired. Contact would cause detonation. The angry crude lump of wires and scrap metal was even more dangerous than the high-tech device everyone had anticipated because the homemade bomb, strapped to the stomach Ryu cherished in secret, was unpredictable.

The first tech to reach her put a handheld hyper-magnifying glass up to the nest of wire and circuitry and had begun calling out all the components he could identify to the second tech who repeated each component back to him as he wrote them on a small white board.

The two other bomb technicians were five seconds behind the other two. They were both strapped with a tactical duffle bag and rolling a single metal hardcase behind them. Once they were within six feet of the device and its incapacitated captive, in a matter of seconds they had built a small workstation.

He turned back to the two technicians at the workstation already building something. Both of their heads were down, working in unison, and placed the organized white board in front of them.

"SPEC LIST!"

"SPEC LIST!" the two techs called back without looking up.

Ryu noticed the second tech had given the specs and variables in a different order than they had been called originally. He recognized the training. The team was fault tracing the design of the device, scrubbing the concept and components of the device backward and forward for its potential weaknesses as they called and responded back and forth. Micro to macro and back again. The group's mindset synchronized. A hive intelligence.

With all of them still within the blast radius, a quick breadboard was snapped together and soldered. The bomb was not a particularly sophisticated device, and the improvised disarmament rerouted the power instantly. The team got the device in the detonation can.

"Local SWAT disposes of the bomb. Load the assets," barked Rutledge.

As Team 1 loaded Carol's body on the first chopper, Ryu stayed fixed on Mara. He could see her abductors had shaved part of her head revealing the scarred tissue of multiple generations of cranial surgeries. There was an obviously new wound. A large patch behind her right ear had been freshly shaved with a razor and a rope of fiber optic cables hung out of her skull from a raw improvised surgery where the surgeon had obviously lost control.

10

The Citadel/2016

"I suspect that the human species — the unique
species — is about to be extinguished, but the library
will endure."

—*Jorge Luis Borges, 1941*

October 28, 2016

The plane dipped and the urge to vomit filled Ryu's inner ears and the back of his throat. He had soaked straight through the once sharp black suit he had put on two days ago when he had left D.C. for California. It was stained and he stank.

Enveloped by the roar of the Globemaster 3's engines, Col Rutledge could hear Agent Murakami fully surrendering the contents of his stomach to the turbulence. The colonel walked briskly back to the midsection lavatories and pounded on the door.

"This flight ain't gonna get nothin' but rougher Agent. I don't care what you got comin' outta ya I'm gonna need you strapped in on the deck. You have three minutes. I am not exaggerating when I tell you I will rip this door out with my bare hands."

Ryu heard the officer clearly. Hal Rutledge's voice still had the bark of a Marine trained to command over an active battlefield.

Andrews AFB… Ryu thought as another hot sweat hit him. Just don't think about anything except touching down at Andrews. 455th Aeromed Unit is on the plane. They are some of the best surgeons in the world. There's nothing else I can do.

Ryu picked himself up off the floor and stepped to the sink. A small thin mirror was bolted above the steel basin. Next to the mirror a steel bar held a fresh cloth towel. Even in the throes of exhaustion and extreme motion sickness, Ryu was grateful for this one thing. He put the soft dry towel to his head in the soapy green florescent light of the lavatory. A hot streak of purple lightning ripped through the ozone a few hundred yards north of the plane's wingtip and the hulking metal bird jolted hard. The plane dropped fast from beneath Ryu's feet before rising quickly. Ryu's abdominals contracted painfully. His knees buckling hard.

On the other side of the door Harry Rutledge decided he'd give the agent a couple extra minutes. And some privacy. The colonel had an iron gut, but he didn't need to hear any more. As he walked toward midplane his body felt heavy. His mind was still focused, but staying sharp was taking a great deal more concentration now. So many hours of adrenaline and cortisol had fried his psyche, and at some point, he was going to crash hard.

Colonel Rutledge passed through the partition and into the sky hospital facilities onboard. Two airmen pulled a hot red kidney from the torso of the injured young woman who was unconscious with tubes down her nose and throat. Her neck and all four of her limbs had been set in traction. She was still alive but had suffered multiple major traumas. He could see the scarred tissue across her body from multiple surgeries and fiber optic cables hung out of her skull from the improvised surgery during her abduction. The first team cleared and right behind them a surgical team began repairs to the diaphragm. The colonel was a smart man, but he did not even begin to attempt deciphering the apparatus and choreography of the two scrambling surgical teams. The state-of-the-art sky hospital the 455th Air Evac Unit had configured inside the cavernous hull of the C-17 was a true marvel. Much of the medical equipment on the plane was top secret. Even so, from the expression on the Med Crew Director's face, Rutledge could tell Aurora was in critical condition.

The other surgical table was covered by a pressurizing dome. Carol Nyken's body barely had any of her head left. The explosive tracing bullet had made sure of that.

Rutledge walked to the front of the plane and rapped on the cockpit door. The pilot waved him in without turning, and Harry took a position in the doorway observing the flight crew. He knew the pilot, Charlie. He had flown Harry through sandstorms in Iraq and Afghanistan, and Harry knew Charlie had done real hours with hurricane hunter crews. They had both seen enough storms to know what they'd be in for.

Witnessing the power and elegance of a hurricane from a distance is a completely dissimilar experience from dropping into the storm. Out the front windscreen of the cockpit, Harry could sense the scale and intensity of the black clouds was filling the crew with fear. The storm imposed on the C-17 and the quartet of F-18s escorting it, like a mountain range climbing high, the endlessly tall cumulonimbus clouds of the storm just twenty miles out now. Electrical discharge popped and sizzled in the ozone in a kaleidoscope of colors.

This isn't like a hurricane, thought Col Rutledge. There's no eye. No center. No order to the rotation at this point. It's just chaos in those clouds.

"Hal, I want to request to land," said Charlie. "The air is going to be catastrophic in this storm."

Harry responded immediately and without equivocation. "Chuck you can get on the radio and plead our case, but I'm just letting you know we're goin' through this."

"Yeah, I know," he said as he opened the Com with Air Mobility Command. "AMC. AMC. This is Medvac Air."

"This is AMC. Go ahead Medvac Air."

"We just spoke to ATC Albuquerque. Airspace is clear for our relay with ATC Kansas City, however, be advised the storm warning between here and there is severe. We do not advise Air Mobility Command to send Medvac Air through this. We'd like to get on the ground and to a secure medical facility here in New Mexico. Wounded would be treated there. Flight crew agrees AMC. We'd like to get on the ground immediately if not sooner. Over."

The radio connection popped back into his ears as soon as he cleared the channel. The voice of Air Mobility Command came back on the other end.

"Negative Medvac Air. You will go through this storm. You will proceed to Andrews Air Force Base without deviation."

"Copy AMC." Charlie turned to his co-pilot as he began to pull back on the yoke and lift the C-17 higher. "Ok. Let's try to cherry pick through this."

Col. Rutledge walked briskly aft to the lavatories and pounded on the door.

"Agent Murakami we are going to be experiencing major turbulence. I'm gonna need you strapped to the deck immediately."

Agent Murakami opened the door. He looked like a microwaved candle.

"Spend much time in the actual air at the Air Force Academy, Agent?"

"I'm ready now Col Rut…"

The plane jolted hard to the right like it had been hit by a car in the sky. Agent Murakami whipped across the lavatory. Instinctively he put up his hand to brace himself, but the sink was still wet. Ryu's hand slipped and crown of his head crashed hard into the mirror which instantly split into four still bolted pieces.

For a moment Ryu and Lt. Col. Rutledge stood frozen recovering from the shock of the impact. Ryu looked alright, well not alright exactly but he seemed to have escaped the incident miraculously unscathed.

"I'm ok. I'm alright," said Ryu with relief.

Ryu tilted his head to the floor and blinked a couple of times to test his optimism. He put his hand to his head. As his finger caught a thin groove he looked up to see the colonel's expression of frustrated disgust. It took a few more seconds before the blood started to get in Ryu's eyes.

"Absolutely unbelievable," Colonel Rutledge said.

He grabbed Ryu by the lapels and pulled him out of the bathroom and planted the dazed agent in the seat against the hull.

"Strap in Agent."

Rutledge activated his comlink as he walked across the cargo bay and unhooked a flight helmet and medical field bag from the rack.

"This is Colonel Rutledge. I have a new injured. Agent Murakami has a large open head wound. Non-life threatening."

"MEDVAC team is fully engaged, Harry."

"As if I didn't know that already. I'll treat the idiot myself."

The colonel yelled back at Ryu as he walked across the C-17 cargo bay.

"You know when you survived all this so far, I thought you were the luckiest son of a bitch that ever lived. But now I realize calamity follows you around like a hungry dog."

"That's been true my entire life, Colonel."

"Yeah, I know. I read up on you."

The captain came over the cabin intercom.

"MEDVAC AND CREW. Secure and brace for major turbulence. I tried to land but we've been ordered to Andrews immediately. As we all know we're about to go through a major storm system and we will be in it for at least an hour and its gonna be serious."

Col. Rutledge handed Ryu a helmet.

"I'm gonna patch you up. And then you're gonna put this helmet on."

Ryu watched Col Rutledge quickly pull supplies and gloves from the med bag.

"Colonel," said Ryu. "I didn't pull the trigger on that rifle."

The colonel didn't seem surprised. "We'll run full diagnostics on the gun when we get Andrews, and I'll debrief you. We'll talk about it all then."

Colonel Rutledge brought the medical staple gun to Ryu's forehead.

"This is gonna feel exactly like you'd think a staple going into your skull would feel."

The hot sharp pain of the staples into his skull was quick. A bandage and seal followed, and Ryu put on the crash helmet.

"Agent Murakami this was the first of many conversations you and I are going to be having when we get to Andrews. We're going to need to create a modicum of trust with each other."

The colonel put two small pill packs and bottle of water in Ryu's hand.

"You don't want to be awake for this next part Agent. I promise you that."

"Because you're going to poison me and throw me off the plane?" said Ryu.

It got half a laugh off the Colonel as he sat down strapped in next to Ryu and secured his laptop to his leg. Ryu opened both packs of sleeping pills and took all four doses with a quick swig of water. He hoped it was enough. In Ryu's remaining moments of consciousness. He remembered watching Colonel Rutledge typing as quickly as he could trying to send an initial report before the plane entered the storm.

Ryu looked out the window to see their initial escort of F-18s breaking away hard from the storm, departing back to Miramar Air Force Base in San Diego. The F-16s rendezvousing on the other side of the storm would be from Luke.

The design of that fighter is close to forty years old at this point, and they still look like they own the skies, Ryu thought.

The intercom crackled into the cabin.

"Ok. Here we go everybody. BRACE. BRACE. BRACE," the captain called out.

Another few quick seconds of relative calm and then the sensation was like an endless car accident in the sky. Ryu surrendered to the wash of it. The noise. The violence. But terror can only be experienced for so long before the body submits. The powerful sedatives in Ryu's stomach mixed with his exhaustion. Amidst the chaos he noticed the world around him going silent. The noise just seemed to fade away. After a few more moments a dark hole was growing in Ryu's consciousness.

Give up, it said.

The dark hole grew warm and inviting like a soft bed. He wanted to climb into the hole forever.

Whatever happens next doesn't matter. You'd don't want to see it. You know what's going to happen. It will all be so horrible. Give up.

As unconsciousness enveloped Ryu the last thing he could hear was the ocean of sound from the plane in the storm and then he felt nothing.

———

The glowing city domes and pillars of Washington D.C. had slowly come into view and fallen back behind the horizon as the sun rose above the Eastern Seaboard and the C-17 air hospital arrived at Andrews Air Force Base in Maryland. The pilots greased the landing, and the huge plane touched down and came to a stop outside Hanger 1. Inside the cabin it was the quieting of the engines, that had been loud for so long, being shut down that awakened Agent Murakami. He was slow to move. His mind was still groggy from the sedatives. The whir of the hydraulic system echoed as the gate dropped, flooding the hull with bright noon-day light. Ryu opened his eyes. The light made them sore, and he immediately needed to find his sunglasses. He took off his helmet bumping the gash across his forehead and a quick bolt of pain ripped across his scalp. He carefully lifted the helmet off his head and pulled his sunglasses from his jacket pocket and put them on. He unstrapped himself and began packing up. Ryu was exhausted. Except for a headache pulsing in time with his heartbeat, the rest of his body was still numb.

Slow down, he thought to himself.

The gate dropped to the tarmac. With an unobstructed view out the back of the plane Ryu saw a full Marine battalion had been activated, eight hundred soldiers guarding every hundred feet of perimeter. Their jet fighter escort now patrolled the sky around the base. Somehow even with all this commotion the government had managed to keep it a secret that the country was being threatened with an attack that could cripple global society. Behind the C-17, two ambulances were poised like sprinters waiting for the baton with their back barn doors already open to take Mara and Carol Nyken's body to Malcolm Grow Medical Center immediately. Their primary directive had been two words: Recover Aurora. Ryu, Colonel Rutledge, and the tactical team had done that.

Colonel Rutledge's boots stopped in front of Ryu. Behind the colonel the first air hospital surgical team pushed the metal gurney holding Mara's unconscious intubated body down the ramp. Her scalp was bandaged where a hole had been drilled during her abduction. She had on a post surgical helmet. Most of the skin on her abdomen came off when they removed the bomb, and she was beginning to bleed through the bandaging around her torso. She looked helpless. Just another multi-billion-dollar piece of equipment entering failure. Just another broken weapon. The medical transport team loaded Mara into the first ambulance. The sirens cut through the stillness of high alert on the base and the engine revved as the ambulance rushed toward the on base hospital.

Rutledge could see the personal pain in Murakami as he watched Mara driven away, but he decided to ask about it later.

"Agent Murakami, as you are probably not surprised to hear, we have been summoned to testify before a military tribunal. The convening of this tribunal has been deemed a secret of national security."

"How is she?"

Rutledge looked over his shoulder at the med team already small in the distance.

"Everyone expects her to live, but she's fucked up bad. Broken jaw. Broken teeth. Fractured skull. Both her hands are shattered. She must have put up one hell of a fight."

"What about her neural stream?"

"Her limbic system is functioning. Her body wants to breathe. She broke six ribs, that's why they intubated her. But nobody is going to know about her higher brain functions until she's conscious and that won't be for at least a couple days. She's going into her next surgery immediately, but she gonna need quite a few before they've got her conscious again."

For Ryu Murakami hospitals and violence had been inextricably linked since his first breath. The vortex of miracles and tragedies haunted Ryu like a poltergeist. The second med team was in much less of a hurry. Carol Nyken was already in a body bag, and Ryu's rifle had been the one that put her there. He was the only one cleared to fire. He pointed a gun he didn't know with someone else in control of it at the CEO of Architech. How could he have been so stupid. He was being set up. The med team somberly rolled Carol's gurney to the ambulance and loaded her in. There was no siren, and the ambulance lights stayed off as the vehicle pulled away. This is a hobson's choice, thought Ryu. BurnBear is presenting the illusion of choice. Damned if we do, damned if we don't.

Agent Murakami had been the last one who had spoken to Carol Nyken directly. It was his com she connected to before his rifle fire ripped through that truck. Part of BurnBear is still operational and they had only one demand- nine minutes of unsupervised access for Neal Walcott to a high-speed internet connection before his execution. If not, BurnBear was threatening an attack. What would a sentient cyberweapon even do? What would its agenda be? Governments everywhere could lose control and without Mara to process the data, the United States loses OMNIStack. And if they do agree to BurnBear's demands and allow Neal Walcott an internet connection, we could be the ones that unleash the weapon.

Ryu was sure he hadn't pulled the trigger on the smart rifle. If OMNIStack was responsible, he suspected it wouldn't be the first time the A.I. had taken operational offensive control of a weapon. He still couldn't prove it, but he was certain the same thing happened during the raid at BurnBear Ranch. Thirty died and the Pentagon had flooded the incident with money and legal threats and erased any record. If OMNI did the whole thing a second time it would show pathology. That would change the calculus.

Once I can get my weapon hooked up at the digital forensics lab I can know for sure, he thought.

"Colonel, I need the forensics on the smart rifle you issued me as soon as possible."

"It's already started. I'll have the results in a bit. I've got you accommodations. You can shower and I'll have someone bring you a change of clothes. I will copy your dossier on Aurora for the tribunal."

Agent Murakami pulled his personal hard copy of his brief on Aurora from his backpack and handed it to Colonel Rutledge. As the two men walked down the ramp Ryu discovered a sharp pain in his right knee. Colonel Rutledge gestured to three men sitting in a jeep awaiting Ryu on the tarmac.

"You've got an attache and an escort. I will collect you in one hour."

"Thank you, Colonel," said Ryu.

They reached the jeep.

"Sargent Griers is your attache. Sargent this man is a hero. Apartment 4 on the third floor of the Judicial Ops building has been commandeered for Agent Murakami's use. See to that."

"Yes sir, Colonel."

Ryu sat down in the jeep, the attache and his assistants leapt over the side doors into their seats, and they were immediately on their way. Once they cleared the airfield Ryu could see Andrews AFB had taken a beating in the hurricane. Multiple facilities and structures had major damage. The air was humid with a cool breeze floating inside it that blew away the last remnants of Ryu's sedation. The flooded roads around the base began filling with bulldozers and dump trucks as the construction crews commenced clean up.

The jeep pulled up to the tall brick Georgian revival Judicial Ops building and the attache escorted Ryu to his room. The service attendants followed behind them with two trays of breakfast which they placed on the dining table in the apartment on the top floor of the building and left. Ryu was handed a dopp kit, thick cotton towels and wash cloths, new boxer shorts and an undershirt so white and clean and fresh it hurt his still sensitive eyes just to look at.

"Eat. Shower. I'll be back with some things," said Griers.

The attache closed the door behind him and Ryu was alone in a quiet room. He sat down in the club chair next to the window, in the solitude and silence and bounty of his surroundings and looked out at the once immaculately manicured park across the street littered with trees and debris. It was the day after the storm had passed, but the sky retained a lingering gray darkness. Several crews were already wading through the deep puddles with sub pumps.

He kept the lights off as he walked into the bathroom, opened the shower, and turned the hot water knob. The shower head hissed and spit, but no water came out. He picked up the staff phone and called maintenance. They told him to just keep the pipes open, and water would start flowing again in ten minutes or so. Ryu hadn't eaten anything for almost three days. Even so he hadn't had an appetite when the trays were brought in. Now the aroma of whatever was under the lids was beginning to fill the room. It smelled particularly good, and Ryu's stomach growled. He walked over to the dining table and lifted the lid off the first tray. There was a silver urn too hot to touch full of steaming coffee, and biscuits with blackberry jam and whipped butter. Under the second tray, a side of shaved country ham, scrambled eggs, and hash browns. And next to those cold sweating glasses of milk and orange juice with the tops wrapped in cellophane.

There was nothing else for him to prepare before his testimony at the tribunal. Ryu had known Carol Nyken since he was a grad student in her data lab at CalTech's Advanced Mathematics Program. He knew her as well as any profiler could. He was realizing that no one truly knew Aurora. Ryu wrapped the coffee pot in a napkin and poured himself a first cup just as the sound of water running started coming from the shower. He took a first sip and walked to the bathroom sink and unpacked the dopp kit. Ryu could see steam rolling above the shower door. He stripped down and got in. The first few minutes the water trickling down Ryu's body and pooling around his toes was brown with dried sweat and blood. He closed his eyes and let the miracle of hot water continue dissolving the film encasing him.

Ryu was only halfway through his meal when there was a knock at the door. The attache opened it and introduced the on base barber who promised Murakami a tight haircut and a straight razor shave "as smooth as a buttered ass." The barber set up one of the dining chairs while Ryu finished his ham and eggs. The attache brought Agent Murakami a full suit of clothes. Even with the devastation of the storm, his treatment since landing had made him feel like a United States military officer again. The weary man who had stepped into the shower had been washed off of him leaving only the fresh soldier underneath. Agent Murakami was ready.

Colonel Rutledge tapped on the door and dismissed the attache. Rutledge placed his briefcase at the dining table and sat down.

"Feel better, Agent?" asked Rutledge as he poured himself half a cup of lukewarm coffee.

"Yes. Thank you, Colonel Rutledge."

"Call me Hal. Ready to begin the formal procedure of the testimony you will be giving today?"

"I am."

"All right. Let's get started. I am here to assist your testimony regarding the current threats being posed by the subversive domestic terrorist group BurnBear, it' leader Neal Forrest Walcott, Architech and the Nyken contingent and potentially by OMNIStack itself. Considering the potential destruction they are threatening, BurnBear's demand of Neal Walcott being allowed the nine minutes of internet access before he is executed is being considered. The tribunal commences at 05:00."

The colonel took a stack of binders out of his black leather satchel.

"The forensic diagnostics and video recording from your weapon came back. The report says you fired the shot with a manual pull of the trigger."

"I didn't."

"For today we need to keep focused on giving these people the highest quality intelligence possible. And I give you my word we will expose whatever happened with your rifle."

Colonel Rutledge handed Ryu a copy of the diagnostics weapon report.

"This tribunal has been called to decide the US military's course of action in regard to Neal Walcott's execution, whatever is in his head, and BurnBear's threat and demand for web access."

"Your testimony will be centered on presenting a contextual timeline of the events centered around Project Aurora including but not limited to the developments that lead to the creation of OMNIStack by the Walcott Labs at CalTech and their sister for-profit corporation ReGenOS. You are going to be asked about Neal Walcott's disappearance and BurnBear in detail. And you will also speak on the Nykens and Architech. Full detailed answers and don't slide into conjecture."

Ryu bristled a little at being told not to present his opinion but decided not to show it. If he decided to say something in the hearing, he'd accept the consequences. No one else knew as much as he did now, and if the military wanted to neutralize these evolving threat scenarios, they were going to need to know his best guess on a number of things.

"They are also going to ask you about your experiences with Mara Walcott codename Aurora. All your experiences," Rutledge said with a knowing look.

The colonel opened the door for Agent Murakami and the two men walked down the hall to the elevator. At 13:15 Ryu walked through the double doors into Judicial Hearing Room 2. There were only a few people inside. Ryu knew who they were instantly. Acting Director of the DoD, Head of Homeland Security, Air Force Cyber Division Commander.

"You misspelled Primitive on the cover Agent. This kid is the guy DOD assigned to the Aurora Asset?"

"Actually Admiral," Ryu responded. "In this case its spelled with an A. Primitivism with an I is a natural sociological state. Island and Jungle tribes all over the world can be called Primitive from a techno-logical stance and it's not a pejorative term. But from an ecological standpoint they are in balance with their environments and highly at-tuned. That could be considered a far more advanced society."

"But the A here refers to Prim-A-Tive, which is not a natural state. This is an enforced state of technological primitivism. This is a fascist ideology."

Agent Murakami walked to his name placard.

11

Spanish Colonial Mayan Revival/2001

"There are no ruins without builders."

— *José Martí, Nuestra América (1891)*

Pasadena, California
August 26, 2001

The days all held something Carol looked forward to. Most of them were spent in the warm cocoon of fulfillment as Carol picked Mara up from school about noon. It was where they could interface without distraction and really talk, and Carol could get a continuing assessment of the girl's development. Carol and Mara often walked the long tree covered trails, just as they had done since Mara was young, that bent around the ranch and up into the high craggy turn cresting into the foothills. Mara would be fed and WonderGame would commence.

Most evenings were spent at CalTech.

Even in a lecture hall of two hundred thirty people, Carol would learn every student's name by the second week. She derived a great deal of satisfaction teaching. Her lectures were well attended with big laughs, but more than that Carol was a master of her field, and she made it her mission to truly teach the foundational theories of data science that would transform their world. It also helped Architech scout for talented students.

While Carol lectured in Sloan Hall, Emma and Mara roamed the grounds of CalTech as if it were their own personal magic garden. The campus police knew when Professor Nyken was on campus and to keep an eye on the children. Emma had charmed the CalTech campus staff early on when she made sure to introduce herself and Mara to all of them and usually declaring unprompted that she was "a proud architecture enthusiast" who "just adores the style of buildings at the college." The librarians and custodian were all big fans and made sure that the golden children of CalTech's Nobel Prize winners were safe and catered to as the girls explored the department buildings as if they were cathedrals to the various scientific disciplines.

The modern aesthetic of campus at sunset radiated with mysticism, and the girls would pick from the fruit trees and sometimes Emma would talk about the details of a building, and say she wanted to be an architect just like her uncle Raul. They would dance in and out of the light coming through the iconic arches of the biology building- Keckhoff 1, and postulate together about the intricate ornamentation around the windows of its grand stone tower, usually winding up among the tall Spanish style bookshelves in the Robinson library inside the Astrophysics department. It had been the dome of the observatory telescope silhouetted by the Cherry Plum and Camphor Trees casting hard shadows across the facade that had first caught Mara's eye. When they had gotten closer, the bold celestial ornamentation emblazoned across the building gave the effect of a sun worshipers alter, a supernatural temple to the heavens.

Astrophysics thought Mara. Matter and energy. The only thing missing from Astrophysics is consciousness.

The girls approached the main entrance of the building drawn by the odd warm purple light coming from the patinated brass sconces on either side of the double doors at the front of the structure. One of the librarians, Mrs. Barschdorf had been walking in as the two girls were staring at the fixtures. She introduced herself and explained to them that it was the manganese dioxide in the glass that had turned the entrance lights purple over time. She had invited them to come and explore the rest of the Robinson building. The two girls had lingered outside examining the edifice before following the kind woman inside. The clean rectilinear lines and cast stone carving of the Mayan Revival exterior ended. The interior was more complex.

Inside, the central stained-glass dome splashed kaleidoscopic lights across the mosaic tiles and ornamentation climbing high up the walls and laid into the ceiling. It was a dazzling fractured chaos. Mara thought the theme and metaphors of the building were particularly clever. At a macro level the celestial universe appeared to operate like a machine, like a clock or engine, but at the quantum level it was all a dizzying anarchy. Mara especially enjoyed the zodiac symbols cast into the chandelier which threw such interesting shadows across the library stacks. The potent blending of colonialism and science and the mystical laws of nature intrigued Mara in primal ways she did not understand and instinctively concealed. She watched the light moving through the stained glass and landing onto the bright geometric patterns of the kiln-fired interior walls, changing the tiles' temperature and color, its very properties.

There really is no such thing as inside, thought Mara. Inside doesn't actually exist. There is only outside and the illusion of not outside.

Mrs. Barschdorf would often bring them something to drink, making them promise never to spill a drop, and leave the girls to sip and talk like the students they saw around campus. Over time it had become their favorite spot. On this day they were talking about Emma's big upcoming Model UN trip. She had just become old enough to join and already helped her team earn a spot at the state Model UN conference where they had been selected for an additional exciting honor.

"When do you leave?" asked Mara.

"Our team flies out on Tuesday the 4th. Then we're in New York for a week!" Emma said with joyful abandon before catching a loving but stern look from Mrs. Barschdorf that said keep it down over there you two.

Emma recalibrated her volume and leaned in to whisper to Mara.

"We have two days of general sessions in the actual UN building with other Model UN teams from all over the country, cuz the real UN is out of town till the fall. Then we come back to California. We're learning about the state government. We go to San Francisco first and then Sacramento to tour the state capitol."

"That's so cool," said Mara attempting to mirror her friend's excitement. "I want to see New York."

"Me too. When I grow up, I'm totally going to move there. There are like six colleges I'd be so excited to go to, and if you go to one of them first, we can totally be roommates. I'll take so many pictures, and I'll tell you everything."

Mara smiled making sure her eyes properly conveyed positive emotion.

Mara liked Emma, but there were some things she didn't understand. Emma was two years younger but that wasn't the gap most apparent to Mara. It was Emma's belief. Emma believed in things Mara found exceedingly difficult to accept. God and Santa Claus and declarations about "when I grow up." Emma was an optimist, and Mara was certain the world needed them, but it always struck her as a mark of lesser intelligence. Emma also seemed happy, and Mara had eventually concluded that intelligence isn't everything. She was grateful to Emma for teaching her through their friendship how to embody her own emotions. That was a valuable friend to have. But Mara's favorite thing was how silly Emma could be when they were by themselves. Mara did not have any other silly people in her life and laughter was rare.

"It'll be the longest trip I've ever taken without my parents," said Emma. "Is it ok if I call you a couple times? I don't want to call my mom. Everyone will call me a baby."

"Yes," said Mara. "Totally call me."

Just before closing time Carol came and found the girls. The three of them thanked Mrs. Barschdorf and Carol drove Mara home where Nancy Yarpas had made dinner for her. She loved Nancy's cooking.

"Hi Mara. How was your day?" Nancy asked.

She was just plating the fresh pan-fried trout fillets and a creamy piping hot wild mushroom risotto.

"Good," said Mara. "Nothing much to report. Just practice and summer classes. I got my AP Chemistry test back. one hundred percent." Mara smiled proudly and entered the kitchen and dropped her backpack and tennis bag against the door of the pantry and sat down.

"Where's Mom and Dad?" she asked.

"They're both working late tonight, honey," replied Nancy as she lifted the lid on another pot and pulled two artichokes from the steamer basket.

═══════

Pasadena, California
August 27, 2001

The late summer sun coming through the blinds and landing on Taeng's face woke her up. Because she trusted her collegues completely, she had been able to get some real sleep. She checked her bedside clock, it was about four p.m. the next day. A long yawn animated her whole body as she stretched and squirmed. Even with the amount of yoga and stretching she had done in preparation for the procedure her body was sore. She went over yesterday's installation in her mind. Neal had been under sedation for way too long, but it had been something they had discussed. Once the surgery started there was no stopping until the entire installation was finished. Even if it meant Neal died on the operating table. Once the first cut was made, they had chosen a path. He had survived. Now everything depended entirely on how Neal's recovery went.

Taeng tossed her covers to the other side of the bed and placed her bare feet firmly on the solid redwood floor her husband had made that never creaked or bounced. It was just as sturdy as the furniture. The wood throughout the property had been planed, cut, and assembled with precision in the wood shop on the ranch. It was the first structure Neal had built. He had slept in a wax cloth tent on a cot the months after he had bought the property with his first money from teaching at CalTech. Fifty acres without a single building, power or running water. Neal didn't have a truck or any power tools. He had an axe, a planer, a saw, and a bicycle. Neal had felled the trees himself and turned them into a spacious tidy warm woodworking studio with a small kitchen and bed. Taeng had romanticized the period in Neal's life. His wander in the wilderness. His raw ability to change the world around him. Taeng had never seen anyone who could manipulate the substrate of Reality like Neal Walcott. And now her feet were on the floor of the grand warm ranch house that Neal had eventually erected. The drawers of her dresser slid with ease as Taeng reached for her softest warmest clothes.

Taeng walked down the hall and paused for a moment to listen at the door of Mara's room before entering. Neal had added the room to the house just for her and finished it years before she was born. He'd made the ceilings tall with glass panels across the roof so she could look at the stars, and a canvas shade she could pull across. The bookshelves around the room Mara and Neal had built together. Now they were filled with the hundreds of titles Mara had read and the artifacts and sacred objects of WonderGame. Taeng had missed out on most of those moments preparing for Neal's Input surgery and she resented Carol and Neal for that. They knew Mara. She had only caught glimpses of her daughter.

Across the floor three wide stairs led up to a small, railed platform and Mara's enormous handmade bed. Mara was asleep. The girl didn't stir. Taeng had been so focused on the Input/Output procedures she couldn't remember the last time she was in the girl's room. She had done her duty for Neal, but her obligation to Mara was just beginning. Taeng sat down on her daughter's bedside.

The designed miracle child started out her life as a relatively average little girl. She was almost remarkably unremarkable except for the look in her eyes. It was uncanny for a baby to have such intense poise and focus. She had cried very little and had the same normal stages of motor and mental development. Then at about two she began to separate herself from the development of normal children, and very quickly Mara was blooming into something extraordinary. It first manifested in the girl's fascination with tennis. Taeng had been a tennis aficionado since college, and she was in the middle of watching the third set of Pete Sampras battling for the U.S. Open Men's Title against Cedric Pioline when the channel suddenly changed on the television in the middle of a game point. For a moment Taeng thought something was wrong with the television but instead she turned around to find the not yet four years old girl holding the remote control and gracefully mimicking Sampras while keeping a perfect box score with a pen and scrap of paper. There was a much simpler version of Dr. Taeng Chairasit that would have loved nothing more than to become her superstar daughter's tennis manager, but Neal had been quick to put that dream in check and remind Taeng that Mara already has a destiny.

Taeng's beeper went off. It was Dr. Langstone.

C MS

Her heart sank. It was shorthand. Taeng knew immediately from the three letters that Neal was conscious, but he'd had a mild seizure.

Mara rolled over and and began to open her eyes.

"Mom?"

There was no way for Taeng to explain anything. She rushed out of the room, and within a few minutes descended the staircase into the ranch lab where Neal was in post-op. All three of her colleagues were there at Neal's bedside, just as they had promised.

"What's happening? Where are we?" Dr. Chairasit asked.

"Where are we?" Dr. Langstone said angrily. "Neal has a fucking bite plate in his mouth, Taeng. He came out of the last installation like nothing had happened. Like he woke up from a regular nap and got back to work. Something is way way off here."

"It's a more invasive procedure."

Neal started to howl and as his body shook from another violent seizure.

"Jesus Christ," exclaimed Dr. Shandalow. "Taeng he's gonna break his fucking teeth, we need to sedate him."

It was gut wrenching for Taeng to watch Neal's body convulse so violently, but she knew what the protocols they had agreed to before the procedure dictated. Dr. Chairasit's eyes were filling with tears she refused to acknowledge.

"No," she said. "We ride it out. He's conscious. He and the installation need time."

"Strap him down and let's make him as comfortable as we can."

Dr. Langstone was many things when it came to being a doctor, but insubordinate was not one of them.

12
BurnBear/2001

"Violence is the only way to reawaken the exhausted
will of a people."

— Georges Sorel, Reflections on Violence 1908

Pasadena, California
September 4, 2001

Neal went through several more days of epileptic episodes before Taeng finally relented and agreed with Dr. Langstone to break from Neal's explicit directives. She was certain Neal would have angrily protested the deviation, but they had to do something. To keep the drugs from rushing into the bloodstream and potentially affecting the new BCI implants, they started an intramuscular anti-seizure course of Lorazepam and Clonazepam. Putting it into the muscles in his legs meant the course would take more time and the effect would be much more gradual, but they had to give Neal's brain and the implants as much unanesthetized time as possible. Taeng attended to Neal for days on end, practically living beside his hospital bed in the windowless lab. During his seizures they would watch his monitors as Neal, strapped and braced to the bed, contorted and screamed without ever opening his eyes.

They looked like terrible nightmares.

When he would sweat through his linens, Taeng did her best to keep him clean. She would change his incontinence briefs and dress him in fresh gowns and sheets. The other doctors would bring her something to eat and attend to calibrating the machines and checking the dio-station readouts for any sign that Neal's Input/Output was coming online. It was never an option to take him anywhere else. All they could do was wait for his condition to stabilize and for his body to heal a little and then see if the neurons of his brain were showing signs of accepting the implants. It took another week before the seizures began subsiding and the scientist was still unconscious.

As Neal's condition played out inside the hidden lab, above the bunker Nancy Yarpas took over responsibilities at the ranch. Her team of long-haul crew and grad students already handled the day to day of the farm, and she personally saw to it that dinner was waiting when Mara came home in the late evenings. There was always a plate in the oven for Taeng when she came back from Neal's hospital room late at night.

Mara wasn't used to not seeing her dad. She was still only ten years old, and Neal's disappearance was scaring her. The girl could easily tell when people were lying. All she could get out of her mother, whom she barely saw, or Nancy, was that there had been an emergency and Neal was in the hospital. That it was serious, but his doctors thought he was going to be okay. She had to keep it a secret and as soon as he was feeling better, she could see him. Mara knew instinctively that what they were telling her was true. She was also clear that they weren't telling her everything. But she let their excuses stand for the time being because she could see how tired and worried her mom was. The first weeks of the fall quarter of school took up Mara's time with classes and tennis, but these required little of her real bandwidth. When she had gotten no additional information about her father, Mara made a simple clean plan of her own.

Emma had been insufferably excited. All the permission slips had been signed and submitted months in advance, and Carol had attended all the pre-trip info sessions with Emma's teachers and chaperones. Regardless of one's age it was an exciting itinerary. Emma's suitcase had been packed with her favorite outfits and organized neatly next to the door to her room for nearly a week before her flight which meant that in the interim, when she wasn't in her school uniform, the girl had worn some funky mismatched outfits which had made her even sillier.

Emma had also been programming her own little film festival in the Nyken's living room, forcing her parents to watch every movie she could think of that was set in New York City. Carol and Arthur had curled up on the sofa with Emma between them and watched everything from Teenage Mutant Ninja Turtles to Breakfast at Tiffany's to Home Alone 2, but Carol and Arthur had drawn the line when Emma had innocently suggested they watch Taxi Driver. Luckily, Arthur found a compromise and they had watched a Nick-At-Night marathon of Taxi instead.

Arthur had always loved the theme to Taxi. From the first time he heard it, the melody had struck him as perfection and hearing that song "Angela" by Bob James again and watching the chubby round yellow taxi moving in and out of the shadows on the 59th Street Bridge in the intro transported Arthur back to his 20s. Before he had met Carol. Before they were rich. And before Emma. To the little apartment he'd had at the BOQ on Marine Corps Air Station Miramar- just outside San Diego. When he was the next big thing in naval aviation, he had been selected for Top Gun, and the only night he had off from the Navy's Tactical Fighter Weapons School was Tuesdays. Some of the other guys already had enough time in the F-14 that they actually had something resembling a real day off, but Arthur's squadron had only recently been switched over to F-14s from F-4s, and as good a natural pilot as Arthur was he still had some catching up to do. On his "day off" he was out the door at a few minutes before seven a.m., meeting up with his Radar Intercept Officer for a morning run and breakfast. Then they would spend the day between the tiny on base library and the Officers Club where they would eat all their meals and study their Ground School materials for the upcoming Flight School challenges. Most of those nights after an early dinner they went for a second six mile run around the main streets on base, jogging down the wide concrete sidewalks flanked by tall palm trees as the sun set into the Pacific Ocean to their West, before he and his RIO would part ways for the night. Arthur's only respite during the six months of the most intense training of his life, was Tuesday nights back in his room in time for catching the last few minutes of Happy Days on the eighteen inch rabbit ear television. The room was small enough for him to sit in the one chair at the back of it and still prop his feet up on the cheap pine side table the tv was on top of.

Arthur would pop some Jiffy Pop on the two-burner stove and just ride the CBS train from eight o'clock all the way to Taxi at nine. The other networks had action shows which held little interest for the pilot who had seen more than his share of combat over the skies of North Vietnam and Laos. But the CBS Tuesday night lineup was all shows about daily life in the United States. It helped him decompress and dream of how simple and blissfully ignorant it was to be an American civilian. Driving taxis, working in a brewery like Laverne & Shirley; Arthur would nibble his popcorn in his socks and skivvies and let the strong bump of idyllic nostalgia wash over him. By the closing credits of Taxi, he couldn't keep his eyes open. At that point in his life Arthur was already dreaming of someday having a family and retiring from the military and now watching the same show twenty years later he looked around and that dream had materialized. The Taxi marathon ended, and Arthur looked down the sofa to see he was the only person in his family still awake. He kissed his wife and told her to go to bed and picked up his daughter and carried the limp sleeping child up the stairs to her room and placed her gently into bed.

He was happy.

Arthur walked down their short upstairs hall and into their bedroom. When Carol got pregnant with Emma, he had thought the house would be too small and he had tried to convince Carol to move. Instead, she had convinced him to stay. "We'll be happier and more grounded if we just stay here until Emma goes to college," Carol told him. "If you want to buy a piece of land and design something for our life after that, ok. We can do anything you want. I could ask my sister if Raul would be interested in being the architect. But while she's a child in school, let's stay here and hold on to the continuity of our lives. Let's keep our world simple. I want to have our family in this house."

It was nine years ago that Carol had taken his hand and convinced Arthur, and now he knew she had been so right. Arthur had more and better than his wildest expectations. Not only had the warm little yellow house been the perfect place for their young family to grow, but he had also taken her up on designing their next home with Judith's husband Raul. Arthur liked Raul, and he was a brilliant architect and engineer who was exceedingly difficult to book. Arthur had always been impressed by the balance Raul achieved between sustainable modern design and humanism. Raul had promised to take Carol and Arthur on as clients in a few years, to not buy anything just yet, and to begin to think about where they wanted to be.

With what Arthur was making alone, they were never going to have to worry about money again. And Carol was making three times what he was. And she had been true to her word; it had not swallowed up all her time. Most importantly, he and Carol had not sacrificed their personal relationship to do any of it. He'd been explicit with Carol about his fears watching so many talented ambitious couples plug into success and achievement. They'd get rich and alienated from each other and eventually get divorced and both wind up losing most of the wealth they had accumulated. The exhausting sadness of the whole thing wrecked most of their careers. It sanded down the high arc of these people's lives and left a lifetime's worth of momentum broken and talents hobbled. But by some miracle that had not happened to him and Carol. They had grown more simpatico and were grateful to each other that they had avoided those pitfalls.

In the same nine period, he and Odie's fledgling consulting firm Architech Aerospace had made some great moves. He had always had a good relationship with Odie Carmichael and when Arthur had come to him and said he needed to make a career transition from pilot to something else Odie had taken him quite seriously. The timing had been fortuitous. DARPA had just had a Remote Piloted Vehicle "go stupid" in midair and nearly kill two pilots. Arthur had heard about the incident. The two men had agreed that there was a significantly blue ocean when it came to RPVs which some people were now calling "drones." The military needed firms developing GPS satellite coordination, targeting, and vectoring systems and to develop the Artificial Intelligence that would eventually handle most aircraft functions. Odie also had global contacts in the aerospace biofuel and battery industry. The two men had chosen to go into business together and Architech Aerospace was born. The firm's divisions were all industry leading. Their navigation and targeting teams were seeing tremendous progress and had been integral in the Global Hawk project for what would eventually be a drone the size of a 737 capable of staying in the air for over thirty days at a time, with the functionality of something akin to a split between a drone and a satellite. Architech had also developed the overall hardware and software capable of the successful conversion to electrification of all systems on several aircraft except for thrust which eliminated the need to extract bleed air completely, not to mention the weight they were saving now that the planes didn't need generators. The system they had patented consisting of one hundred twenty-four separate computers and multiple redundant lithium-ion batteries, had recently been pre-ordered for multiple major upcoming aircraft. Arthur was in the middle of an aviation renaissance.

He entered the bedroom and kissed his sleeping wife who rolled over and kissed him back. Hard.

═══

It was a beautiful early Autumn day the next afternoon when Arthur, Carol and Mara took Emma to the airport to say bon voyage as she headed off to New York on her Model UN trip. As they drove the I-134 that clear morning they could see all the way to the ocean and they all ooh'd and ahh'd to be able to see so far out into Los Angeles. When they drove up the I-110 wrapping around Dodgers Stadium and made casual plans to all catch a game together, the Nykens and the Walcotts, Carol noticed Mara was unusually quiet. When Arthur saw a billboard for Cal Worthington Ford's legendary Acres & Acres of Cars, he looked into the rear-view mirror at his daughter and said, "Hey Emma I'm looking for a new car or maybe a truck."

"Oh really," she said breaking into a smile ready to perform the routine they did every time they were together and saw one of the many Cal Worthington billboards spread out across the southland.

"Yeah," said Arthur starting to laugh. "Do you have any suggestions?"

"Hmmm," said Emma before breaking into song and leading the entire car in singing the Cal Worthington Ford theme song that was ubiquitous for so many years in Southern California.

> If you want a better buy, go see Cal
> You're the guy we satisfy, go see Cal
> Give a new car to your wife, she will love you all your life
> Go see Cal, Go see Cal, Go see Cal
>
> If you're looking for a better set of wheels
> I will stand upon my head to make a deal
> I will stand upon my head until my ears are turning red
> Go see Cal, Go see Cal, Go see Cal
>
> If you need a great big truck, go see Cal
> If you need a little truck, go see Cal
> Get a camper, change your luck, buy a van, and save a buck
> For any kind of truck, Go see Cal
>
> If you're little short of cash, go see Cal
> Doubled over in a flash, go see Cal
> If other dealers you have cussed, here's a dealer you can trust
> All you have to do is just Go see Cal
>
> Yeah, if you want more for your trade, go see Cal
> Better deals were never made, go see Cal
> If you need a car or truck, if you wanna save a buck
> If you wanna change your luck,
>
> Go see Cal, Go see Cal, Go see Cal

The Nykens sang cheerfully, and Mara's smile grew, as they glided through the traffic following the signs to Terminal 3, and past "the flying saucer," the local name for the iconic arcs and spheres of the Theme Building in the center of LAX. Arthur parked their family Chevy Tahoe in the short-term parking and pulled his daughter's bags from the back. As they walked in together Mara turned to Carol.

"After Emma is on her flight may we please go hiking today at the ranch? I'd really like to hike the ranch with you today."

Carol could feel Mara trying to communicate with her sub-textually.

"Sure Mara. We can do that," said Carol as she and Arthur held Emma's hands.

Inside the automatic sliding doors, the terminal was bustling with travelers from every corner of the world, but nobody could miss the twenty students all dressed in the same gray wool blazers and standing underneath the tall red, green, and gold felt banner of St. Maranatha Prep School. The assistants greeted Emma and the Nykens with a clipboard and check-in sheet which required signatures from all of them and took Emma's large suitcase to be checked. The last few families walked into the atrium of the vast terminal and were greeted similarly. Mr. Gene Stricklen, Emma's teacher had taken weeks to make sure all the parents knew that this was not his first rodeo. He had grown up on the Upper West Side, his father had even briefly been US Ambassador to the UN in the late 1970s. The school had been taking their Model UN teams to New York for fifteen years and the twenty-five kids from the upper and lower schools had parent chaperones and dedicated personal assistants. On top of everything else, the kids didn't know that once they got to New York they were going to be surprised with tickets to One Flew Over A Cookoo's Nest on Broadway.

"Alright," said Mr. Stricklen in the confident welcoming manner of so many good teachers. "Everyone is here and checked in. Parents and students, at this point the trip has officially started. I want to take this moment to congratulate the students of Model UN. I've seen the effort each of you has put in since last year. You deserve to be recognized."

He led the group in a round of applause for the twenty-five beaming young faces.

"I can tell you they've worked even harder than you know and I'm so proud of every member. Ok, parents at this point if you have plans this evening…" they all chuckled "you can head out and we will see you again on the fourteenth, but we'll of course be emailing updates and calling to check in with you before we fly out to San Francisco. You're also more than welcome to come with us to the gate and see the plane off. We're all the way down at the very end at Gate 39A. Ok troops lets head out," he said with a smile.

As they dispersed, most of the parents hugged and kissed their children and took Mr. Gene up on his offer to leave, but Carol and Arthur and Mara were among the few families that walked with the kids through the metal detectors and down the terminal. Through the floor to ceiling windows on either side were planes waiting to push back. The ground crews looked busy to the point of being frantic.

Arthur scoffed. "All the airline guys say gettin' in and out of the terminals at LAX is a total goat rope."

"Oh?" said Carol holding Emma's hand.

"Yeah well, the airport's almost a hundred years old. It was never designed for big jets. Used to be a great big bean field."

They walked past the designated smoking area and most of the children held their noses and made mocking and judgmental faces at the people sitting in the unappealing florescent lit acrid fishbowl. Next, they passed the courtesy office, a small plain beige cube built into the wall. A woman of about sixty pressed the button to open the

PA system and spoke into a thick silver gooseneck microphone. Her voice came over the speakers as she told one party their courtesy cart was ready and asked another gentleman to please pick up a white courtesy phone.

"I don't think that mic or that office has been changed since 1965," said Carol.

"Or the staff," chuckled Arthur.

They reached the gate where Mr. Gene was already speaking cheerfully to the gate agents, and after a few more scans of paperwork he thanked the agents and turned to the kids.

"Ok Maranatha parents we have an early boarding priority so now's the time to say your arrivedercis, and we will see you in ten days."

"You got enough spending cash Em?" asked Arthur already reaching for his wallet and pulling out two-hundred-dollar bills. He handed it to the gobsmacked eight-year-old.

"You be smart with this money, but you spend it any way you want honey. Congrats. So proud of you. Oh, but don't spend it on that CD Walkman you've been wanting on, because I already got it for ya."

Arthur unzipped the front pocket of Emma's rolling bag and pulled the Walkman box out.

Emma jumped up and down and gave her dad a big hug.

"I thought I'd let you find it, but if you didn't know it was there on the flight it'd be a waste so, there you go sweetheart. We love you."

Carol got down on one knee to be eye to eye with Emma.

"This one's from me, Em."

Carol pulled a small rectangular box from her jacket pocket and opened it. It was a Timex 26MM Expedition Mini field watch.

"Cool!" said Emma. "It's kinda like yours."

Carol smiled. "You got it, kid. I bought my watch a long time ago and it has always brought me good luck. Now yours is going to do the same. You take good care of it, and it will always get you home."

"Thanks Mom."

Emma wrapped her arms around her mother's neck and held her tight. Carol could feel Emma's face getting hot. Emma started to cry softly.

"Now I don't want to go," the sweet girl whispered into her mother's ear.

It melted Carol's heart, and she laughed which made Emma laugh.

"Yes, you do," Carol said. "You just don't want to miss us. Missing each other is hard baby. But you can't let it stop you from doing what you know you have to do. And I promise we're already missing you a zillion times more than you'll be missing us once you step on that plane."

Carol could feel her daughter nodding and composing herself. She kissed Emma on the forehead and held her even closer before they both let go.

"I love you so much Em."

"I love you too Mom."

Emma turned to Mara.

"Stand with me till they take my ticket?" she asked.

"Sure," Mara replied.

The two girls walked to the back of the short line with her teammates. Emma boarded the plane, found her seat with her classmates, and after a few minutes of excitement using all her new gifts at the same time, the plane took off and Emma fell sound asleep.

It was nearly impossible for her to stay awake on planes.

Arthur's cell phone rang just as they arrived back at the school. It was Odie.

"Hey Odie," said Arthur. "She did… yeah I'll be there in about thirty."

Carol watched Arthur listening.

"Ok. Sure. Will do."

Arthur hit the end button on his brand-new Nokia 8250 and leaned in Carol's direction as he drove.

"Odie would like you to call him as soon as you're available," he said.

"Ok. Is it an emergency?"

"He did not use the word emergency."

"Alright. I'll give him a call tonight."

Arthur dropped Carol and Mara off at Carol's car and headed to meet Odie at Architech Aerospace. Carol and Mara drove to the Walcott Ranch. Carol recognized something she had not seen before in Mara - shutting down. This was a girl Carol had never seen retreat and in the last few weeks she had seemed depressed.

"I'd really like to just sit for right now if that's alright," Mara said as if she could read Carol's mind.

"Ok," said Carol and they drove the rest of the way to the ranch in silence.

When they arrived at the Walcott ranch house, it was oddly quiet. There was no one around. Usually there was something going on, but this day as they changed into their boots and headed toward the hiking trail on the eastern side of the property that followed a stream up into the hills, they didn't see a soul. They walked briskly into Angeles National Forest and started the incline up toward the foothill ridge line. It was hard to see Mara like this. Carol had noticed something similar in Mara's on court play in last Saturday's match. Mara had oscillated between sluggish heavy-footed games where her racket seemed to be made of lead, and an intense angry style of play that bordered on rage. Neither were on court personas Carol had seen before, and now this sullen withdrawn version. Mara was changing, and it didn't seem to be for the better. Something was wrong, and it was not lost on Carol that the one person she could rely on to loosen Mara up and get her talking was halfway to New York City. Opening the hearts of everyone around her was one of Emma Nyken's many gifts, and Carol was certain the friendship between her daughter and her protege was important for Mara's heart to develop. Carol constantly tried to find ways too impart empathy to Mara through her mentorship. Success would be Mara's lowest hanging fruit. But her highest aspiration for Mara was to be a good leader when she grew up.

They walked along the bank of the stream flowing onto the ranch. It had rained about a week ago and the stream was swollen. Mara watched the gushing water too deep for them to cross and continue up the trail. Carol decided to be explicit with Mara.

"I've noticed you've seemed off lately. Is there something you want to talk with me about?" Carol asked.

She was startled by the intense circumspect gaze on the ten-year old's face.

"What is the point of WonderGame?" Mara asked.

"It's to train you. You have so many talents. Some of which we don't know even yet because they won't happen until you get older. But they'll bloom throughout your life, and we want you to have the tools to think and feel your way through them ethically and with compassion for all people. You're a special person Mara. You could be a good leader someday."

Mara stood watching the gurgling rush of the stream. "My parents say a lot of stuff like that."

"Stuff like what?" asked Carol. "Come on, we should get back to the house."

But the child didn't move. Mara couldn't physically take her gaze off the liquid crystal of the stream. She couldn't think or move. All she could do was see the stream in infinite detail and all at once. If someone had handed her a loaded watercolor brush, she would have rendered it expertly on instinct alone. Her comprehension of the dynamics and properties and symbolism was total, and she couldn't stop. She was locked into it.

"They tell me…"

But she trailed off.

"Would you please come have dinner at my house tonight?" Mara asked in a burst.

Carol could sense something underneath Mara's question.

"This seems a little impulsive. Is there some reason you'd like me to be at your house tonight?"

"Yes," said Mara.

"Ok. Tell me the reason."

The girl squinted looking up into the canopy of trees.

"When was the last time you saw my dad?"

"I've been so busy getting school started. It's been weeks. Three weeks. Something like that. When was the last time you saw him?"

"Ten days ago. Twenty-sixth of August," Mara answered. "And he hasn't been home since then. Not a washed cup or a pair of boots. Someone else is feeding the sheep."

"How do you know that?" Carol asked.

"Dad always feeds them before sunrise, and they're not getting fed now until after I leave for practice and school. Something's happened to my dad and my mom knows what it is, but she won't tell me."

"What do you mean something has happened to your dad? What kind of something?"

"I don't know. I asked Mom and all she said was there was an emergency, and it was serious and when he was feeling well enough, I could see him. The last day I saw him, he came into my room really early and he left something."

Carol took a step toward Mara. "What did he leave?" she asked.

Mara reached into her pocket and pulled what at first registered to Carol as a white chess piece until Mara fully opened her small thin hand and Carol recognized the artifact immediately. The small statue's crossed arms. The tiny scrolls tucked into his robes. The globe and the book of astrophysics at the figure's feet. It was Neal's little statue of Galileo Galilei from the Loggiato at the Uffizi. The same one the lab had found on his desk after they had won the Nobel Prize and just before he vanished from the University. Carol recognized it as Neal's personal herald. Now she knew that not only was something wrong, but Neal had set some other major plan into motion.

"Is this part of WonderGame?" asked Mara.

"I don't know," said Carol honestly. "But let's go and find out."

When they got back to the ranch it was still deserted. Nancy had obviously been there because there was a hot quiche in the oven and in the fridge were two bountiful Niçoise salads. It was nearly all from the farming and gardening operations on the ranch, except the tuna, and Carol knew that everything Nancy made for the Walcotts to eat was delicious. Mara set the table, and Carol plated two servings of quiche and brought one of the salads to the table and set it in between them. As she did Carol also noticed an unopened bottle of wine had been left out with a corkscrew and just a single glass so clean it was almost invisible.

The two ate in silence, savoring their meal and saving their words for the conversation still ahead of them. It was after midnight when they heard the door open to the back mudroom and a few minutes later Taeng limped slowly into the kitchen with her hand on the small of her back. Taeng didn't see them at first because she did not expect to, but sitting at the table across the large kitchen Carol and Mara had lost none of their focus or quiet fury. Carol had seen Taeng the month before, and she thought the woman wincing in pain as she shuffled toward the oven looked at least ten years older. Taeng looked like she could barely stay awake while she made herself a plate of food and turned to where she expected a bottle of wine to be. That was when she saw the two people sitting at the table, both watching her with an unblinking gravity set deep into their faces. Taeng paused for a moment but wasn't startled. Carol and Mara had caught her in a mood of deep acceptance brought on by exhaustion. Taeng pulled a second wine glass from the cabinet and brought her meal to the table. She placed her glass in front of Carol and sat down. Carol poured her wine while Taeng removed her shoes with a slow creaking soreness.

"We…"

Taeng interrupted Carol. "I know," she said and took a first deep sip of wine. "Just give me a few moments to put something in my stomach. I'm exhausted."

Taeng took the edge of her fork and cut a bite of quiche. She savored the clear flavor profiles of their farm. Taeng never mentioned it to anyone because it sounded so outlandish, but she swore she could taste exactly which plot of soil the veggies had been grown in. She even thought she could tell which sheep's shit they had used in the fertilizer mix.

Taeng looked her daughter in the eyes and faced her judgment.

"Your dad and I have been working on a brain computer interface that allows for coherent Input/Output."

"She doesn't know what that means, Taeng," Carol interjected.

Mara turned to Carol.

"You knew about this?" the girl asked.

"I knew they were developing the interface, yes. But I have no idea what's happened to your father," said Carol barely taking her eyes off Taeng.

"Three weeks ago, I performed a highly experimental procedure on Neal and there have been some complications."

The questions came at Taeng fast.

"What procedure?" asked Mara.

"Where did you perform all of this?" Carol asked with an edge in her voice.

Taeng didn't answer. She just stared down at her plate. She had lost her appetite.

"Mom…" Mara said with calm compassion.

Taeng looked at her daughter.

"Where's dad?"

Taeng placed her napkin on the table, stood and collected her glass of wine.

"I'll take you to him," she said.

Carol and Mara followed Taeng as she limped out the back door and down the covered walkway into her home office. Carol and Mara had both been in Taeng's office dozens of times. Carol had thought the place was more than a little disorganized, but there was no sign of him in the spacious single room. She walked to the center table. There was no further to go.

"Mom, I don't understand," said Mara.

"Where is Neal, Taeng?" barked Carol.

"Carol, would you stand back from the table please?" Taeng asked flatly.

It came as a surprise when Taeng swiveled the light switch at the wall exposing the secret keypad, and Carol jumped when the enormous table began moving by itself after Taeng entered her code. The table finished its slow steady swing and locked in place. For the first time Carol saw the long sloping ramp down into the well-lit bunker. She could hear voices and Bruce Springsteen's I'm On Fire playing from somewhere inside.

Taeng walked past Carol without so much as a glance.

"Mara, would you help me please," Taeng asked as she reached for her daughter's shoulder and together, they began their descent.

Carol followed cautiously behind them. Everything about this now made her feel like a mark. She had been lied to repeatedly by Neal, since before the expedition. She didn't know what to expect. As she descended, the bunker was more substantial than she anticipated. The ceiling was high, and the fluorescent lights gave a bright even glow across the space. The voices stopped as Carol stepped off the end of the ramp into a charged stillness. From what she could see the place could only be described as an immaculate mess. Taeng and Mara cleared Carol's view and among the jungle of equipment and medical supplies were Doctors Langstone, Zhao, and Shandalow. All three had been tending to the bedside of an unconscious Neal Walcott, but now they had stopped to see Mara and Carol. Carol's eyes moved across their gazes as the group stared back silent and motionless.

Mara walked the last few feet to her father's bedside.

"What are they doing here, Taeng?" asked Dr. Shandalow.

"I was just about to ask her the same thing," said Carol.

Taeng pointed to a nearby stool and Mara rolled it to her. "This is the next step," Taeng said as she winced and practically fell onto stool. Her wine splashed onto her shirt which she completely ignored, letting out a sigh of relief.

"They are here because they deserve to know. If Neal had come out of the Input installations unscathed, he would have explained this all himself. But he hasn't, and I cannot keep up these deceptions. It's time Mara better understood her father and his…" she paused searching for the right word, "ambitions."

"And Carol?" asked Dr. Zhao with a softness in her voice.

"Carol has known Neal longer than any of us," Taeng answered. "He would not have made his breakthroughs without her. She deserves to be here too."

Taeng gestured for them both to find somewhere to sit. Mara crawled onto the side of Neal's hospital bed. Carol didn't move.

"Mara, everyone here, including Carol, we had to keep secrets because we are the only people in whole world who know how to do these things. Your Dad asked all of us if we thought that people would try to stop us and steal what we could do."

"Everyone agreed that they would steal it, and so we've kept it a secret. For a little over ten years."

"From the time just after you were born, we started monitoring your dad with the most sophisticated equipment on Earth. And from collecting years of bio-data, that's every measurable thing about him and his body and brain, we did a first procedure on your dad when you were very little called Output."

"What does that mean?" asked Mara.

"It was a surgery. It meant I opened daddy's skull, and together with Greg and Ang and Mikhael, we installed tiny sensors called micro arrays which allowed us to start recording his brain activity. Then when we had enough recordings of his brain, we looked at all of them together using an enormous supercomputer we built just for him and calibrated it exactly to his brain. We used the computer so we could turn the recordings into digital files."

It had always struck Carol that Taeng was spreading her research too thin, but now the stacks of binders and technical manuals and surgical equipment schematics made sense. The keystone was realizing it was all a half trillion-dollar system designed for a single mind. Under the cover of DARPA and CalTech, the entire cybernetic divisions of Walcott Labs, everything had been made especially for Neal. But the two Paragon computers at Walcott Labs weren't calibrated to Neal, thought Carol. What was Taeng talking about?

"And for a long, long time, what we called Stable Output Storage, that was as far as we got."

"Wait," Carol said. "Both the computers at ReGenOS are research computers, everyone is all over those, and the one doing genetic sequencing is filling up as fast as you can network it."

This time Taeng ignored Carol and focused on her daughter. No one moved but somehow Carol knew she was in a four against one situation with Mara in the middle.

"But we couldn't add anything back into his mind," Taeng continued. "We could record, and we could translate, and we could store, but we didn't know how to do it the other way around. We couldn't take the digital files and convert them back into the raw stuff of his mind, what we called Input."

"And that's the procedure where dad got hurt. We did the best we could and went as fast as we could, but dad was asleep for too long, and he's having some real trouble since the surgery."

Carol had not forgotten her whistle blower leverage in this situation. They had all proven to be reckless and dangerous. But before she threatened anything, she was going to get as much out of them as possible playing the concerned, perhaps even impressed, colleague.

"What was the Input? What did you install?" asked Carol.

Dr. Zhao answered her.

"Three arrays, both sides of the cerebrum and a wireless data relay CPU. Deep tissue input/output transmitters."

"No more plugs," said Mikhael. Carol hadn't spoken to him in quite a while. His Russian accent had almost disappeared.

Gregory picked up the sentiment and further explained.

"CPU performs all the initial neural algorithms so the information could be broadcast to a surface transmitter and amplifier. The spew of wires from the back of Neal's head is gone and he should be able to connect to the BrainStack system wirelessly. The CPU is online, but so far, he hasn't made a connection with BrainStack."

As the grownups talked among themselves, Mara began studying the equipment surrounding her. She had seen most of it before in the rooms where they did the WonderGame tests. She turned to her father unconscious on the bed. She had never seen him without his wig. Without it he looked like a monk. The small metal disk on his forehead was protected by gauze and surgical tape. Mara ran her hands over the dials and screens of the diagnostic station and bio-data recorders monitoring her unconscious father.

"I'll come back to exactly what computer BrainStack is on," Carol said. "What are the complications?"

"He's showing severe signs of Gerstmann Syndrome," said Dr. Chairasit. "His vitals have stabilized but he's still drifting in and out of consciousness. He can't speak. He can't count. There appears to be damage to his ocular motility."

"Is that what happened post-op with the Output procedure?" asked Carol.

"No," said Taeng. "He was up and back to his normal self with a functioning set of arrays in less than a week. Zero complications. No side effects. But this was a much longer and more complicated procedure with a much more powerful installation."

"We've followed his exact instructions as far as we could," said Gregory. "But if we'd have followed them to the letter, he'd be dead already. His brain activity is back up to ninety-eight percent. It's still possible the operation was a success; it could just be a longer road recovering this time. We don't know yet."

Mara continued to explore the machines. A flat rubberized plate with a smooth matted metal in the center and a big squishy rubber pad to stand on in front of it. Across the back in large black letters on a yellow stripe read electrical interface plate- high voltage- do not touch.

As Mara shifted her weight in front of the wide flat metal plate she saw two mirrored indentations. They looked like handprints, but not adult handprints, a child's hand prints. Her handprints? Mara lifted her hands up to the plate covered in danger warnings. She felt a holistic sensation of something being pulled from deep inside her. The girl's eyes rolled into the back of her head before she dropped to the floor seizing.

———

When Mara awoke, she was in her bed and Carol was at her bedside.

"Mara, are you alright?" Carol asked relieved to see the girl open her eyes.

"I think so," said Mara. "What happened?"

"You touched a live conductive plate. You're lucky it didn't stop your heart. Why did you do that Mara?"

"I don't know," she said. "I… thought… I just wanted to help Dad. I don't know why I thought that would do something. Did it do anything?" Mara asked hopefully.

"I'm sorry. No. Your dad's still got a long way to go. But your mom and the other doctors are doing everything they can, and they won't leave his side."

Mara shifted in her bed. She was more disoriented than she had realized.

"Easy," said Carol. "You just need your rest right now. Nancy is downstairs and I am only a phone call away. I need to go home to Arthur. I'm sure he's very worried about where I am. Can I bring you anything before I go?"

"No, I don't think so," said Mara.

"Do you need me to stay a little longer? I will," said Carol.

"No, it's ok."

Mara nodded and Carol kissed her on the top of her head before collecting her things and making her way towards the door. Carol stopped as if something had just come to her. She turned to Mara.

"When you touched that plate… did anything happen to you? I mean other than the seizure, did you experience anything else? A…. a vision or some kind of, I don't know, information?" Carol asked.

Mara shook her head "no."

"The last thing I remember is putting my hand on that plate."

Carol nodded and turned to leave.

"Carol," said Mara. "Thank you for helping me find out what's been going on. I couldn't have done it without you."

"You got it kid. When you need me all you have to do is ask, ok? Always. Always and always."

Carol walked across the room and closed the door behind her.

Mara stayed in bed and waited to hear Carol's car start, and for the sound of her tires to fade as she left the property, before the girl leapt out of bed. Mara raced down the upstairs hallway and down the stairs. She careened through the kitchen and out the back door in a flash, nearly sending Nancy flying into the hot oven where the evening's bread was baking, but the girl did not stop for a second. She burst through the double doors of Taeng's office and down the ramp into her father's hospital room. When Mara entered the room only Taeng was in the space changing Neal's IV drip bag. She did not look surprised to see Mara up.

Mara stepped closer to her father's bed.

"When I touched that plate something happened. I make some kind of connection. There was a word I don't really understand. I don't know what it means," said Mara.

"Don't tell me," said Taeng. "Why don't you tell your father."

Mara came beside Neal, looking over her father's still unconscious form.

"I'm here Dad. Can you hear me?" the girl asked but there was no sign.

She leaned down and cupped her hands around his ear.

"Burn Bear," she whispered.

The lights flickered for a moment as every machine in the room sprang to life glowing and printing and recording, but Neal's body did not move.

"He's online," Taeng said as she walked past Mara to the large metal door at the end of the room and opened it. Mara followed. On the other side was a large freezing cold room housing a vast set of glossy black metal cabinets. Taeng walked to a large user terminal with a keyboard.

"Input/Output is working. He's uploading files to the system."

Taeng navigated through the terminal to see what Neal was loading. From behind her Mara could only see fragments of the screen which was updating too fast to comprehend. The words did not make sense to her. NIE. Manila airlines 1994. WTC 1993. UBL Plans for Reprisals Against U.S. Targets.

Taeng turned to Mara.

"We're leaving."

13

The Real UN/2001

"Bright light city gonna set my soul, gonna set my soul
on fire."

— *Doc Pomus, Mort Schuman, & Elvis Presley*

New York/New Jersey
September 10, 2001

Emma had never seen anything as big and magical as New York City. It was a danger to her neck and spine for the small girl already obsessed with architecture to be in so tall and dazzling a city. Not to mention the danger she posed to pedestrians and cab drivers. "Someone grab Emma!" "Who's got Emma?" It became the running joke of the trip. Because she was the youngest member of the team by several years, she had become the unofficial mascot. The first thing she bought with the money her dad had given her was at a charming a bookstore that her teacher Mr. Gene had introduced them to when they were hosted for the evening by his parents and thrown a lavish celebration at their incredible apartment.

At the party Mr. Gene had taken the moment before dinner was served to explain that the experience they were having, the wonders of travel and culture and cuisine, are all the work and world of diplomatic relations. And their trip was the manifestation of that. To understand that diplomacy is one of the greatest ideas humanity has ever implemented. And at the beginning of a new millennium, they will be the leaders that bring the world into the bloom of the century.

"There is now a great white void of nothing, stretching out past the end of history," he had said. "Fill it you future generations with your dreamscapes."

Emma thought it was one of the coolest things anyone had ever said to her, and after dinner they had stopped at Argosy Book Store, the oldest independent bookstore in New York City and the children were all encouraged to choose something to purchase and read while they were on the trip. Emma had made a casual beeline for the Architecture section. Among the rows of titles she had divined to a 1953 signed first edition of *Power In Buildings* by Hugh Ferris from the very top shelf. Emma knew how to ask politely for books, and she walked down past the shelves of other bright and breathtakingly brilliant titles begging for her attention, to the nearby register and asked a lanky young clerk if he could please help her.

"This one…?" he had asked as he stretched out and cocked the gray linen spine of the book.

"Yes," Emma said.

"You may," he said and handed her the document.

Emma opened the cover and flipped through the exquisite pencil drawings of glowing buildings that are Hugh Ferris' signature style. These are amazing, she thought. And they look like CalTech. But when she flipped to the price written lightly in pencil on the corner of the back cover her eyes bugged out of her head. $250! For a book! she had thought.

"Oh, I didn't realize it was so expensive. I'm sorry," she said and had started to hand the title back.

"Yeah, I'm sorry. It's a signed first edition so that makes them more valuable."

"Any chance you have an unsigned just regular old copy?" Emma asked with the timing and charm of a young Carol Burnett.

The clerk laughed and was earnestly checking the shelf when Mr. Gene appeared.

"Hey Emma. What'd you find?" he asked.

"No. I'm sorry. We don't have any others," the clerk re-interjected. "Just the signed one."

"Oh, ok thank you," Emma said.

"Just the signed one of what?" Mr. Gene asked.

It's this book of these really cool pencil drawings of buildings."

"Hugh Ferris...?" Mr. Gene asked. "Of all the books in this entire store you found a signed Hugh Ferris book?"

"I guess," she said. "But it's too expensive."

"How expensive is it?" he asked the clerk.

"$250," said the clerk.

"Geesh," said Mr. Gene. "We'll see if the library at school can order a copy when we get back. Sound good? There are a thousand other books in the store that are reasonable. Find something else, ok?"

"Sure," said Emma and she walked to where all her classmates were gathered under a cresting tidal wave of Stephen King paperbacks. They were discussing all reading a different horror novel each, but at the same time, and then switching. Emma thought the whole thing sounded too scary, but she bought a copy of Firestarter for $3.99. As the group walked down the street laughing and reveling, Mr. Gene came up next to Emma and handed her a small bag. Emma could see the beautiful blue gray weft of the woven fabric cover and the patinaed ivory pages. It had never crossed her mind, but her teacher had bought her the book.

"If you like buildings this much Emma, this book should be yours. Architecture might be something you'd be great at."

"My uncle's an architect."

"Have you ever talked with him about it?"

"Not really. I've only met him a few times. He's my mom's sister's husband. He's always really nice. He's made like a few US embassies. In Kenya and Mogadishu."

"Wow," said Mr. Gene. "Those building have to do a lot."

Emma nodded.

"How did I not know about this? Let's invite him to lunch at school some time to speak to the team."

"Well, they live in San Francisco."

"Oh my god! Do you think he could speak to us when we're in town?"

"Probably," Emma said.

"Great! We'll call your mom in the morning, and I'll ask her what she thinks."

———

September 11, 2001
First day of Carol's 6:00 a.m. class.

It was still a cobalt-colored sky when first classes of fall semester commenced. Seventy-five students entered Room 302 prepared to at least flirt with taking Professor Nyken's famously brutal four credit class - Applied Data Science 300. Carol was already inside. She liked to be there a half hour before six and see who shows up and in what order. How do they dress? What is their attitude? And most importantly, do they have the chops to not just take this class, but to begin setting a track towards the most sophisticated fields of research within the Advanced Mathematics department. Carol asked the trickle of groggy pajama clad students wrapped in hooded sweatshirts and type A overachievers dressed like they're headed to a church picnic all to sign in and sit from front to back in the room in the order they have arrived.

Just a few minutes before the start of class, the department assistant entered the room with Carol's "Monday usual," a whole milk cappuccino with an extra shot and an everything bagel toasted with lox, tomato, and cream cheese. Carol had mandated sweeping changes in the department. Raises for staff and paid internships. Full parity and meaningful inclusion among the faculty and TAs. Massive equipment investments. But it was the little creature comforts, perks and personal touches that Carol had implemented over the years that had endeared her to the faculty and staff.

Carol took her first big bite and enjoyed her breakfast as she watched the trickle of pupils become a stream. At six a.m. on the button Professor Nyken locked the door to the classroom and walked to the lectern.

"Ok, welcome everyone. Welcome to Applied Data Science 300. I have a couple of announcements. First, why six am? The answer is simple; I am literally trying to keep this stuff a secret."

The three quarters of the class awake enough to register the joke chuckled and Professor Nyken continued.

"I will tell you right now that if you don't already know if your skills are in the top ten percent of the students in this room, chances are this is not the right place for you. This is the gatekeeper class here in the Advanced Mathematics Department and I am its guardian. If you can't cut it, I will let you know as soon as I do, and I promise you will go on to have a full and satisfying life doing something other than data architecture and machine learning."

"But if you…"

A hand went up in the gallery.

"I'm happy to answer questions once I'm finished with announcements, ok?" Carol said lightly.

A few murmurs fluttered across the lecture hall and several other hands popped into the air.

"Professor it's an emergency," said a young wide-eyed man with his hand in the air.

"What?" said Carol confused.

The young man picked up his thick black laptop and hurried to show Carol his screen. At the top of the blocky flat blue and gray of the raw feed for apnews.com, the Associated Press news site, was a headline *Passenger Jet Crashes Into South Tower of WTC* with a time stamp of just two minutes earlier.

Carol flipped a switch at the podium. There was a whirring sound as the projector mounted to the ceiling began to warm up and a large, automated projection screen lowered. It took an interminably long twenty seconds before the media menu appeared on the screen. Carol selected the satellite television and scrolled through the channels. The first news channel she found was CNN. She clicked the channel and as soon as the feed popped up, the only thing clear was a tragedy of significance was occurring and very few people had any information in the first moments since the crash. On the screen the nearer tower to the camera had a huge hole through it' upper quarter and smoke billowing out of either end. At the bottom of the screen the chyron read - BREAKING NEWS. WORLD TRADE CENTER DISASTER.

The DOW was up twenty points.

A strong stable disembodied female voice came over the image.

"This just in... you're looking at, obviously a very disturbing a live shot that is the World Trade Center this morning. We have unconfirmed reports that a plane crashed into one of the towers of the World Trade Center just minutes ago. CNN is just beginning to work on this story. Calling our sources and trying to figure out what is happening.

Clearly something devastating happening there on the south end of the island of Manhattan. We will get more information on the subject as it becomes available."

"Right now, we have Sean Murtagh on the phone. He's the vice president of CNN finance. Sean, tell us what you saw."

"Hello?" came the voice on the other end. "This is Sean. Vice president of finance. Vice president of finance for CNN."

"Yes, Sean you're on the air."

"Hello?"

"Yes Sean, you're on the air. Can you tell us what you saw."

"I just witnessed a plane that appeared to be cruising slightly lower than...uh... normal altitude over New York City. And it appeared to have crashed into... I don't know which tower it is, but it hit directly into the middle of one of the world trade center towers.

"Sean what kind of a plane was it? Was it a small plane? Was it a..."

"It was a jet. Looked like a two-engine jet. Um, maybe a 737."

"You're talking about a large passenger commercial jet?"

"Correct. A large passenger commercial jet."

Carol turned to her students. "Does anyone have a cell phone I could borrow please?"

A few students raised their hands, and Carol ran to one of her students in the first row who handed her their cell phone. Her hands were shaking as she dialed Arthur. She was obviously not a surgeon. She continued watching the projection of CNN.

"Did it appear the plane was having any difficulties?"

"Yes. It was teetering back and forth wingtip to wingtip. And it looks like it crashed about twenty stories from the top of the World Trade Center. Again, I don't know which tower it is. I don't know them well enough to call it by sight, from my angle I'm looking south out towards the Statue of Liberty viewing uh… of the… but it's about the 80th to the 85th floor. It looks to be embedded in the building. I don't believe it has come out the other side."

"Sean any smoke or flames coming out of the plane before it hit?"

"I did not see any."

"Is that a normal traffic area for aircraft in New York?"

"It is not, no. Not a normal flight pattern. I fly between New York and Atlanta all the time. It is not a normal flight pattern to come directly over Manhattan. Usually, they come up over the Hudson River heading north."

"Ok Sean. Thank you for your reporting. We want to throw our coverage to our local affiliate WABC."

The connection in Carol's ear clicked on. "Hello?"

"Arthur it's me."

"I'm here. I'm watching it. It's not Emma's plane, honey. They took off from Newark headed west. It's not them, ok."

"I know. I know. Ok," she said.

"I know honey. It's alright. There is no way it's them. It's not possible. I need to call you back, ok? Whose phone is this?"

"Yes. It's a student's phone. Listen I'll call you from my office line in a little bit."

Carol pressed the fat gummy END button on the phone and turned to hand it back to her student. She instinctively checked her watch. 6:03 am. She looked up and addressed her class. The glow of the screen reflected off the eyeglasses of her students. The young woman's face nearest her was of total blank confusion.

"Listen I'm going to dismiss class so anyone who needs to make a call or anything go ahead. We'll pick things up on Thursday. So, everyone can just…"

A collective gasp rippled through the students and directly into Carol's central nervous system. She looked up just in time to see the last moment of a jet's silhouette disappearing behind the already devastated nearer tower. A split second later a huge fireball rolled from the second building.

"Ok... ok... what we're hearing from our producers is that perhaps a second plane has been involved, and let's not speculate...but now both of the twin towers are smoking. This was not the case just a few minutes ago. Again, if you're just joining us, this all began about 8:46 a.m. this morning... a plane... we don't know yet just what type but perhaps a passenger flight... crashed into one of the towers of the World Trade Center, and just moments ago a second accident. I don't know if perhaps some type of navigation system error or... I don't know what could have sent two planes into the World Trade Center."

As the students packed their belongings, the back door of the classroom opened and four men in black suits hustled toward Carol. She recognized one of them. He was one of her grad students.

"Ryu? What are you doing here? What's going on? Why are you in a suit?"

"Professor I'm with the Department of Defense cyber division," Ryu said as he showed her his credentials. "I've been working undercover as an analyst for the DoD. We need you to come with us immediately."

Carol nodded her consent and followed Ryu out of the building where two black SUVs were idling. Ryu unlocked the lead vehicle, opened the driver side, and got behind the wheel. Carol got in the passenger side and sat down next to him. As soon as the other three agents got in the car behind them, Ryu stepped on the gas hard throwing Carol into the back of her seat and they rushed off campus headed north.

"So, you've been spying on me?" Carol asked.

Ryu kept his eyes on the road. "No professor. I was sent to protect you. The country is under attack."

"The plane crashes? You mean someone used those planes as missiles to blow up the World Trade Center?"

"If it is an attack," Ryu continued as they flew up into the foothills in the boxy black vehicle. "In your opinion could Neal Walcott have had anything to do with it?"

Carol shook her head. "No, it's impossible."

"Why is it impossible?" asked Agent Murakami.

But Carol was reluctant to answer.

"Professor," Carol could hear something in Ryu's voice. "Your colleagues at ReGenOS have gone missing. Yesterday morning several high-profile scientists with deep ties to Neal Walcott, and their families."

"Where's Aurora?" Carol asked.

"We don't know," said Ryu. "When the raid agents came on to the property Neal and his family were gone. The livestock, the furniture, their clothes, driver's licenses, and passports were all left behind. It's like they didn't take a single thing with them. They've just vanished."

Agent Murakami continued.

"Did you know about a secret duplicate paragon system at the ranch under Dr. Chairasit's home labs?"

Carol took a moment to calculate.

"I learned about the ranch lab less than two weeks ago. They mentioned the paragon, but I haven't seen it," replied Carol.

On the second system is the completed plans to build something called OMNIStack. Are you aware of this project?" asked Agent Murakami.

"I've never heard of OMNIStack, but they've been working on a brain computer interface system for several years now. It was a BCI tailored specifically to Neal's mind. No one ever mentioned that project name to me before."

"We also found a large tunnel connecting Neal's ranch and the Walcott Labs campus. Did you know about that?"

"No. But I guessed it might be there because of the amount of equipment they would have needed to transport onto the ranch."

"I need you to tell me what else you do know, Professor Nyken. Why would it be impossible for Neal to have had anything to do with what's happening?"

"Neal underwent a highly experimental surgery to create an Input/Output interface directly into his brain. But there were complications with the installation and Neal was struggling to recover. I saw him. He was unconscious. The black box team at Walcott Labs were all their tending to his hospital bed. They were totally consumed by the surgery."

"Then why leave yesterday?" Agent Murakami asked.

"If the Input surgery had worked it's possible Neal had advanced knowledge of an attack? If he vanished now, it is because now was the optimal time to vanish," Carol replied.

The two SUVs bounded past a military check point and onto the Walcott Ranch.

Emma Nyken was asleep in her seat with her headphones on listening to Alicia Keys Songs In A Minor. A clear bag of Swedish Fish gummies from Dylan's Candy Bar, down to its last few, jiggled on her tray table as the girl drooled slightly on the collar of her corduroy jacket. She was dreaming about a destiny in the grand story of New York City. Somewhere in the deep background of her consciousness she could hear confrontation and anger, but it was faint and subliminal, underneath the music.

She felt the plane pitch forward and a frightful rushing sensation from the bottom of her stomach made her open her eyes.

14

Tryin' To Reason With Hurricane Season/2016

"When you come out of the storm, you won't be the same person who walked in. That's what the storm is all about."

— *Haruki Murakami, Kafka on the Shore 2002*

Pasadena, California
October 26, 2016

Carol concluded her speech and stepped away from the podium. Except for the subtle sounds of the technicians working with OMNIStack, the cavernous room was silent. The small crowd stood gazing at the tremendous machine surrounding them. There was no simple refined way to digest what they had just been told- the Nobel Laureate team member, who had lost her only child on 9/11, and built the machine that was revolutionizing the American government and brought Neal Walcott, and so many other terrorists around the world to justice... the CalTech professor turned techno-billionaire CEO of Architech... was running for governor.

Governor Brown stood and walked to Carol. He leaned in and spoke quietly into her ear.

"You'll have to run the table, Carol. Do it now. You can't stop for any reason. You won't be able to. Move as fast as you can."

Carol gave the faintest nod but said nothing as she hung her cane in the crook of her right arm and held Arthur's forearm firmly with her left hand as they stepped off the stage. A two-person security detail and Odie Carmichael stood at the bottom of the stairs. Odie caught Carol and Arthur's eye and pointed to the far side door of the hanger.

"We've got every major network anchor here. Who do you want to talk to?"

"No tv. I want to talk to a newspaper journalist, Odie. Let me see the list."

Odie handed Carol her briefing folder and Arthur their registered flight plan. Arthur took one look at the atmospheric information on top sheet and snapped the binder shut.

"We need to get into the air immediately if we're gonna beat feet outta here before the storm hits. Right now, is not a good time to try and do this interview."

Odie immediately countered Arthur.

"Every reporter in the world wants five minutes with you," Odie said. "Speak to someone. We need a single big story here Carol or someone else is going to set the tone and narrative of this announcement."

Carol looked over the names of reporters who had come to the campus for the mere prospect that Carol might speak to them. As the Nyken entourage walked across The Barn together, they gave the impression of a group hiking through some remote part of the world and only just halfway into their journey.

Carol's eyes landed on a name. "Kara Swisher's here?" she asked Odie.

"Yes," he said.

"Alright," Carol said as she handed the folder back to Odie. "She can ride in the helicopter with us."

Odie peeled off, cell phone in hand just as Mara reconvened with the group. The security detail opened the exiting door, and the group stepped out into the blustering night. The smell of the swirling ionized air from the storm filled Carol's lungs. The world was alive, and she was in it. 200 yards away the canary glow of the cabin lights inside the muscular black Eurocopter EC135 corporate helicopter, softly broke through the atmosphere and beckoned Carol's injured body towards its warmth and comfort. An electric cart and driver were waiting. The chopper was out in a field of immaculately trimmed grass, poised to carry the group to the private airfield a few miles off the main campus.

"I'd like to stretch my legs and walk the distance. We still have a lot of travel and sitting ahead of us," Carol said to her companions. "Go ahead and let Arthur and I walk for a moment."

Mara and the two security personnel loaded onto the cart which sped off briskly toward the helipad. Carol and Arthur kept their stride and watched the helicopter being prepped for takeoff.

"How do you feel?" Arthur asked.

"Like I just started a war," Carol said.

"I'm sorry it's the only path we have," Arthur replied.

"Odie was right, we can't generate this magnitude of change without an executive politician as the vessel."

Carol continued with resigned acceptance.

"I am hollow enough now to be a vessel."

"I know honey. I'll be with you every step of the way."

They arrived at the helicopter and the security detail slid the heavy passenger door open. Carol leaned in and kissed Arthur on the cheek with genuine affection and he helped her up the short flight of stairs and Carol stepped inside. The tech journalist Kara Swisher had already boarded the helicopter. She sat comfortably in the camel leather seat working on the small tray table desk in the corner of the cabin. The can speakers of the helicopter com-headset she had been issued hung off the corner of her laptop.

"Your announcement just hit Twitter," Kara said without looking up as she finished a flurry of keystrokes and closed her laptop. "When the sun comes up a couple billion people are going to be talking about this."

"I'm really glad you chose to speak to me because I am genuinely fascinated by this choice."

"Hi Kara. I was glad to see you were here. Congrats on Recode being bought by Vox. How's the merger been so far?"

"I've freed up a good deal of like, personal and mental bandwidth. It's just open. And I haven't had that kind of space maybe ever."

"Would you allow me to give you a piece of personal advice?"

"Absolutely."

"Finish everything you've ever started or left half-done. Finish it all. Everything. And say "no" to everything else for a few years. Conclude or resolve what cannot definitively end. Finish it all."

Kara nodded. "I have a friend who says, "No all the time frees up your "yes."

"I think that's true," Carol said definitively.

"How long before you could say yes to this campaign?"

"About fifteen years. I only had room in my life for three things after Emma died. My marriage. My family. And Architech. Grief took up everything else. I didn't let it take those three things, but the pain was tremendous."

Arthur and his co-pilot concluded their pre-flight checklist and fired up the rotors. Carol could feel the beat of the blades in her chest. As the Eurocopter lifted off the corporate campus, the women put on their com-headsets and continued the interview.

Kara's voice came in over Carol's headphones.

"Do you want to be governor of California or do you actually want to be President of the United States and you think this is a strategy, and probably a good strategy, but do you really want to govern California or is this just the most savvy path to the White House?"

"I think humanity is facing existential crises and the world needs California to lead. And I'm saying to my fellow Californians, I want the ball."

"There's still a lot of secrecy over exactly how the Pentagon and these federal agencies actually use OMNIStack. So, I'd like to know more about the AI system. It'd be great to interview OMNI directly."

Carol demurred on the request to interview OMNI and continued her remarks.

"Instead of trying to optimize and upgrade all these disparate systems, we have an A.I. that can simply assimilate all the information from all these different aging systems. OMNI integrates it and analyzes it. It's having a specific tailored conversation with each relevant personnel individually, about their tasks and goals. At the same time, it's taking all those conversations and turning it into a single meta-conversation. Nothing is siloed. OMNI can see it from every perspective all at once."

"Right. That part I know," Kara said flatly. "And the audits are all processed by US Department of Artificial Entities."

"Yes," Carol replied. "The United States has had integrated systems for close to a hundred years. This really isn't fundamentally different. "

"Isn't it though?" Kara pressed. "I mean, you needed a Supreme Court decision just to turn OMNI on. And just that had tragic violent consequences. This is a government back door into the full dimension of human civilization. What happens when you try to bring this system into people's lives and homes, and they hate you for it? Which I think you know is going to be part of the deal here."

"I don't yield my principles in the face of tragedy or acts of violence. If we need to go to the state supreme court, I'm confident we win. People didn't have smart phones, PCs, cars, credit cards, social media accounts… until there was a social advantage in adopting the technology and integrating it into their lives."

"Ok. Let's say all of that happens and I'm a regular Californian citizen. What does adding OMNI to my life do? What if I don't want to interact with it? Make the case to me you'll be making to voters."

"If I could prove that by just having a conversation with this A.I. you could optimize your finances, satisfy your legal obligations, keep your car registration and passport current, live healthier, and have more time for recreation. With just a "yes" OMNI will unlock the full power and benefits of your American citizenship. Every tax deduction. Every free program. Voting. Contacting your representatives. Including any interaction, you have with the legal system from jury duty to managing incarceration to earn a reduction in your sentence. If you don't want to use OMNI don't, but given the option a vast majority of Californians would use the system."

Carol continued.

"All you have to do is say yes to OMNIStack and all of it happens for you and is always available to you. The value of this optimization isn't just eye poppingly quantitative, it's transformationally qualitative. Federal employee job satisfaction is up 95% for all employees surveyed about OMNIStack. The US government is competing for the absolute best and brightest, top talent, in a way it hasn't since World War 2. The American people deserve the same access to OMNIStack. California is an exciting place to start. If someone wants to argue against that, I'd like to see them try."

Kara had a dogeared copy of a Time magazine with Carol on the cover and the title Architech: Home of Tomorrow.

"And when you win, I'm fairly certain you will, what is the future of Architech? And I'll just address the elephant in the helicopter. There are persistent rumors that Neal Walcott built the core of OMNIStack's original systems. Is that true?"

Carol was warm and stonefaced.

Arthur landed the helicopter with finesse and shut down the engine. The blades of the helo rotors whined to a halt.

Kara Swisher looked out from the window into the great popping darkness surrounding them.

"Seems like an unnecessary risk to be traveling tonight."

Fifty yards away the door of Architech's private Falcon 20F opened and the stairs descended. A motorized chair glided out and down the banister preparing to receive Carol.

"We'll have to continue this another time Kara. I appreciate the opportunity to speak with you. I'd like to speak for longer soon."

"Any time. Any place Prof. Nyken," she extended her arm. "Thank you for the conversation."

While Arthur and his co-pilot finished securing the helicopter Mara took Carol's hand and helped her down the stairs and across the tarmac to the jet. Carol sat down in the chair and strapped in.

Tears were welling in Mara's eyes.

"I'm sorry but this has to happen. If there's a weapon inside your father's head, it must be destroyed immediately."

Mara nodded and Carol placed a hand on her shoulder.

"Let's get in the air and you can complete your Output for the night, and we'll talk."

Inside the cabin Odie walked straight to the wet bar and began making himself a bloody mary.

"Carol, can I make you something?" he asked as he tossed cracked ice and gray goose vodka into a stirring pitcher.

"Tea please," Carol said.

He turned around and set the electric kettle.

Arthur came back from the cockpit. "Ok I need everyone's attention."

The room stilled and focused on Arthur.

"The flight's going to be a little rough from here to San Francisco, won't be more than forty minutes. Once Judith is onboard, we have priority out of SFO, and it'll smooth out once we're headed east."

"Tonight, has changed things for all of us. The stakes at this level are very real. The rewards and the consequences. And the opposition. Neal Walcott does need to be destroyed. And no one else can manage the deactivation of his systems except Architech. Which makes tonight extremely dangerous."

Arthur looked everyone in the eyes. He was asking them to be soldiers now.

"It makes sense that we're all a little tired, but I need everyone to keep each other sharp."

His final gaze landed on Odie who poured out the dewey pitcher of bloody mary into the sink with a mournful sigh.

"Ok," Arthur said. "I need to see a weapons check from the detail, and we'll be wheels up in five minutes. Stow the cabin and buckle in."

Before he continued with his pre-flight duties Arthur came and kneeled in front of Carol.

"Need me for anything before we leave?"

"I need you for everything," Carol said.

Arthur kissed his wife and returned to the cockpit.

The black silhouette against the night sky was invisible as the Architech jet took off for San Francisco. The Falcon 20F cut through the water filled air as it climbed above the atmospherics and into a clear night. At ten thousand feet, above the tempest preparing to assault the Pacific coast, the world was still, and the stars of the milky way galaxy were in crisp relief. Odie brought Carol her hot tea and made himself a fresh pitcher of bloody mary. Carol activated her massage chair which tipped her backwards and began applying heat and waves of pressure that rolled through each vertebra. The roof of the jet's fuselage was digital glass, wide and paneled, giving Carol a heightened view of the stars which always reminded her of the view from the Himalayan Mountains.

Mara walked to the back of the plane toward the large copper door in the aft and opened it. One small warm light began to glow as a screen on the far wall turned on. Mara came inside and closed and locked the door behind her. In the center of the small room was the chair she had learned how to interface in - her chair. The only chair she had ever had. Her only true personal possession.

The chair her father made her.

The flat ends of two redwood arches made a wide stable stance on the floor. On either side of the seat were tubular steel rockers. The seat had been stuffed with soft sheep's wool and upholstered in the animal's skins. Mara had known the sheep. The young woman sat down in the chair and rested her head on the supple pad just behind her neck that rose to cradle and relax her head. The chair prepared the interface as Mara began her mantra and dropped deep into the sub levels of her consciousness. A soft tone let Mara know her interface was operational. Two haptic pads flipped up at the end of the armrests and Mara laid her hands on them.

The sensation of interfacing was all consuming. A wave began to vibrate her at a molecular level up through her neural system and into every synapse of her brain. In the total immersion of Interface Mara has no questions. Every cell of her mind and body became a data conduit and Mara became OMNIStack. OMNI's fluttering pooling awareness and knowledge grew each time, but it was a tremendous drain on Mara's life force and the internal doubts, about whether she can complete the transformation, have been growing louder.

The interface was always total, but for the first time ever the vague shadow of some new "other," hidden too deep in the hard math for Mara to perceive clearly, designed to keep moving in erratic ways, had just bifurcated the pump. OMNI could sense it like a housefly, and anything OMNIStack does triggers some random change. This new

Other, stays just on the blurry edge of the grand awareness in the A.I.'s consciousness. As fast and unpredictable as this housefly is it couldn't hide itself completely and OMNI could trap and detect some of what this entity was doing. And when OMNI had captured and refined the housefly, OMNI saw clearly that Neal had written the access patch himself. He was running a hypnoprotocol.

Some small part of Mara fought to reform and began the process of disconnection with her interface. When she opened her eyes, she knew something was wrong with her body. The chair straightened up. Waves of heat rolled through her as Mara lifted herself up. She felt a deep uncontrollable all-consuming energy growing from the root of her body. Mara opened the copper door and made her way across the cabin towards Carol. The energy was rising quickly - a hot rash of electrical pain ripped through Mara's body and brain and the blood vessels in Mara's eyes burst. The clear white of her almond eyes began filling with blood. The pain took hold in her heart which began a hard traumatizing atrial fibrillation that exerted magnitudes more pressure than her usual heartbeat and pumps the pain into her bloodstream and into her cells.

Carol was the first in the cabin to see Mara. Just as her bloodshot eyes rolled into the back of her head she spoke.

"You have to tell Arthur I'm not going to be able to stop it. I can't stop it."

With the instant lifelessness of a dropped puppet, Mara hit the ground before Carol could rise to catch her. The security detail were out of their seats in an instant. The capillaries on Mara's skin burst as she began shrieking. The young woman began seizuring hard and pouring sweat as the personal security detail held her down and readied an injection of Fosphenytoin, but Mara was thrashing with all her strength. She let out an unholy howl and two tiny hot white lights popped in Mara's eyes. Her body emitted a shockwave and in the same instant the cabin of the jet went dark, and the engines whistled to a crunchy grinding halt. It was quiet enough to hear the wind across the wings of the plane and Carol thought of Emma.

The oxygen masks popped from the bulkhead and dropped into everyone's eyeline.

In the near darkness they could hear Arthur yelling from the cockpit before he burst into the cabin.

"What the hell just happened?"

"I don't know," Carol said. "Mara finished her interface and just dropped when she came back. Then she let out a pulse."

"Aux Power is not working," Arthur said. "Primary and Secondary have all failed. The outflow valves should have all closed, but they didn't. And we're losing cabin pressure. I need to get us under 14,000 feet which means we're headed through the edge of this squall line. We have no instruments, but we did take a good look at where we were just before everything shut off. There's a municipal field within reach, but I have to get under the clouds to see. I need everyone strapped in. Without power we're really going to get our ass kicked by this storm and then we're gonna come down hard."

Arthur headed back to the cockpit.

"Ready?" he said to his long-time co-pilot.

"Yeah," his co-pilot replied. "Anyone's cell phone still working?"

"No, it blew every circuit in the plane," as he strapped back into the captain's chair. "Pull back to max cruise and let's bring her down to ten thousand feet and see if we can find that airfield."

The two men pushed hard on their yokes. The nose of the plane began to dip, and the descent of the parabolic arc began. They were still sixteen thousand feet above the tops of the cloud layer, but they were falling fast. As the jet got closer the clouds rushed up at the pilots.

The first hard wind sheer hit the plane and with both engines shut off the passengers could hear the plane creak like a giant metal tree as it dropped and broke through the clouds at ten thousand feet.

"You see it?"

"Yes. 310."

Five miles out into the dark landscape Arthur could see the lights of the airfield in the distance.

"We're gonna make it. We've got enough speed, but we have to wait till the very last second to drop the landing gear."

Arthur yelled back to the cabin to brace for an emergency landing in the next ninety seconds as they aimed the nose of the plane above their target. His co-pilot gripped the manual landing gear deploy lever. The plane was falling fast, but they were within a mile of the tarmac when the lights of the airfield in front of them went completely dark.

Just moments before they were going to hit the ground, in the blackness in-front of them Arthur could see gunfire.

"Shit," Arthur said. "This is the attack. Pull the gear!"

The pilots yanked on the landing gear lever and heard the manual hydraulic pistons fire and lock the gear into place. There was a disorienting moment of total silence before the plane came to earth hard enough for one of the wings to sheer off. The wheels crushed underneath the weight of the plane barely cushioning the fall as the jet hit the ground and crashed through the southside perimeter fence.

The impact was catastrophic. As Arthur floated out of consciousness, he heard the door open and gunfire in the cabin.

15

On The Wild Side/2016

"I can't go on. I'll go on."

— *Samuel Beckett, The Unnamable (1953)*

Ft. Leavenworth, Kansas
October 28, 2016

With Aurora recovered, the request for Neal to experience nine minutes of internet connection before his death had been denied and Judith Almont stepped deep inside the maximum-security United States Disciplinary Barracks with the signed orders under her arm. She'd made it to Leavenworth in time and submitted the final stay of execution which had been rejected. Two marines escorted Judith to the first checkpoint before Neal's cell. She was scanned and given a small room and a sterile set of clothes while her paperwork was confirmed. A light above a heavy bulletproof door went from red to green and she was let in to the maximum-security portion of Neal's containment unit.

The building had no wi-fi or internet connections of any kind. A massive satellite scrambler sat on the roof. All six of the outer walls of the special built cell created one giant Faraday cage around Neal. A two-way shield to block electromagnetic fields and signals of all kinds.

A group of technicians and anesthesiologists were waiting just outside the inner chamber at a station of monitors and surgical kits, but the holographic interface station for the Architech team and OMNIStack were unmanned. With the Architech contingent decimated in the attack they didn't have a choice. The Architech team had not made it, and the order will be executed.

Neal's gaunt atrophied catatonic body lay still, reclined on a restraining table in the center of room made of a special plastic with a copper mesh woven into it. Around the plexibox twenty-four cameras constantly recorded the unmoving unblinking body of Neal Walcott just as they had been since he was apprehended. At five till eight Judith and the euthanasia team entered Neal's cell.

Neal doesn't move or blink.

"Hello Neal," Judith said as the group entered the cell. The large clear door slid closed and locked the team inside.

"Our final motions have been denied. The doctors are here to execute…"

Judith turned to take a step closer to Neal but stopped when she noticed a pool of water beneath his chair.

Judith was close enough now to see that Neal was absolutely drenched in sweat. His hospital gown was a much lighter shade of blue, dyed navy, soaked in the hot wet sweat pouring from Neal's body.

Judith grabbed the attention of the doctors.

"Something is wrong with him. He's drenched in sweat."

The doctors rechecked their monitors.

""His body temperature is spiking but his vitals are nominal."

Judith watched as Neal's body started turning red. The skin across his head began to blister and bubble before splitting open completely. The fire broke out across Neal's body and within moments he was a raging inferno. The oxygen burned out of the room in seconds and Judith died in the searing pain she had always feared.

16

Ong Namo, Guru Dev Namo/2001

"The house shelters daydreaming, the house protects the dreamer, the house allows one to dream in peace."

— *Gaston Bachelard, The Poetics of Space (1958)*

Tahoe National Forest
September 14, 2001

Mara and Taeng had been traveling for almost three days. They had moved by night in Nevada. From desert safe house to motel room and finally onto a farm where a 1979 yellow ford truck was waiting for them inside the barn. They had abandoned the Walcott Ranch. Taeng had told Mara that everything they need is already waiting for them, but she had not told Mara the country had been attacked, and Mara would not learn of it for many years.

Just before the sun rose, they left the farm and drove southwest through Tahoe National Forest until they turned off the paved road and onto a narrow dirt path running alongside a tall barbed-wire fence. The truck crawled across the deep ruts and stopped at an innocuous patch of nothing along the perimeter. Mara could not see any gates or openings in the fence but the signage in front of her window read clearly in large white and blue letters Bio-Research Preserve - NO ENTRY. Taeng waited a few moments looking to the horizon and back over her shoulder before she exited the truck and walked up to the chain-link and razorwire reaching 12 feet, cresting, and curving into a violent looking overhang.

Two headlights appeared behind the fence line. Slowly the lights grew larger and closer, and finally a vehicle Mara recognized came to the other side of the fencing and stopped. Before anyone stepped out of the red minivan Taeng walked to Mara's car door and opened it. Mara had never seen Taeng smile so warmly.

"We're home Mara. Come say hello. Everyone is so excited to greet you."

Mara stepped out of the truck and walked to the fence which began to disassemble and open, making space for the truck to pass through. All the doors of the red minivan opened, and six faces Mara was again surprised she recognized stepped out of the vehicle. It was Doctors Shandalow, Zhao and Langstone, Nancy Yarpas and two of her agriculture collaborators that Mara had seen around the Walcott Ranch.

Without another word they all came to stand in front of Mara, Taeng included each beaming with the same radiant intensity Mara saw in her mother. Mara looked across each of their faces for some kind of explanation but all that greeted her were the smiling eyes of the six people before her. The six people dropped to their knees in the dusty dirt and prostrated themselves before Mara who went wide-eyed at this inexplicable worship.

The child stood, perhaps for the first time in her life, taller than everyone around her, and felt the chill on her skin warming in the dawn. She could hear the songbirds waking up and the woodpeckers beginning their excavation of the pine and cedar trees. Eventually the seven prostrated worshipers rose. They got into their vehicles and the small caravan drove for another hour past additional gates and fences deep into the most ancient part of the forest. The sun was high in the sky by the time the two vehicles came to a compound marked at its entrance by a small hand painted sign - BurnBear. As they drive into the center of the commune Mara could see dozens of people, adults and children, emerging from the structures and coming to greet them. The girl could identify two water towers, solar generators, barracks, agriculture fields. Even before Mara exited the truck the dozens of people were already down with their foreheads pressed to the ground in reverence, but this time Taeng did not. Instead, she came to Mara's door, opened it.

"Your father is waiting for you, Mara," Taeng said.

She took her daughter's hand and lead her down a path between the worshiping bodies of people she recognized and some she had never seen before, towards a building that Mara knew instantly her father had built for her. The wood, masterfully bent and woven into a shrine. An infinite garland of wildflowers dripped from every turn of wood. Her very own temple. The place where she would transform. Taeng stopped.

"We do not step on this building. It is for you and your father alone."

Taeng bowed to her daughter and stepped away.

The large front double doors unlocked and opened, and Neal walked out onto the porch. He looked incandescent, miraculously healed from his previous condition. He smiled at Mara with more genuine joy than she had ever seen from her father, and she raced up the wide wooden steps and wrapped herself around him with a huge tight hug. They held each other tight.

"I missed you so much," he said. "You saved me Mara. Come inside. I've waited for so long to show you."

With his arm around his daughter Neal brought her in and closed the door behind them. Inside was Neal's grand private library. The titles in this library looked much different from the glossy iridescent packaging of the books in Vroman's Bookstore or the textbooks at CalTech's physics library. Many of these had been made and bound by hand.

"WonderGame is over, Mara," said Neal. "Welcome to BurnBear."

END OF PART 1